Meet Me in the Woods

By

C.R. Reece

A Wild Ink Publishing Original

Wild Ink Publishing

https://wild-ink-publishing.com

Cover Design: Jessie Knuth

Editing: Nicole DeVincentis, Andie Smith

For those who fight the most terrible monsters—their inner thoughts—and still stay soft.

Playlist

Prelude: "Creature Fear" by Bon Iver

Track 1: "Meet Me in the Woods" by Lord Huron

Track 2: "715 – Creek" by Bon Iver

Track 3: "Son of Sam" by Elliot Smith

Track 4: "Motion Sickness" by Phoebe Bridgers

Track 5: "Savior Complex" by Phoebe Bridgers

Track 6: "Wait By The River" by Lord Huron

Track 7: "Heroes" by David Bowie

Track 8: "She Lit a Fire" by Lord Huron

Track 9: "This is Me Trying" by Taylor Swift

Track 10: "Pretty Pimpin" by Kurt Vile

Track 11: "These Are My Friends" by lovelytheband

Track 12: "Salem" by Bon Iver

Track 13: "Moon Song" Phoebe Bridgers

Track 14: "Research" by Big Sean

Track 15: "All the Pretty Girls" by KALEO

Track 16: "Read My Mind" by The Killers

Track 17: "Seven" by Taylor Swift

Track 18: "Somebody That I Used To Know" by Gotye

Track 19: "It's Cool, We Can Still Be Friends" by Bright Eyes

Track 20: "Mastermind" by Taylor Swift

Track 21: "I Know the End" by Phoebe Bridgers

Track 22: "The Yawning Grave" by Lord Huron

Track 23: "Closer" by Kings of Leon

Track 24: "Little Dark Age" by MGMT

Track 25: "Heads Will Roll" by the Yeah Yeah Yeahs

Track 26: "This Place Is A Prison" by The Postal Service

Track 27: "Photograph" by the Verve Pipe

Track 28: "Bury a Friend" by Billie Eilish

Track 29: "My Beloved Monster" by Eels

Track 30: "Sisters of the Moon" by Fleetwood Mac

Track 31: "Blood Bank" by Bon Iver

Track 32: "The Night We Met" by Lord Huron

Track 33: "Invisible String" by Taylor Swift

Track 34: "In the Air Tonight" by Phil Collins

Track 35: "Tornado Warnings" by Sabrina Carpenter

Track 36: "Twilight" by Elliot Smith

Track 37: "Season of the Witch" by Lana Del Rey

Track 38: "Possum Kingdom" by The Toadies

Track 39: "Which Witch" by Florence and the Machine

Track 40: "And He Slayed Her" by Liz Phair

Track 41: "Vampire" by Olivia Rodrigo

Track 42: "Burn the Witch" by Radiohead

Track 43: "Murder in the City" by The Avett Brothers

Prelude - "Creature Fear" by Bon Iver

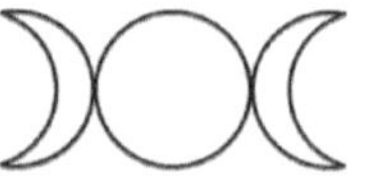

HE COULDN'T FEEL his legs, but he knew they were moving as quickly as he could force them through the darkness. The sensation of his muscles burning would have brought a welcome respite from the ice-cold fear flowing like freezing river rapids through his veins, but his nerves, numbed by fear and the brutal cold, refused to awaken. Despite this, his legs continued to pump faster than they ever had before, darting over the shadows of fallen tree limbs as the path curved downhill. He slipped over blackened, dead leaves soaked from the midnight dew, but managed to keep himself moving forward with an agility only the fight for survival could evoke. His labored breaths, echoed in rhythmic ghostly white clouds, were visual reminders that he was still alive, even if for only a few more precious moments.

Fear had distorted everything. Or maybe it was the eerily quiet velvet midnight sky. Either way, he couldn't feel his feet touch the earth or the air hit his lungs as he hurtled himself into the woods, away from the place he once called home.

What had he just witnessed? The black eyes glowing in the darkness that couldn't possibly be human. The copper scent of blood everywhere. Even now, he could taste it in the back of his throat.

He stopped, hiding behind the safety of a towering tree's bent trunk, to see if he had been followed by the beast that would surely haunt his dreams, if he lived so long to sleep again. Scanning the shadows of dark spaces in between the tightly crowded trunks of the thin beech trees, his fatigued eyes played tricks on him. Dark outlines of human-like figures crept behind trunks, while flashes of glowing eyes peered out through the breezeless midnight air, but perhaps his mind was just playing tricks on him and they were simply fireflies dancing in the night.

Smacking his palm to his mouth to hush his own labored breathing, he strained to listen for any movements other than his own. He forced his eyes to close despite his fear, but the blood pumping through his ears was the only sound he could hear. He strained to see through the darkness. Nothing but the moonlight flickering playfully through the trees, reflecting its golden light onto gently rolling water. The narrow creek gurgled in the distance, a gruesome reminder of the bloody gasps he had just heard.

He leaned over, resting his hands on his knees, his wool trousers soaked with sweat, and attempted to catch his breath. A twig snapped on the path behind him. Involuntarily, he swiveled around. Nothing but blackness in between shadows of the tree trunks. He heard another brutal snap. This time, it wasn't from the twigs on the trail. It was from deep within his skeletal frame. A sudden white, hot flash of pain registered under the base of his skull.

If he hadn't died instantly, Wesley's last view of Earth would have been looking up at the midnight crescent moon sparkling through the silvery leaves of the largest bent tree running along Moon Creek.

Track 1: "Meet Me in the Woods" by Lord Huron

Lowen

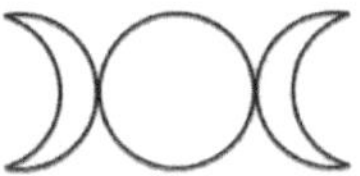

LOWEN PARKED HER car in a small, empty lot next to the darkened woods, a chill of ominous foreboding tingling up her spine. The antique, purposely yellowed invitation in her lap beckoned her to read its words one more time, and she had to admit, the elegant calligraphy was a nice touch.

Congratulations on being selected for the annual Moon Creek Harvest Moon Ritual. Meet us in the woods tonight.

Sincerely,

The Moon Creek Town Council

Lowen rolled her eyes, shaking away the unsettling feeling

gnawing at her gut, and threw the letter on the passenger seat. Stepping out of her car, she admonished herself for parking in the smaller, empty lot on the opposite side of the meeting spot where her two best friends and the other selected students awaited. Not that navigating the trails would be a problem—even if their darkened paths were barely visible under the October night sky.

Lowen knew the woods as well as she knew the freckles on her nose. The tree canopies had always been her blanketed sanctuary when she felt alone and anxious, the trails were her training ground for running long distances to clear her mind, and the creek's secret song helped her through her bouts of dark thoughts. These woods were as much of a home to her as the small cottage house she shared with her mom and sister.

The afternoon sun had given way to a cool evening, and as she navigated the familiar trail, she felt pockets of cool air forming around her bare arms. She should have brought a sweater, she thought to herself, as she quickened her pace. It was only about a three-minute walk to where Taylor, Noah, and the other chosen high school seniors were meeting, but the anxious thrumming of her pulse urged her to get to them faster. She could already hear everyone's excited laughter in the distance, causing a rush of unexpected excitement to tingle through her body. She hadn't felt anything besides the heavy weight of depression lately. Plus, she knew the Moon Water Ritual was a joke. It was just another odd tradition created by a quirky town of bored Midwesterners. She and Noah had been making fun of it since middle school. Despite all of this, she felt her pulse quicken under her skin as she rushed down the path until she saw it looming ahead of her like an exhausted spine surrounded by perfect postures.

Lowen stopped for a moment on the familiar trail, gazing at the tall bent tree, the one she had laid beneath earlier that morning. It would have been a strange thing to do even once, but this was the third time this week. She acknowledged it was an alarming habit—depressed or not—and had kept it a secret from the small circle of trusted people in her life. She stared at the unremarkable brown earth, searching for some reason for why she had gone to that specific location three times this week, and let her body crumple onto the soft earth.

Now, as she scanned from the soft dirt ground to the tall, bent tree looming before her, she wrestled to remember something in which she felt in her soul she had forgotten. Perhaps she was going crazy. Like for real crazy. The kind she didn't even want to discuss with her therapist or her mom. The thought of not being in control of what her mind and her body were doing as they worked simultaneously to force her to collapse on a trail in the middle of the woods was frightening—scary enough that she knew she wouldn't tell a soul. She'd rather fully go off the deep end all alone than mention it to anyone.

A snap from high in the trees brought her back to reality. She looked up, pointing her phone's flashlight toward the treetops to find the culprit of the noise, but nothing moved. She had been looking for the owls, the elusive newcomers to Moon Creek. To Lowen, they were harbingers of something to come. When she pictured their amber eyes glowing in the dark, she knew in her bones they were a warning.

The local news reported on the owls a few days ago, informing the residents to be aware and courteous to the many new faces visiting their quaint town. Traffic patterns, restaurant waits, and hotel bookings could be impacted. Bird watchers from all over the Midwest would soon be travelling to Moon Creek to hopefully get a look at the rare birds, as they never travelled so far east. Known to only reside along the Pacific coast, all the way to Mexico, the birds were easy to discern due to their dark brown feathers and spotted head and chest. For Lowen though, the spotted owls weren't merely a migratory mystery; they seemed to be the beginning of something new. She couldn't quite shake the heavy feeling in her limbs reminding her that the owls' appearance coincided with her own magnetic pull to the woods. If only she could see one, perhaps she would realize they were just birds and shake the unsettling cold gnawing at her bones.

To her dismay, the owls remained hidden from her, so she continued down the trail, but the feeling of being watched tickled her spine and rested on the nape of her neck. The woods felt out of the place somehow, but she couldn't quite put her finger on it. Something was out there, past the trail and into the shadowed forest, that didn't belong. The chill tickling her spine intensified.

"Get a grip," she muttered out loud as she came to the parking lot on the south end of the woods. Pairs of headlights illuminated the shadowy figures as she approached.

"It's creepy out here at night, isn't it?" a familiar deep voice said. "You're crazy for walking through there alone."

Lowen smiled at the gentle teasing and released a deep breath. Her best friend, Noah Messing, stood regally with his signature playful grin and bleached blond hair at the entrance to the woods. She admired the easy presence he had expertly acquired. He kept his angular jaw slightly elevated which, along with his height, allowed him to cast downward glances toward the peons skittering below him. For the Harvest Moon Ritual, Noah wore matching black eyeliner and nail polish.

"Yeah, I thought it wouldn't bother me, but walking through the woods at night was honestly a little unnerving," Lowen said, glancing back at woods, as if willing something to move so she wouldn't feel so paranoid.

Instead, Noah drew her into a familiar embrace, one that was utilized more for lazy comfort than intimacy or protection. Their bodies fit together perfectly; she rested her head into his chest, and he laid his chin on top of her head.

"Anyway, where is our resident woo woo girl?" he asked, while they scanned the woods as one combined unit searching for the missing link to their trio. Lowen could feel his words vibrate atop her skull, lulling her into a rare moment of relaxation.

As if summoned into existence by the mere mention, Taylor appeared from behind the hood of her trunk. Lowen couldn't help but feel envious when she saw her. Taylor didn't look the part of someone whose favorite hobbies included reading horoscopes obsessively, cursing as much as possible and attempting to cast love spells; she looked simultaneously athletic and graceful in her black leggings, white crop top, and oversized jean jacket. In her arms, she carried a large cardboard box with no sign of discomfort or struggle. Noah nudged Lowen's arm, breaking her from her habit of becoming a silent observer, a pattern she relied upon when she began to feel overwhelmed in social situations.

"I can't believe we're doing this. We really need to start questioning the sanity of everyone in this godforsaken town," Noah said, rolling his eyes.

Despite his attempt to communicate the lameness of the impending event, Noah's eyes twinkled in genuine curiosity. The kids of Moon Creek had heard the Moon Water Ritual lore growing up and now that they were seniors, the handful had been chosen. Every year on the night of the September full moon, or what they called the Harvest Moon, thirteen seniors were chosen to walk deep into the Moon Creek woods to a place where the creek flowed without the obstruction of the trees and the moon shone down into the water. They would take their jars, filling them with water charged by the glow of the full moon. The magical water was said to hold special powers of luck and strength for those who ingested it.

In more recent years, the teens would bring back their filled jars and give them to the senior football players before their first game. On the night of the game, the players would huddle and chug their moon water before going to the field as a source of luck. The whole thing was kind of gross—who knew what was in that water—but no one questioned the risks. It made a strange sort of perfect sense for a small town to take something occult-like and turn it into a superstition for their football team to win games.

Lowen wasn't sure if anyone really believed it worked. The football team's record for losing was proof enough, but still, the thought of being part of the tradition was exciting—especially considering Lowen, Noah, and Taylor had all been randomly selected by the high school's student council. Lowen had always felt like a nobody in town, especially at school. Sure, she had Noah and Taylor, but her friend circle didn't stretch much further than that. Her two friends were great at being well-known and outgoing, with Taylor playing almost every sport and winning class president while Noah earned the lead in almost every school play and musical. They had always been a crutch for Lowen in social situations, where they knew so many other kids and carried on conversations with ease, allowing her to gratefully fade into the background.

"Okay guys! Does everyone have their jar?" Taylor asked in her usually loud, assertive voice.

The selected teens began to gather around her, as she had

officially become the leader of this ridiculous ritual—which was Taylor's natural role in all things. The student council had given her the mysterious box one week ago with the jars and instructions for the night. She set the box on the ground next to her, opened it and began pulling out thick, emerald-green velvet fabric. She extended an elegant arm and handed Noah the first piece of fabric. As he unfolded it, they all realized it was a robe.

"Costumes? I would have accessorized if I would have known," Noah deadpanned, as he pushed his arms through the massive sleeves. "And a hood? Chic."

Not only did the robe touch the ground, but its enormous hood covered Noah's head and made him all but disappear into the backdrop of the dark green woods.

After handing out all thirteen robes, along with thirteen lanterns that each person lit, Taylor opened the instructions resting in the bottom of the box. Looking around at her classmates, Lowen felt as if she had time-traveled into some parallel dimension. Their long robes covered their jeans, sweatshirts, and sneakers, and their hoods covered their haircuts and makeup. Even the flashlights from their iPhones were replaced by lanterns. The aesthetic was so jarring that everyone became uncharacteristically quiet at the same time, as if their costumes had shifted their belief in the moon's ability to produce magic.

Taylor, recognizing the sudden apprehension of the group, took out the envelope from the town council with the instructions for collecting the moon water. She read aloud:

Go to the place in the woods where the creek flows,

Where the trees part and the harvest moon glows.

Step into the water and turn it red,

Keep this blood pact or witness the undead.

"What the actual eff?" Noah whispered to Lowen.

Taylor, seemingly perplexed, flipped the so-called instruction page over.

"Oh! Here are the actual instructions," she said, a look of relief washing over her face. "They are probably just trying to freak us out."

She began to read the instructions to the group:

1. Follow the Tulip Trail east to the creek. When the trail splits, follow the narrow, unmarked trail south.

2. The tree clearing around the creek for the ritual will be obvious. The full moon will shine directly onto Moon Creek without obstruction.

3. Climb down the bank and into the water. Create a full circle.

4. Four knives are hidden in the inside pockets of four robes. Use the knife to cut at a diagonal along your left palm, one quarter inch deep. Start from the base of your thumb to the base of your pinkie.

5. When you are finished, pass the knife clockwise to the next person.

6. When the 13th person has finished, everyone must simultaneously place their left hand in the creek and repeat:

Moonlight, protect us.

Moonlight, take our blood.

Keep the unknown in the darkness.

And keep the evil in the mud.

7. Collect your moon water in your jars.

8. Tell no one about the specifics of this ritual.

Thank you for your sacrifice.

Taylor stopped reading and looked up at Lowen with wide eyes.

"Is this for real?!" a cheerleader named Blaire, with long brunette hair very similar to Lowen's, asked. "Is this some kind of sick joke? It has to be a joke, right? It's, like, really specific."

Instinctually, each person reached into the inside of their robes. Four teens drew out small silver knives about five inches in length with intricate details of moons, trees, and thin winding lines on the handles. A shiver ran down Lowen's spine. She was relieved her fingers didn't wrap around cold metal.

"I don't think it is a joke," Taylor said, her voice uncharacteristically soft. "The council seemed very serious when I came to pick up the box. They made me swear I wouldn't open it until I was with everyone tonight."

"Let me see that paper," Lowen said, gently taking the instructions from Taylor's hand.

"Keep the unknown in the darkness. And keep the evil in the mud," she read again. "Has anyone ever asked a family member who has done the ritual in the past about it?"

"My mom did it her senior year," Blaire said. "She told me to keep an open mind before I left tonight. I just thought she was telling me to believe in the magic of moon water, not that I was going to have to cut myself!"

"Come to think of it, my uncle was a little cryptic about it, too," Noah said. "I told him a couple weeks ago that I was selected and he and my dad exchanged—a look. I just assumed it was more of their judgmental hatred seeping out."

"What are they hiding from us?" a boy with shaggy blond hair asked, his voice tight with fear.

"I'm not sure, but let's head down to the spot in the creek and check it out before the moon reaches its apex," Taylor suggested, pointing ahead to the shadowed trail. "What's the worst that can happen? We all chicken out, grab some water, and go? At least we can say we got the moon water."

As the group followed her down the trail, Lowen couldn't shake the frigid chills running up her spine. Someone was watching her, she was certain. If this Moon Water Ritual was truthfully a protection spell, she just might need it.

Track 2 - "715 ~ Creek" by Bon Iver

Lowen

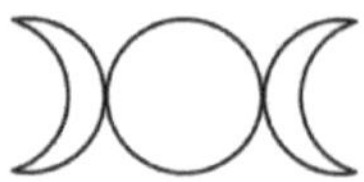

THIRTEEN HIGH SCHOOLERS in hooded emerald-green robes walked one by one down the darkened trail, illuminated only by orange glowing lanterns, to an unobstructed clearing in the gently babbling Moon Creek. The black water was illuminated by the glow of the full moon, making it appear silver. The once individualized group became a cohesive unit, silently holding onto one another as they took off their shoes and socks and slowly slid down the muddy embankment into the shin-deep frigid water. They looked up to see the pale moon slowly creeping through the sky to the very center of the circular clearing above the creek.

As if on command, the teens wordlessly spread into a circle in the creek bed.

"What now?" Lowen asked, looking around nervously at the other twelve faces she had known her whole life.

"How about a vote?" Noah offered. "We can still back out of this."

"How about we just get this over with?" Taylor responded, a hint of frustration in her voice. Lowen saw Taylor's eyes dart quickly from the glowing moon to the hand in her robe pocket.

"If we do this, we can't tell a soul," Noah said. "People will think we're crazy."

"Maybe we are," Blaire muttered.

Her chocolate brown hair had fallen from the huge hood of her robe, making her look like a small child. Adults had always confused Blair and Lowen because of their similar lanky build and long brunette hair. Lowen wondered if anyone could tell them apart now in their matching robes.

"All right, the moon is almost at its apex. Let's hurry," Taylor said, her voice sharp with an edge of impatience.

Lowen watched as Noah, along with the other three who drew knives from their robes, pulled out the silver blades from their pockets.

"On the count of three," Noah whispered. "One... two... three."

The first four pressed the blades into their palms, starting from the base of their thumbs to their pinkies. Lowen could hear hushed whispers and sighs as she squeezed her eyes shut, just as she did every time she had blood drawn or scraped her knee as a kid. It would be a miracle if she could make it through this ritual without passing out.

As the instructions stated, each of the first four passed their blades clockwise, the creepy routine continuing in tense silence. The second group of teens made the same cuts into their palms and passed the knives clockwise again. Dread pooled in her belly as Lowen realized she was the thirteenth person and would have to finish the ritual alone. Blood pulsed like an incessant drum playing a death march in her ears as she tried to breathe in the night air in large gulps.

Pull it together, Low. Everyone else is totally fine. It's just a little cut, she said to herself.

Taylor, standing next to Lowen, finished rinsing the blade of the knife in the creek and tapped her elbow to Lowen's to signal it was her turn. Lowen knew if she looked into Taylor's eyes she might cry or run or vomit, so instead she focused her gaze on the knife, its ornate handle seemingly from another time. Wrapping her cold fingers around the handle, she shakily flipped her left palm up into the moonlight, pushing the knife down into her palm below her thumb. She applied enough pressure so she could feel her skin pop under the weight of the blade. She quickly swiped down, and a hot, crimson stream suddenly flowed down her hand.

"Are you okay?" Taylor asked, her voice echoing a million miles away.

Lowen couldn't speak, her head feeling as if she had submerged it under the cold babbling water of the creek. Darkness began to obstruct her vision, the image of the creek bed becoming a scene from an old television show that was gently fading to black. As she felt her eyelids close and let herself drown into the peaceful relief of unconsciousness, she sensed that whatever the ritual was supposed to do had worked, as if a heavy blanket had finally been lifted from over her head. She hoped someone would catch her before she hit the frigid water below, not that any of it mattered all too much as the soothing whispers of unconsciousness washed over her. Instead, she welcomed the quiet bliss of leaving this world for a while. What happened to her physical form was none of her business. Perhaps it was just the sweet escape of fainting, or maybe the magic of the ritual had truly worked, because Lowen could swear she felt her body and soul separate for a brief moment as her world faded to black.

From high in the treetops of Moon Creek, a hopeful smile crept across the stranger's face.

Meet Me in the Woods

Track 3 - "Son of Sam" by Elliot Smith

Sebastian

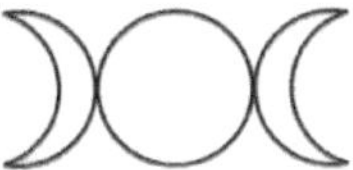

THE RETURN TO Moon Creek made Sebastian restless, possibly even a little manic. His body jittered, causing him to pace back and forth on a precariously thin branch high up in the trees, as if he were a caged lion anxiously walking a well-worn, narrow path.

Perhaps it was the crisp farm-scented midwestern air. Or maybe it was the memories of what he had done here so long ago haunting his usually well-guarded thoughts. Regardless, a restless and tad bit unhinged Sebastian was dangerous, and even he had enough self-awareness to realize he needed to get this frenzied energy out of his system before he did something truly terrible that would cause his presence in town to be discovered.

With that thought lingering in the chilled night air, Sebastian casually hopped down from the tall tree, strode through the woods with his hands tucked casually in his pockets, and then drove to a rest stop a few towns over to grab a bite to eat.

Meet Me in the Woods

Track 4 - "Motion Sickness" by Phoebe Bridgers

Lowen

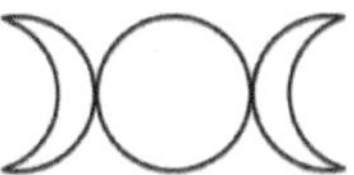

HER EYES FOCUSED momentarily on the blurry jar of moon water sparkling in the sunshine on her nightstand. Lowen couldn't control her eyes shutting again, plunging her back into her dream. Naked branches swayed in the breeze far above her, their black trunks shooting up like gnarled bones into the night. Twinkling stars dotted the sky, so close she felt as if she could reach up and grab one. The moon, full and silver, cast a gentle glow upon her face. Lying on her back, the crushing weight of anxiety no longer compressed her chest. Instead, her body was light enough to float, to become stardust swirling above the woods she knew so well.

Suddenly, her peace was interrupted by the moon becoming unnaturally bright. Too bright. No longer did its light shimmer a quiet silver but instead had transformed into a violent bright white. The warmth radiating from the sky signaled that night had contorted today, foregoing its usual soft and slow transition. The brightness made her squeeze her eyes shut in her dream, like she hadn't seen rays of sunshine in years. Her eyebrows arched in an unfamiliar pain as her vision blurred. It was too warm. Too bright. She dizzily scrambled to find the shade of a tree, but the leaves had already fallen, mocking her as they lay dead on the dry ground. Beads of sweat trickled down her back as fear seized her lungs.

Wake up, she urged herself.

Wake. Up.

Lowen pried open her heavy eyelids, forcing them to focus on the familiarity of her lavender floral quilt in the safety of her childhood bedroom. Acidity hit the back of her throat as she pushed herself up from her pillow. Rubbing her eyes, she attempted to erase the lingering dream from her mind. The small jar full of crystal-clear moon water reflected the rays of sun from her dresser. It looked so small and unassuming now. She half-expected it to be tinted a reddish hue after witnessing her blood flow from her hand and drip off her elbow into the clear creek water. Someone had plugged her phone into its charger and placed a half-full glass of water and a bottle of Advil on the nightstand beside her. The thought of her dripping blood triggered her wounded hand to instantly throb to the beat of her heart. Pulling up her arm from her blanket, she saw a fresh bandage had been applied. She reached for her phone, where five new text messages awaited her: two from Taylor, three from Noah.

Taylor: Just checking to see how you are doing. You passed out so fast! Thank God Noah caught you before you fell all the way in the creek

Taylor: Call me when you wake up! Don't miss the whole school day… the game is tonight

Noah: u okay? u owe me. I saved your life :)

Noah: call me when u wake, love

Noah: PS: we told ur mom that u accidentally cut yourself on a rock :)

Lowen slowly pulled herself out of bed, suddenly aware of the dull headache throbbing behind her eyes. It was already past eleven o'clock. She could still get to school and show up for the second part of the day. Everything took twice as long with the bulky wrap covering her left hand, but after taking a moderately quick shower, followed by throwing on a pair of oversized gray sweatpants and a blue crewneck sweatshirt, twisting her long dark hair into a bun on the top of her head and sliding on flip flops, Lowen finally made her way downstairs. A note on the kitchen island greeted her next to a gigantic chocolate chip muffin resting on a paper plate.

Dropped off your sister at school. Taking a client to look at some properties. Call me right when you wake up so I can check how you are feeling. Stay home from school if you need to, and make sure to eat and drink lots of water!

Love you,

Mom

Lowen grabbed the muffin, poured the remaining coffee from the pot into a mug, slung her backpack over one shoulder, and walked out the front door to the driveway. She felt grateful for her friends and family, but she also couldn't help but feel irritated. They always took care of her, and she was appreciative they did, but it sucked she was the one who needed the help all the time.

Why can't I just be the normal one for once? she thought.

The sun beamed down brightly on the concrete driveway, forcing Lowen to squint until she was inside her car. Its rays burned her skin, as if someone had turned the sun's power too high. As she grabbed her sunglasses, she wondered if the combination of bleeding from her hand and fainting last night made her sensitive to the light.

What an odd dream, she pondered as she thought back to the heat of the sun in her mind. *What does it all mean?*

Track 5 - "Savior Complex" by Phoebe Bridgers

Wesley

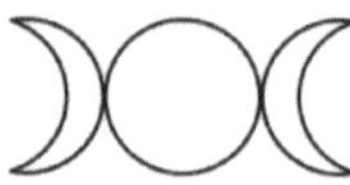

THE SAME THREE terrible dreams haunted him as they played on a monotonous loop each night, like a television with no off button. He found them so old and repetitive they didn't even have the quality of having happened anymore but rather felt like antiquated childhood fables found in a familiar book. This dream was different though.

It jolted Wesley James awake and disoriented him so much, he had to take a moment to remember where he was. He sighed with relief as he realized he was safe in his home in the historic district of Uptown New Orleans. His four-post bed made of dark mahogany wood sat facing an ornate fireplace with a flat screen television above it. Large windows lined the wall to his right and were covered by flowing black velvet curtains that draped onto the original hardwood. The curtains made it impossible to tell what time of day it was, but added to a dark, comforting ambiance. It was a masculine and beautiful room, yet lonely.

Wesley closed his eyes to physically will the mental picture his subconscious had created to return. Nighttime. Woods. A chill in the air. From his vantage point high in the trees, he looked down at the brown earth below him. A white-hot light struck. Shutting his eyes, he could feel the warmth as the light turned everything behind his eyelids red. From the cool darkness of night to this sudden flash, Wesley could feel the warm sunlight tickling his skin.

Wearing only gray sweatpants, Wesley swung his bare feet to the cold floor below. He had kept the original hardwood floors and multiple fireplaces intact when he bought the two-story house that was originally built in 1872, but completely renovated the kitchen and bathrooms to sleek, contemporary designs. He walked to his custom closet and found a V-neck t-shirt, slid it over his head, and stepped without a sound down the winding grand staircase. He had worked methodically to update the place for years, room by room. With each room he renovated, Wesley paid close attention to every minute detail—from light fixtures to cabinet hardware. The house was an ongoing project, one he never considered to be finished, even after years of tearing out and replacing drywall.

As he padded through the old house, darkened in the glistening morning hours by thick velvet curtains on each and every window,

Wesley thought fondly of his time in New Orleans, as if he were about to say goodbye to the city that embraced all things strange and treated him so well. He would miss the long days of working on the house, followed by the humid nights of wandering the quarter to partake in a French Seventy-Five and cup of gumbo.

Wesley had never found a place other than his familial home, a farm tucked away in the Midwest, where he felt such an innate sense of belonging. He had immediately soaked in the darkness of the city: the voodoo magic, the floating cemeteries, the warm cultural embrace of death followed by celebration after celebration. He didn't feel lonely in New Orleans because the city itself had become his friend. It was a living and breathing body, humid and smelling of sugar and crawfish and garbage and seawater. It slept through the heat of the day and came alive at night with a sensual pull, attracting travelers and residents alike to revel in its darkness and succumb to their carnal urges.

If he really thought about it, he loved the city because it made him feel superior to it and its inhabitants. He lived a buttoned-up existence of working on his old home with his own hands, reading novels cover to cover each night, and quietly wandering Bourbon Street without partaking in its alluring pleasures. With heavy nostalgia already weighing down on his shoulders, he sighed, pausing for a moment before entering the sun-drenched kitchen. He wasn't ready to say good-bye.

Early morning daylight poured through the window above the kitchen sink. He reached his arm toward the diagonal rays timidly, and let the warmth tickle his pale skin.

He did it, he thought, instinctively pulling his arm away from the window. Pausing to soak in the green gardens in his backyard speckled with orange and red flowers, Wesley was overcome by the sadness at the thought of leaving them behind.

It only took thirty seconds for Wesley to organize his thoughts. Skipping two stairs at a time, he rushed to shower and pack his brown leather duffel bag. Twenty minutes later, his black Audi pulled out from the driveway and hit Interstate 65 North, headed toward Moon Creek, because despite all of the horrific memories hovering like toxic mist around the small town, he knew the curse had been broken.

Track 6 - "Wait By The River" by Lord Huron

Lowen

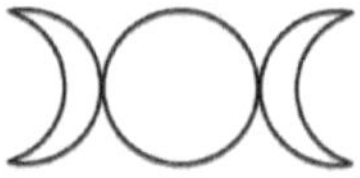

LOWEN HAD EVERY intention of going into school late, but as her mind wandered on her drive, her car took her to another destination: back to the woods of Moon Creek. It wasn't until she had absentmindedly turned into the empty parking lot that she registered where she had driven.

Well, I already missed the beginning of the day. Might as well blow it off and rest, she thought.

Making the decision to skip school instantly relieved the tightening in her chest. Anxiety would always linger like a ghost who couldn't quite move on, but the clear blue September sky felt infinite, breaking Lowen free from her personal prison. If the sun had been obstructed by a single cloud, the day would have felt chilly, but the bright sun made it feel like there was no temperature at all— just perfect, weightless air all around. Lowen wandered down the familiar trail on which she had walked, ran, biked, and skipped since she was a small child. She felt peaceful despite what had happened the night before. The daylight brought back familiarity, and the sun sparkling through the trees made the woods playful and safe once again.

The sound of a twig snapping from behind startled Lowen, shattering her fleeting illusion of security with one pop. She whirled around quickly but saw nothing. Staying perfectly still, her heart beat against her ribcage. She knew in her body someone was following her. Rustling green leaves from low shrubbery off the trail in the densely wooded area caught her eye. More snaps of twigs and leaves crunching. Lowen thought about running back to her car; a white-hot flash of terror jolting through her nerves. Fear wasn't something she inherently carried but since her strange habit of lying down involuntarily in the woods and the eerie night of the Moon Water Ritual, it hung around her shoulders like a smothering scarf she couldn't remove. Would she make it to her car before whoever was out there caught up with her?

So, this is fight or flight, she thought sarcastically.

And then she saw him moving quickly in the woods.

"Jesus," Lowen sighed as his furry tail leapt over a fallen tree trunk. Clearly, last night's festivities had gotten to her more than she wanted to admit. She gestured obscenely to the squirrel as he made his way up a slender tree.

As if by some sort of dark, familiar magic, Lowen suddenly felt the magnetic pull from deep behind her bellybutton. Her eyes became heavy, her feet picking up and moving themselves. Before she knew it, Lowen was under the slender bent tree. She allowed herself to sit on the soft, brown dirt of the trail, leaning her back against the tall, curved tree's trunk. Without a fight, she closed her eyes, drifting into a quiet liminal space as the sunlight danced between the canopy of leaves overhead.

She dreamt in black and white, mostly black though. The night air was deathly quiet as her legs moved quickly underneath her. White tree branches stretched their ghostly limbs along the trail in the woods. Her heart thudded against her breastbone and she wondered if it would crack her chest wide open if it beat any harder. She gulped for air as she ran faster and faster. Whatever—or whoever—she was running from had finally caught up to her, its bony fingers clutching her shoulders tightly.

Then nothingness. Quiet, somber darkness.

Lowen opened her eyes groggily. After a few moments, she remembered where she was and forced her heavy legs to stand.

Maybe I should start seeing my therapist again, she thought bitterly.

A wave of disappointment crashed through her body at the admittance, as if she had failed an important exam. She wasn't ready to believe all of this was in her head, even if her magnetic pull to the woods was unexplainable. She wasn't ready to take all of the blame, and she certainly wasn't ready to see the look of worry in her mother's eyes when she told her what was going on in her head.

These dreams mean *something. The Moon Water Ritual* did *something. All of this is connected,* she decided. *And I'm going to figure it out.*

With a new invigorated sense of purpose, she walked away from the bent tree and made her way down Tulip Trail, back to the spot in Moon Creek where she and her classmates conducted what she could only describe as a ceremony the previous night. The creek water had lowered and now only her feet were covered by the gently flowing stream. Lowen slid her feet out of her flip flops, stepping cautiously into the ice-cold water. She didn't really know why she was going back to the scene of the crime, but part of her hoped she would remember what happened after she cut her hand and passed out. She knew intellectually that the white flash she experienced must have been due to losing consciousness, but something deep inside told her something happened in that moment—something she couldn't explain. Something supernatural.

An object caught Lowen's eye at the bottom of the shallow, clear creek, close to where she stood in the water. The black and white stood in contrast to the soft, brown bottom of the creek bed. She reached down to pick up a smooth, black rock that fit in the palm of her hand. Etched hastily on the flat side were two words: THANK YOU.

A chill crept up the back of her neck as she looked around, the familiar feeling of being watched, but all was still in the trees and on the trail. Lowen swiftly climbed up from the creek, grabbed her flip-flops and rushed barefoot down the path to her parked car. She needed to get the hell out of Moon Creek Woods, and fast.

Track 7 - "Heroes" by David Bowie

Noah

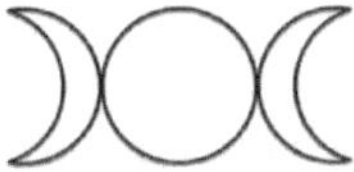

"IT'S MOMENTS LIKE these that make me feel like I'm living in a cheesy '90s teen show. Like, does it get any more cliche than small town Friday night football games?" Noah asked, rolling his eyes.

"What? I can't hear you. Stand up!" Taylor yelled, with more than a hint of annoyance in her voice, as Noah was the only one in the student section sitting on the bleachers.

He wasn't surprised Taylor was decked out in Wolverine gear, complete with black lines painted across her cheeks and shiny pom poms. Even if the display of school spirit made him want to puke, Noah couldn't help but be completely entranced by Taylor's effortless enthusiasm. He watched with admiration as she shook the two black and silver pom poms, yelling loudly as the Wolverine football team made their way across the field.

"Call me a cliche again, Noah, and see what happens," she bent down and whispered, smiling mischievously as she shook a pom

pom into his face.

Noah looked down at his phone, a ball of worry knotting in his stomach. Neither he nor Taylor had seen Lowen at school all day, and she still had not called or texted about the game tonight. It wasn't like her to go so long without communication.

"She'll be here. She has to take photos for the yearbook," Taylor said, as if reading his mind. "I'm sure she just decided to sleep the day away."

Since they were small, Taylor's ability to clock exactly how Noah felt became a superpower she took seriously. One strained look on his face was all she needed to swoop in and save the day. It was a notable act of love and empathy; Taylor came off as bossy and biting to everyone else, never smoothing her rough edges for anyone but him. But sometimes, he just wanted to worry. Or be angry. Or feel sad without the incessant rush to make him feel better.

Noah sighed, taking a swig of whiskey from the flask he hid inside his jacket. With a small whimper, he stood up next to his friend on the bleachers. They cheered, one enthusiastically and one as if it were a chore, as the two teams met at the center of the field.

Sebastian

Sebastian chuckled at the thought of being at a high school football game in the middle of nowhere Indiana. How absurd. The late September sunset blazed vibrantly, and as he stepped out of his car and onto the asphalt of the high school parking lot, he took a moment to admire its brilliance. The bright pink sun was illuminated by the deep purple sky and lavender clouds. He thought about leaning against his car and savoring each second of vivid color until it set beyond the horizon, but the lure of the crowd cheering changed his mind.

"Four dollars," a middle-aged woman sitting behind a plastic table, demanded without looking up as she watched the game streaming on her phone.

"Good evening," he said, looking her up and down as he walked up to the table.

She wore a Wolverines ball cap over her bleached blonde hair, with a sweatshirt proudly declaring "PTA MOM" across the chest.

Obviously, he thought with a smirk.

He watched with amusement as the woman physically startled at Sebastian's presence. She took in the sight of him as they all did, drinking up his height, his smooth skin, his midnight black hair, finally transfixing their attention on his intoxicating emerald-green eyes. He watched as confusion clouded her intrigue. Was he too old to be a high school student? His youthful glow screamed teenager, yet his mannerisms and confidence seemed to belong to someone far older.

"Oh, you must be new to town. I haven't met you, and I've met everybody," the woman said, extending her hand in a girlish manner. "I'm Linda Dillon."

A smile stretched across his face as Linda batted her lashes like a coy schoolgirl.

"I've visited once or twice, but yes, I guess I am fairly new to town." He took her hand into his left palm, covering it intimately with his right. "I'm Sebastian. It's a pleasure to meet you."

Before he could further charm the PTA mom, Sebastian was nearly knocked off balance by something, or rather, someone. A small body bounced off his back like a pinball. Before he could even turn around, the person ran past the ticket counter toward the football field.

"Lowen!!! Watch yourself! Do you have a ticket?" Linda yelled.

"Yeah, I have my press pass! I'm sorry, Mrs. Dillon! I'll be sure to get lots of pictures of Nate," the girl yelled back, zigzagging her way through the crowd with a camera bag swinging from her shoulder.

"I'm so sorry—we have taught these kids to have some manners, but what can you do? By the way, Nate is my son. He's the starting quarterback for the Wolverines this year," Linda bragged, staring intently into Sebastian's eyes.

"I'm sure you are very proud," Sebastian said, handing the woman a five-dollar bill.

He licked his bottom lip slightly, knowing Linda was no match for his charm. He had to stifle the chuckle rising to his throat as she sat frozen in her plastic chair. Reaching over the table, he leaned in closer to the woman, close enough to hear her pulse under the thin skin of her wrist, before pulling a carnival ticket from the thick roll sitting in front of her.

"Thanks for your help this evening," Sebastian said, winking as he turned toward the bright lights of the football field.

"H-h-have a nice time tonight," Linda called after him, as Sebastian strolled slowly toward the stadium lights with his hands in his pockets, whistling a song from long ago.

Lowen

Even though the fall evening chilled the air enough to see one's breath, Lowen's clothes were drenched in sweat by the time she made it down to the football field. After leaving the woods earlier in the afternoon, she went home instead of going to the rest of her classes. The immediate and overwhelming feeling of exhaustion hit her the moment she sat in her driver's seat in the Moon Creek Woods parking lot. The mixture of fear and confusion from seeing the etched rock had dissolved into utter fatigue, causing her to sleep through the entire afternoon and run late to take yearbook pictures of the football game tonight.

Lowen now felt sweat drip down her spine as she bent over to grab her camera from her bag. She struggled to free her arms from her flannel and now stood on the sidelines in a white tank and jeans. She lifted her long hair off her sticky neck and pulled it into a bun before taking a deep breath.

Okay, you've got this, she reminded herself.

Back in reality for the first time since last night at Moon Creek, Lowen sighed with relief. After such strange events, the normalcy of a football game, surrounded by so many people, allowed her to focus on the present moment. Squinting, she adjusted her lens as she crouched down to get some shots of the players on the field. She moved stealthily around the huge players on the sidelines to get the shots she wanted, weaving around their sweaty bodies with confident ease. Once Lowen found an unobstructed view of the stands, she turned around to capture images of the cheerleaders and the crowd. A buzz vibrated in the back pocket of her jeans.

Noah: There u are. Look up and to ur right

Lowen: Oh heyyyy! I see u. I'll come up as soon as I'm done xoxo

Noah: Save me

Lowen: Say cheese

Noah: Absolutely not

Lowen focused her lens, snapping photos of Taylor and Noah and laughing as Noah flipped her off. She then widened her lens to capture the entire student section. Pivoting her body to the right, she shot photographs of parents and community members in the less rowdy section of the stands stretching along the flat, violet horizon. No one noticed her as she spied on them through the safety of her lens, and the peaceful invisibility let Lowen's shoulders relax as she caught their animated reactions to each play.

As she adjusted her focus and snapped a shot, a pair of eyes caught Lowen's attention through her lens, their hue a jaw-dropping vibrant green. The eyes stared directly back at her, as if they had melted away the barrier of her lens. Lowen lowered her camera, taking in the owner of the mesmerizing eyes; he definitely did not go to school with them. He wore a white T-shirt and blue jeans but didn't seem cold sitting in the September breeze. She squirmed as he refused to break his stare, the two of them in a silent standoff. Instead, he smirked. Embarrassed and unsure of what to do, Lowen looked down and tinkered with her camera before turning her back to the stands where the stranger sat. She loved feeling invisible from behind her camera but this stranger had burst the imaginary bubble. Lowen swore she still felt his eyes lingering on her back, like his gaze traced invisible fingertips over her skin. She unconsciously tucked the stray hairs behind her ears, suddenly wishing she had worn something nicer.

Turning her back to the stranger and once again facing the football field, Lowen attempted to regain her focus on the task at hand, although the strange thrill of the man watching her never completely left her mind.

At least this time I know who is watching me, she thought.

As she tried to focus on the game, Lowen was surprised to see the Moon Creek Wolverines playing football like they never had before. The intensity and physical power were thick in the air with pads violently crashing as anguished grunts and intimidating growls were unleashed on the field. The cheers from the crowd seemed to bounce energy infectiously down to the players on the field and then back up to the stands.

A group of seniors would already be getting a keg ready for a bonfire in the Moon Creek woods to celebrate. Lowen simultaneously documented the night with her camera and texted her friends to find out what the post-game plans were. Her anxiety from the Moon Water ritual and the rock she had found thankfully melted away with the familiarity of normal life. After sneaking multiple glances, she realized with disappointment the stranger had disappeared from the stands. Even without the thrill of a new handsome mystery man in town, Lowen looked forward to the warmth of the bonfire, surrounded by people she had known her whole life.

Sebastian

The magenta sun set completely beneath the horizon, and darkness fell once again over Moon Creek. The combination of the chilly night sky, the smell of buttery popcorn and sizzling hot dogs, and the echo of girls laughing while football pads clashed against one another gave off the impression that perhaps tonight, anything was possible.

Sebastian sat silently in the stands, taking in the game and all the players.

Track 8 - "She Lit a Fire" by Lord Huron

Lowen

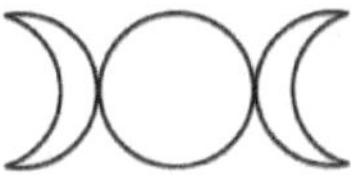

A PALPABLE INTENSITY sizzled in the night air at the bonfire, as if a frenzied energy had followed everyone from the football field into the woods. After all, it wasn't often that the Wolverines won a game. The blazing orange fire roared, the silver kegs foamed, and the music throbbed as the bass bounced off the quiet trees, no one stifling the clamor of celebration. Adults never made a fuss about post-game bonfires; they were a rite of passage and the small community felt safe knowing their neighbors would watch out for each other's kids.

"You made it!" Noah said, extending his long arms to embrace Lowen.

His tall, lean body teetered a bit, just enough for Lowen to clock he had already partaken in the festivities.

"Just in time, I see," Lowen said, smiling weakly as Noah twirled his fingers through her hair. "How many drinks have you had?"

Noah motioned to his lips, pretending to zip them shut as he swayed like a fragile tree branch. Lowen sighed with relief when Taylor came into view, her goddess-like silhouette illuminated from the glow of the fire, as she walked toward them with two red solo cups in her hands. The other, she held by her teeth.

"There you are," Taylor mumbled between the lips pressing the lid of the cup. She handed Lowen and Noah their plastic cups and then wrapped a long arm around Lowen's shoulders in a half-hug greeting. "You had us worried today."

"Yeah, sorry about that," Lowen said, looking down at the cup holding mostly foam. "I guess I just needed to get some more sleep."

"Well, anyway. To the Moon Creek Wolverines," Taylor said, raising her cup.

The three friends pressed the cups of cheap beer together for a cheers.

"And whatever got into them tonight," Noah said, his words slurring. "Such manly men."

In unison, the trio side-eyed a pack of football players as they vivaciously laughed, drank, and pushed each other. Their energy seemed to be increasing, getting louder and more physical as the minutes ticked by.

"The vibe is a lot, isn't it?" Taylor asked, reading Lowen's mind. "Maybe the moon water really worked. You know they chugged their bottles before the game? It's so gross."

"Honestly, all of this is a little too much for me right now and I'm exhausted," Lowen said, gesturing vaguely at their crowded surroundings. "I think I'm going to bounce before any drama starts."

"Not a bad idea," Taylor said quietly.

To her surprise, Taylor didn't put up too much of a fight about her leaving, even though she had just arrived. Perhaps she could tell Lowen had been off since the Moon Water ritual, or maybe she had the same sinking feeling as Lowen. Regardless, she was relieved to not be guilted into staying.

"Take care of him," she whispered to Taylor as they hugged goodbye.

"Always," Taylor whispered back, not taking her eyes off Lowen.

Lowen wrapped her arms around Noah, allowing him to rest his chin on top of her head.

"Be careful," she said.

"Always leaving us," Noah slurred.

Lowen walked past the group of football players as they

reenacted their plays from the night. She could pull out Nate's laughter from the pack; it was the same as when they were ten years old. Nate, even though he was like a stranger now. A stranger who knew all her childhood secrets. The mortifying thought lingered as she zigzagged through the crowd. She knew she could easily slide behind a group of football players whose backs were facing her. From there, it was only a two-minute walk to her car. She looked down at her phone as she walked, creating an excuse not to make eye contact with anyone.

Out of nowhere, Lowen felt the air knocked out of her lungs, her phone flying from her grasp. The strength of the hit knocked her feet off the ground as her body fell backward in the direction of the bonfire. The heat on the back of her shirt rang a sharp warning bell that her body would land close, if not into, the fire. Lowen braced herself for the fall and the pain that would undoubtedly follow.

At the last possible moment, she felt hands reach out, grabbing her forearms to pull her body in the opposite direction. As the hands let go of her arms, they wrapped around the small of her back. Her head and shoulders lunged forward into a hard, broad chest. Both bodies tumbled, hers falling on top of the other person. Lowen couldn't move for a moment. The shock and pain of the hit left her lying frozen on top of a stranger. A stranger who smelled like spring rain and cedar. She inhaled deeply, lifting her head to find she was staring at a face with eemerald green eyes and a mischievous smirk.

As she untangled her arms and legs from his, she noticed the stranger wore a gaudy, yet beautiful necklace with a huge gemstone matching the hue of his twinkling eyes. Lowen and the stranger stared at each other without saying a word for a moment. He subtly cocked his head to the side, as if trying to untangle her thoughts. His face became a puzzle piece she knew somehow fit in the mosaic of her life. The rest of the world faded away to pesky background noise until she heard her name being shouted repeatedly.

"Lowen! Lowen! I'm so sorry," Nate called out, running over to her. "I didn't see you walking past. Are you okay?"

It was only then Lowen realized what had happened a moment ago. Nate, imitating one of his football plays, plowed into her body. The flames had been so close to burning her.

"Don't worry about it. I should have been paying more attention," she mumbled, acutely aware the stranger was still staring at her as they both rushed to stand up.

"I'm so sorry. I guess we all just got a little hyped after the game. Can I at least walk you to your car?" Nate walked slowly toward her as if she were a wild animal he might scare away.

"It's not a big deal," Lowen lied, as she tucked her hands into her hoodie pocket to conceal their tremors.

With her back to the stranger, she could feel the heat of his body close to her skin, someone wore than the fiery depths she almost witnessed. She couldn't bear to turn around and make eye contact with him, so instead she kept her gaze focused on Nate.

"I'll walk her to her car."

The tone left no room for argument.

Lowen turned around to see the stranger standing mere inches from her, with her shoulder blades lining up to his chest. She looked up into his green eyes, but they were intensely fixed on Nate.

"You saved her, man. Thank you," Nate extended his hand to shake the stranger's. "I don't think we've met. I'm Nate."

"Like she said, it's not a big deal," the stranger said, his voice icy despite Nate's typical affable approach.

Lowen and Nate looked at each other, and Nate raised his eyebrow in silent communication.

The stranger merely turned to Lowen and motioned toward the parking lot.

"Are you sure you're good, Lowen?" Nate asked.

"I'll be fine," she said, smiling at Nate reassuringly as she began walking a few steps ahead of the green-eyed man.

A flash of heat surged through her body as she walked away from the woods and her friends, at last alone with the stranger. When they finally distanced themselves from the crowd and the light of the bonfire no longer glowed on their faces, Lowen slowed to walk in step with him.

"I saw you at the game earlier," he said, his voice smooth and piercing in the quiet of the night.

Lowen knew she should be nervous or cautious or *something*, but she couldn't muster any feelings of self-preservation with him.

"I saw you, too," she said, noticing his smirk as she spoke.

She thought back to the warmth of flames so close to her skin. "It was a big deal," she admitted. "What you did back there, that is."

"Are you injured?" he asked, his eyes desperately searching for an answer. "Will you be okay to drive yourself home?"

She squirmed, averting her gaze to the ground and tucking her hands into her hoodie's pockets, unaccustomed to such intense focus. "I'm fine," she said. "Can I ask who you are? I've never seen you before tonight."

"Who are you?" he countered, his smirk widening as if they were playing a game to which he only knew the rules.

"I'm Lowen," she said, pausing to turn to the stranger in the parking lot and extending her hand.

"Sebastian," he said, swallowing hard as he placed his hand in hers.

She held her breath as electricity jolted through every nerve fiber in her body. Time seemed to stand still as they stood, hands clasped, staring at one another. After a moment, Sebastian pulled away, leaving Lowen to regain her balance on the ground that seemed to tilt on its usually sturdy axis. Heat rose to her cheeks as she averted her eyes from his, only to notice the green glow coming from his chest.

"That's quite the necklace," she said, pointing to the large jewel around his neck.

"Thank you," he said, the words floating in the air above them like spirits in the night.

His lips pulled into that smirk again. The one she was sure would make her knees buckle.

Lowen unlocked her door, sliding shakily into the driver's seat. Looking up at Sebastian, she searched for the unspoken parts of their odd conversation. Instead, all she saw were playful eyes and a matching grin.

"I almost forgot," he said, pulling something from the pocket of his jeans. "You dropped your cell phone."

"Thank you," she said, taking the phone from the hand he extended. "I would have been lost without it."

"I get the feeling you're the type of person who is never truly lost," he said, as he carefully closed the car door before stepping back and tucking his hands casually in his pockets.

As Lowen put her car in reverse, she smiled politely, aware he was going to watch her until her car was out of sight. He had saved her. Had been a perfect gentleman. Had even found her phone. But still, something nagged at the back of her brain, tickling like an oncoming sneeze. Halfway home, it hit her.

Thank you.

That knowing grin.

The black rock was etched with two little words.

As if a lightbulb had gone off in her brain, Lowen knew without a doubt it was Sebastian who had left her the message in the creek. Every fiber in her being screamed at her that despite how crazy it sounded, it was the truth. *I get the feeling you're the type of person who is never truly lost.* Now, she had to figure out what game he was playing and more importantly, why.

Track 9 - "This is Me Trying" by Taylor Swift

Wesley

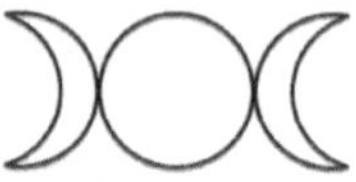

HE DIDN'T REALIZE how much he had missed the crisp air on September mornings; his body had grown so used to the thick Louisiana humidity that his lungs thanked him for this gentle reprieve. The leaves were still green, but the first subtle signs of change were happening at the very tops of the tallest trees. Their leaves had shifted to bright yellow and red hues and fluttered out from high above when the wind gently nudged them. Even as they fell to the earth, dead, they still looked beautiful. Wesley wondered why the annual death of trees was something people found beautiful—even comforting.

Probably because they know they will come back in just a few long, dark months, he thought.

Would people be okay with death if it wasn't so permanent? What if the price to pay for impermanence was that of irreversible change?

After driving twelve hours north, Wesley arrived in Moon Creek in the middle of the night. He booked a hotel room for one week in the center of the small town on Main Street, neatly unpacked his luggage, and tried to get a few hours of sleep. Attempting to relax and distract himself, he opened the local newspaper, hoping the black and white words would lull him to sleep.

"TOURISTS TRAVEL FROM ACROSS THE MIDWEST TO SNEAK A PEEK AT OUR NEW LOCAL CELEBRITIES," he read as he stared at the blurry photograph of an owl staring wide-eyed back at him.

Perfect, he thought to himself as he smiled knowingly. Perhaps an old friend would make a visit after all.

Wesley set his alarm for seven o'clock with a plan. The next morning, he walked to the local general store to buy a pair of binoculars, marveling at the renovated brick building that still stood after all this time. Still in the crisp hours of morning, he parked his black Audi at the Moon Creek woods. Although it looked familiar, so much about the wood's surroundings had changed. The asphalt parking lot itself, along with the wooden signs labeled with trail names and arrows, was all new. But the tall, thin trees, the smell of wet moss and decay, they were the same as they had always been. A sharp heaviness filled his chest, stuffing itself into the places he was allowed to become hollow after all these years. He had the sudden urge to turn around and drive far away from this godforsaken town but instead buried the acidic taste of raw grief deep down for a few more minutes.

Dressed in jeans and a dark green pullover hoodie, Wesley took his binoculars and followed the wooden signs marking Tulip Trail. Cold sweat covered the back of his neck, his hands becoming clammy as memories attempted to overwhelm his conscious mind. He shook away the images, forcing them back to their home within his nightmares. Within minutes, he found the exact spot he had driven twelve hours to visit and silently begged the ghosts he usually shoved into the darkest parts of himself to join him in the woods.

Lowen

"Mom, I'm going for a run," Lowen yelled up the narrow wooden staircase lined with portraits of Lowen, Margot, and her mother in various stages of their shared lives.

"Okay. Make sure you take your phone," her mom shouted from the shower, the surprised relief palpable even with a staircase and shower curtain separating them.

Lowen lied to herself as she tied her shoes that she was going for a jog to get back to normal life, before one of the biggest waves of depression threatened to wash her away a few months ago. But if she were being honest with herself, she would admit that she hoped her run in the Moon Creek woods would allow her to see Sebastian again. If he really had left the rock, perhaps he would be there. The mixture of apprehension and intrigue made her palms sweat, but she made a promise to herself that if she did run into him, she would not let her nerves show. She would be charming and very much the opposite of the frazzled, frozen mess she had been at the bonfire.

There was also the magnetic pull. The one leading her to the bent tree hovering like a wounded soldier in the woods. She tried to shake it off, but something deep within her bone marrow was trying to lure her back there. It tugged at her subconscious, beckoning her to follow the trail and seek answers to questions she didn't even know how to ask.

After a ten-minute mile jog to the woods that burned her lungs, Lowen stood at the entrance of the trail, placing her hands on her knees to catch her breath. The jog had been hard, but had also invigorated her, waking up bones and muscles that had hibernated when the deep blue waves of depression washed over her. With the sun sparkling overhead and the crisp air flooding her lungs, she couldn't help but feel hope rise like a balloon in her chest. After eighteen years of living in the same place with the same people, something bigger—something a little dangerous—seemed as if it were on the horizon. She couldn't put her finger on it, but the woods whispered to her that everything was about to change.

Lowen walked down the familiar path of Tulip Trail, allowing her muscles to relax after pushing them too hard, too fast. She knew each root erupting from the earth, knew each fallen tree trunk to hop over, and knew she could take the trail through the thickly wooded part of the park until it wound down by the creek. From there, Tulip Trail looped back up a steeply graded hill that would bring her back to where she began. She felt her body adjust to being in the woods; the sweat from running in the sunshine was now cold on her face and her eyes adjusted to the shadows from the canopy of leaves blocking out the sunlight.

In the distance, Lowen noticed a hiker walking toward her on the trail, his orange jacket standing out against the dark bark of the tree trunks. Even from a distance, she could see he was a large man and that he was staring directly at her. She looked down at the dusty trail, but every so often looked back up to find him still staring. As they passed each other on the trail, she glanced at his round, ruddy face.

"Good morning," he said, smiling too sweetly.

"Hi," Lowen muttered. *Serial killer*, she thought.

Wow, I can't even pass someone on a trail without thinking they are going to murder me, she thought. When had she become so paranoid? *Since you realized you were a girl,* she thought, smiling sadly to herself.

She chewed on this thought as she walked; men could carelessly walk through the woods without worrying much. Meanwhile, she had to carry her cell phone and mace and only wear one AirPod at a low volume so she could hear a potential threat coming. The constant feeling of being hunted was so pervasive in her daily life, she couldn't quite imagine it any other way. Whether it was walking through the mall with Taylor and feeling men's eyes boring holes through their clothes as they walked by or it was picking up food at the diner and vigilantly checking that no one was following her back to her car, Lowen always knew what it meant to be a girl in this world.

Lowen continued down the trail, allowing her breathing to slow as she followed the mental map she had drawn for herself. She was in the quiet part of the woods, the part where not many people visited. The part she usually loved the most, but that felt almost too secluded right now. The man in orange had left her on edge, the hair on her arms standing in instinctual warning. She wished she had chosen the trail leading to the opposite entrance, the part of the park where most Moon Creek residents parked, where a playground had been built, and that was accessible from one of the busiest roads in town.

Alone with her persistent stream of thoughts, Lowen almost didn't hear the sound of leaves crunching behind her at a distance. When she heard them again, she turned her head but continued forward. The man in the orange jacket was now behind her.

No biggie. I'm sure he just turned around to head back where he came from, she told herself.

Her heartbeat quickened, knocking violently against her sternum. Despite her fear, she didn't want to seem hysterical, so she only looked behind her every so often, turning her head quickly so he wouldn't notice. The man was large, with a round face, reminding Lowen of the moon. His black hair was buzzed short, close to his scalp, and his face was clean-shaven. Despite his size, the man moved with surprising grace and speed, his wide legs gliding over the sticks and rocks on the trail with ease. Was it all in her mind that he was quickly closing the gap between them? Too quickly.

Lowen noticed his short arms swinging faster as he continued following her, his quiet steps pushing to a near-jog.

A hot wave of sweaty fear washed over Lowen's skin. Her heart pounded in her ears as she looked behind her again, the man's arms and legs moving faster than they had been just moments before. How could he possibly move so fast? She wondered if she began to run if the man would run, as well. She imagined a rabbit being torn apart by a coyote, the life leaving its eyes as it finally surrendered the chase.

Lowen swallowed, her throat dry in the thin air, making the decision to continue walking in the direction of the playground. Surely, mothers would be pushing their kids on swings, cars would be driving by, life would be going on as usual. If she could make it there before the man reached her, that was it. She glanced behind her again to see the man was gaining unnatural speed, despite still maintaining a walking gait. She could hear the puffs of his breath now.

Run, she thought. *You have to run.*

Lowen finally understood why rabbits stood frozen in fear. As much as she demanded her legs move faster, she was frozen in the quiet, unassuming movement of walking, as if her body believed that if she continued to act like nothing was wrong, nothing would be wrong. But it was all wrong. She glanced over her shoulder again, the man so close now she could see plainly the violent resolve reflecting off his black eyes, as if she were nothing more than an ant to squash.

As panic crept into her throat, seizing her airway, Lowen noticed the shape of a person standing ahead. Only his back was visible to her, but his jeans and green hoodie were like a lighthouse beckoning to her. With binoculars held to his eyes and his head tipped back, the man stared up into the tall trees, a quiet calm floating around him like a mirage in the desert. It took everything in Lowen not to scream out to him, to rip through his peaceful silence like a chainsaw.

)))●(((

Wesley

Wesley lowered his binoculars as the serene woods erupted into chaos. Her labored breaths sucked the air out from between the tree trunks. Her thundering heartbeat drowned out the gentle trickle of the water flowing between the rocks. The scent of her fear, wild and animalistic, overpowered the wet leaves and decaying wood. Her body was only a few feet from his when their eyes finally met. Huge brown eyes locked with his, communicating panic. For a moment, he couldn't move, couldn't breathe. It was her.

A flash of orange over her left shoulder forced Wesley to look away from her. A large man stalked toward them, and even from the distance separating them, Wesley could see his black pupils overshadowing any other color of his eyes. He flashed the man a warning glance, allowing his eyes to glow golden for an almost imperceptible moment, before directing his attention back to the girl.

"Babe," Wesley said, casually extending the arm holding the binoculars toward her. "Come see what I found."

He wrapped his other arm around her waist, guiding her body in front of him to block her from the man plowing toward them. Their bodies were so close now that he could see her pulse racing in the large blue vein running down the side of her neck, the blood moving wildly like a raging river in a storm. Wesley closed his eyes, grinding his teeth together until he could think clearly again, shaking away the faint scent of strawberry drifting from her hair.

"Hold the binoculars to your eyes," he whispered. "I've got you."

Her hands shook violently as she reached out for the binoculars, her soft fingertips grazing his skin.

"How was your walk?" he asked, his cheerful voice a little too loud.

"Oh, you know," Lowen answered, imitating his jovial tone.

Wesley listened, straining to hear the man in the orange jacket's footsteps padding on the forest floor, but only the girl's thundering heartbeat, sloshing and irregular as it attempted to calm its beats, filled his ears.

"Is he gone?" she whispered, the binoculars still against her eyes.

Wesley glanced behind them.

"He turned around and headed back in the other direction," he whispered in her ear.

She remained frozen, her back inches from his chest, staring up at the tallest limbs of the tree.

"He's gone," Wesley said, touching her elbows as he gently guided her to turn around.

"Are you okay?" he asked, awkwardly stepping back several paces and tucking his hands into the pocket of his green hoodie.

"Um, yeah. Thanks," she said, tucking a strand of brunette hair behind her ear as she looked down at the ground.

Wesley paused awkwardly, unable to find the words he had rehearsed a million times over. How was he, a mere stranger in the woods, going to tell her who she was and that she was in danger? He couldn't do it. Not yet, anyway.

"Do you need me to walk you somewhere?" he asked, before adding. "I don't mind."

"No, that's okay," she said, kicking the dirt with the toe of her sneaker. "I'll call my friend."

She doesn't want my help.

He always wondered what it would be like to meet her. If something magical would happen, as the ancient spell had suggested.

I guess not, he thought.

"Um, thanks again," she said, turning away as if the encounter bore no significance whatsoever.

"No problem," he said, his voice trailing away as she took her cell phone from her pocket and dialed a number.

Wesley didn't know what else to say. He knew the man in the orange jacket would not return after Wesley had shown who he was with a quick flash of his eyes. He knew she was safe as she slowly walked back down the trail, her head bent down to look at her phone. Isn't this why he had come all the way back here to begin with? Wasn't her safety enough?

It is enough, he thought to himself. *It has to be.*

The curious thing about housing both a heart and a mind

though, was that although Wesley knew he had done enough by simply keeping the girl protected and returning to the shadows, his heart screamed for him to want more. But after such a long time of being alone, he didn't quite know how to go about getting something he wanted, so instead, he watched her walk away.

Lowen

Lowen let the warmth of the sun thaw the chill that had traveled all the way to her bones as she sat on a bench next to a mother watching her son go down the slide. She couldn't help but glance into the shadowy woods, not only to make sure the man in the orange jacket wasn't coming for her, but also to get another glimpse of the bird-watcher who saved her. Something about him seemed so familiar. She wondered if she should call the police but didn't really have any proof she was in actual danger. Was the man really chasing her? Or was it all in her head?

"Saved by two hot strangers in less than forty-eight hours? Do tell and give me tips and tricks to becoming a fellow damsel in distress."

Noah smiled as he rolled down his window all the way, his familiar face almost causing Lowen to burst into tears. He stopped his car in front of her, reaching over to swing open the passenger side door for her, but despite him lightening the mood, Lowen couldn't shake the feeling she was being watched from the woods as they pulled away.

Track 10 - "Pretty Pimpin" by Kurt Vile

Sebastian

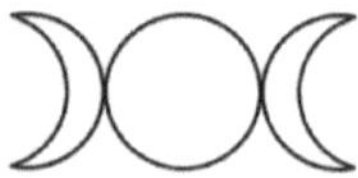

SEBASTIAN CASUALLY STRETCHED his body like a cat upon the buttery leather couch in his newly rented house. It had only taken him one weekend to find a home in Moon Creek, buy furniture, and pay good money for people to take care of the details. He rented this particular house for three reasons: the massive stone fireplace in the expansive living room, the newly renovated bathroom with excellent lighting, and the fact that the house sat at the very border of town, quite a distance from the main roads and other houses. He needed his privacy, and the proximity to her would prove to be invaluable.

Kicking up his boots onto the glass coffee table, he reached for his phone to turn up the volume on the classical music streaming through multiple hidden speakers in the house. Sebastian tilted head against the back of the couch, closed his eyes, and smiled. Not only did he meet her, he "saved" her. He had waited so patiently for the right moment at the bonfire that he promised himself a special treat afterward if everything went according to plan. Or if everything went sideways. He deserved a reward either way.

How easy it was to manipulate their meet-cute, he as the hero, she as the damsel in distress. He smirked, remembering how he had become a tangled knot of limbs on the ground with her.

After so much time searching for her, imagining her, needing her to break that damned spell, Sebastian found himself surprised by her tangibility. Her humanness. He had regarded her as a thing. A simple means to an end. But now, hearing her raspy voice, gazing into her eyes that flashed with stubbornness and untapped strength, he realized she was so much more.

Whoever she had been bound to be, he was going to be stuck with her, so to be pleasantly surprised by Lowen's beauty and her complexity was an exhilarating bonus.

Sebastian opened his phone and found LOWEN in his contacts. After she had left the bonfire, Sebastian gently nudged the information he needed, including Lowen's phone number, from the boy who almost knocked her into the flames. What was his name again? Nate? Ah, yes, Nathaniel. So trusting to give a stranger someone else's number.

And with that, Sebastian texted simply, but with careful

consideration:

"Hey."

He closed the screen on his phone and remembered the fleeting feeling of *something* when he talked to her that night. He had felt off balance, as if the ground had tilted slightly underneath him. It had been a very long time since a person had made him feel that way. Sebastian stood up and paced the floor of the living room before pouring a glass of wine and sipping it until he felt like himself again: balanced, strong, alone, and superior to, well, everyone.

Track 11 - "These Are My Friends" by lovelytheband

Lowen

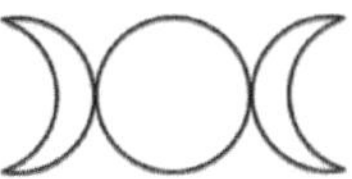

LOWEN SAT IN her empty Lit Classics class on Monday morning, intrusive thoughts buzzing in and out of her ears so quickly that she hardly had time to even make sense of them. The man in orange. The bent tree. The black rock in the creek. The flash of light during the Moon Water Ritual. Sebastian's presence. The man with sandy blond hair she swore she had met before. Her haunting dreams.

The bell hadn't yet rung and her classmates still fluttered in the hallways like butterflies, refusing to be pinned down to their chairs until absolutely necessary. Lowen felt disconnected from their laughter; exhaustion and darkness seemingly weighing down her muscles and bones. Nothing had felt right since the Moon Water Ritual.

How is it that not one, but two, perfect strangers happened to help me in less than forty-eight hours? she wondered.

Fear and intrigue pricked her skin until goosebumps formed.

She wanted desperately to share her thoughts with Taylor and Noah, but she wasn't sure she could explain to them what was happening. Nothing made sense to her, only that the puzzle pieces were laid out on the table in a jumble, and she needed to find the rest and snap them into place to see the whole picture. The Moon Water Ritual, a midnight black corner piece. The vivid dream, a blindingly bright centerpiece. Sebastian, a dazzling green piece with a razor-sharp edge. The menacing man in the woods, orange and flat. Each piece fit together in a mysterious puzzle, yet so many were still missing. And then there was the piece containing Lowen, with its irregular edges and round notches allowing it to fit into all the others. When she thought back to the many times in her life when she didn't feel whole or didn't feel like she knew who she was, she now felt like those answers were within her grasp. She was connected to all of this.

Lowen's phone vibrated in her pocket, shaking her from her thoughts.

Taylor: my house tonight for a lil witchy fun

Noah: I'm in

Taylor: this one's for u, Lowen. You better get your bony ass over by 8pm.

Lowen smiled to herself as she typed, "k". Taylor had dabbled in witchcraft after following some accounts on TikTok. Within weeks, the three best friends were burning sage and mixing oils in Taylor's expansive bedroom, with its enormous four-poster bed draped with sheer cream curtains and faux fur rugs, regularly. Nothing, not one supernatural thing, had ever come from it, but it beat everyone staring at their phones when they hung out. Instead, it reminded the trio of the unrestrained fun they had back when their imaginations actually worked. The three found themselves more often than not sitting cross-legged on Taylor's bedroom floor while chanting words that made no sense and giggling as they divulged ridiculous manifestations for their futures by the glow of candlelight.

"Good morning," Dr. Clarke announced, taking his seat atop his desk as he pushed his tortoise-shelled frames further up his nose.

As Lowen tucked her cell phone back into her bookbag, she realized the new teacher was beginning to grow on her. Sure, he dressed like a teenager and his sandy blond hair desperately needed a trim, but he was enthusiastic and seemed genuinely excited to teach. With the rest of her senior year schedule consisting of blow-off classes, Lit Classics was the one she actually looked forward to.

"Today, we are going to start a little research before we dive into our novel, *The Alchemist,* and that's by finding out a bit more about some real-life supposed alchemists. First, let's go over the basics we discussed last week. Give me one goal of alchemy."

"To turn a base metal like lead into gold or silver by using the Philosopher's Stone," a girl near the back of the class called out.

"Very good. What else?"

"To find or create the Elixir of Life to provide immortality or cure diseases," Lowen offered.

"A potion for immortality. Who would take it?" Dr. Clarke asked with a grin.

He then hopped off his desk and walked over to the chalkboard and began writing a list of names from a sheet of paper in his hand.

Nicolas Flamel (15th century)
Isaac Newton (1642–1727)
Count of St. Germain (d. 1784)
Johann Christoph von Wöllner (1732–1800)

"Now, here's the deal. You get to choose one of the names from this list. You have today in class and tonight at home to do your research. Be prepared to discuss your findings tomorrow. Here is a list of prompts to help guide you during your research phase."

While Dr. Clarke passed out papers, Lowen looked at the list of names.

Count of St Germain it is, she thought.

Grabbing her MacBook from her book bag, she lifted the screen tiredly. Why was she so worn out? It felt as if all the energy had been sucked from her bones. After a quick login, she typed "Count of Saint Germain" into Google, scrolling past Wikipedia and clicking on the next link titled, "The Immortal Counte de St. Germain".

Interesting.

"Is it possible for a man to live forever? According to many, Count de Saint-Germain did just that. Supposed alchemist, Saint-Germain was rumored to be born in the late 1600s and has popped up throughout history, affiliating himself with some of the most historic figures, including Catherine the Great and King Louis XV."

Just as she settled a little deeper into her seat and let the world around her fade, the bell rang to announce class had ended. Packing up her things, she smiled awkwardly at Dr. Clark, leaving the quiet room for the explosion of high school chaos in the hallway. As soon as she rounded the corner, Noah grabbed her wrist, and Taylor flashed her a perfect, yet mischievous grin. Both had their backpacks slung over the shoulders and jackets in their arms.

"Skip day!" Noah blurted out, a little too loudly, the scent of vodka lingering in the air.

"I can't skip. I missed Friday," Lowen reminded him.

"Come on, I'll forge an early dismissal note for you. We have witchy plans, and I'm painfully bored with this place," Taylor whined as she leaned against her locker, her long, black hair cascading down her slender back like a Disney princess.

Lowen knew she didn't stand a chance against the united front, their eyes whispering, "You know you want to." A fake note was signed and delivered to the front office before the next bell could ring, and the three friends were blessed by the morning sun tickling their skin and the smell of unrestricted freedom before third period even started. A skip day was exactly what she needed, she thought to herself, as she ran with her friends through the student parking lot before someone caught them. Feeling lighter than she had in days, Lowen sat in the backseat of Taylor's Jeep with a goofy smile stretched across her lips as she reached for her phone from the front pocket of her bag.

Unknown number: "Hey."

"Caught you! No phones today, Lowen. You know they interfere with the mystic realm," Taylor said, her catlike brown eyes staring playfully at her from the rearview mirror.

Lowen heard Noah snort from the passenger seat, his head leaning against the window as if he were about to take a nap. She rolled her eyes for Taylor to see, but clicked off her phone screen, tossing it onto the seat next to her. She didn't really want to look at it, anyway. The day, sunny and blue, was just too gorgeous to stare at any more screens, so she closed her eyes while letting the breeze tousle her hair as Taylor tore down Main Street, finally opening them again when the Jeep turned into the parking lot of a tiny blue house that had been converted into a crystal shop.

"Supply time, kids!" Taylor sang, opening her door and sliding out before Lowen and Noah had a chance to unbuckle their seatbelts.

The inside of the small shop was deliciously dark and smelled of patchouli incense. The shopkeeper, a man in his late forties, quietly greeted them without looking up from the book he was reading behind the counter.

"We need rosemary, lavender oil, a white candle, and some more sage sticks," Taylor ordered as she began walking in the direction of a shelf holding dried herbs and flowers in glass jars and plastic baggies.

As she went on the hunt for supplies, Lowen and Noah pretended to help, but huddled next to a table displaying a wide array of colorful crystals, some towers, others no larger than pebbles.

"Are you doing okay?" Noah asked, his dilated pupils the telltale sign that the alcohol was already taking hold.

Lowen smiled sadly because despite, or maybe because of his own personal demons, Noah always had a sixth sense when it came to her inner turmoil. Here he was, asking her how she was doing while clearly something was going on with him. She hadn't seen him this bad ever. But she also knew better than to push before he was ready. After all, she hadn't been great these past few months, either, and Noah had never confronted her. Lowen weighed how she should answer his question, deciding after a momentary pause to be completely honest, hoping that Noah would feel comfortable doing the same.

"Is it weird that I feel like all of this stuff was supposed to happen? Like, I feel like I'm on a train where the tracks were already built, so I'm supposed to just ride it out to some unknown destination," Lowen said.

"I'm pretty sure Taylor is on the hunt for answers today," Noah said, nodding toward Taylor as she placed herbs in a little basket to take to the counter for checkout. "We've been talking about all of the weird shit that has gone down since the Moon Water ritual and she really thinks she can figure it out."

"As long as there is food, she can do whatever she wants," Lowen said, as she pretended to inspect a heavy rose quartz, relieved her friends understood more than she gave them credit for. As her mind relaxed and her body slowed from its perpetual state of fight or flight, her stomach growled, reminding Lowen of how little she had eaten in the past few days.

"Pizza or hamburgers?" Taylor asked, smiling at Lowen as if she could read her mind while sliding her card through the reader.

"Do you want us to chip in?" Noah asked.

"Are you crazy?" Taylor responded, raising her eyebrows as if she were asking for a challenge. "You know my parents won't even notice. So, what will it be? Pizza or hamburgers?"

The trio piled back into Taylor's Jeep, making their way through town to her massive estate to eat junk food, play around with magic, and maybe find answers to the weird happenings haunting Moon Creek.

Track 12 - "Salem" by Bon Iver

Taylor

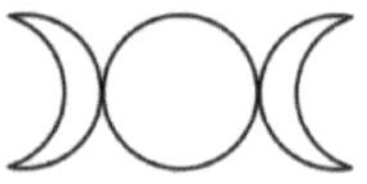

TAYLOR OPENED THE door to her bedroom, a stupidly large room obnoxiously furnished and decorated for a princess and watched wistfully as her two best friends made themselves at home. A quiet blanket of peace swept over her body, knowing the two of them would always be by her side. The rush of sentimentality made her roll her eyes, even as salty tears started to sting. She leaned against the door frame and let her mind wander as Noah and Lowen bantered back and forth, completely unaware of the tsunami of emotions crashing over her.

Taylor Bell envisioned herself as the soup in the children's story, "Too Many Babas", except the babas were the gods who created her and they never actually fixed the soup at the end. One god sprinkled too much of this ingredient, another god was too stingy with that one. Combined, she was a messy creation: a fun, little experiment to try on an otherwise boring day of being gods. She didn't realize this until kindergarten when all of a sudden, she was outside of the comfort of her mother's arms and father's protection and forced to become another bobbing head in a sea of five-year-olds within the archaic confines of the Moon Creek Public School System. Not white enough to hang with the white kids, not black enough to hang with the black kids. Too rich, too entitled, too loud, too smart. Not approachable enough, too intimidating.

That first day of kindergarten was hell. Taylor's world spun around her as she recognized she was the only biracial child in her very small, very homogenous town. Throughout her life, she always looked back to that day as when her hard shell began to form. Like a turtle, she formed a spiky, hard, indifferent exterior, keeping the world away from her fragile interior.

The second day of kindergarten was heaven because those gods must have felt bad, so they decided to throw her a lifeline—or two. But it didn't start out that way. After pretending to be sick to her parents, but failing to will a fever into existence, Taylor reluctantly walked into her classroom and sat down stiffly at her desk with her chin high, unable to look anyone in the eye, nevertheless acutely aware she would never sink to put her head down on her desk. Even at five, she won every game she played.

Taylor watched as her classmates laughed and screamed and ran around the room, completely oblivious to her unfolding identity crisis. A boy with white-blond hair and a crusty nose that seemed to constantly drip ran toward her and stopped at her desk, looking at her before wiping his nose with his sticky fingers that looked like they hadn't been washed in weeks.

"Ewwww," he screamed as he ran away, completely oblivious to the irony of his statement.

A group of rambunctious kids in the back of the room giggled, apparently in on the boy's antics. Taylor, paralyzed with embarrassment and rage, stood up quickly to go to the restroom, but didn't make it far before she vomited in the hallway. She straightened her spine to stare at the splattered pool of her undigested waffles and orange juice when she heard a small voice behind her.

"Are you okay?" a girl asked.

Taylor turned around to see an awkward, birdlike girl with long brown hair walking slowly toward her. Even at five years old, Taylor saw the kindness and empathy settling deep into the girl's brown eyes.

"I'm Lowen," the girl said quietly, looking down awkwardly at the tiled floor of the seemingly infinite fluorescent-lit hallway.

"I'm Taylor."

"Want to be friends?" Lowen bit her lower lip as she asked, keeping her eyes fixed on her shoes.

"Yes," Taylor choked out around the lump forming in her throat.

The two girls smiled at each other for the first time, before another small voice came from the open doorway of their chaotic classroom.

"Today is gross," a dark-haired boy with blue eyes said, looking at the two girls as if he were making a promise to them. Scrunching up his nose, he studied Taylor's puke splattered on the floor before introducing himself. "I'm Noah."

Breaking the trio's unspoken spell, their teacher appeared in the empty hall, briefly surveying the mess on the floor. To the woman's credit, she barely batted an eyelash when she saw it. Bodily fluids were a common workplace hazard for a kindergarten teacher.

"We will call the janitor to clean this up. Come on now, back to the classroom, you three," she said, opening her arms like a mother hen scooping up her chicks.

It was the first time, but certainly not the last, Lowen, Taylor, and Noah would be called "You Three". A crash hurried their teacher back into the chaotic classroom ahead of them, leaving a slight breeze and the faint scent of her floral perfume in her wake. The trio looked at each other for a moment.

Despite the horrendous beginning, the bullying and the vomit, something sweet and fresh rose to the surface of Taylor's little belly: happiness. She'd made friends.

"Taylor. Earth to Taylor! What is this spell supposed to do?" Lowen asked as she sat cross-legged on Taylor's cream faux fur rug, still birdlike in so many ways, yet so much stronger and braver than she once was. She was organizing her lunch in front of her: a cheeseburger in the center, fries neatly placed on a napkin to the left, and her diet Coke to her right.

"I will never get over how you have to organize your food," Noah said, as he laid on his stomach at an angle across Taylor's massive bed, his chin propped up above crossed fingers.

"Laugh all you want, but if you make it pretty, it feels healthier going down," Lowen explained sarcastically.

"We are doing a spell to find out what people are thinking," Taylor explained, allowing herself to gently come back to reality.

"Will this work instantaneously or do we have to be in front of the person?" Lowen asked earnestly, her eyebrows pinching together.

Man, one of those new, hot strangers must have really done a number on her, Taylor thought, smirking to herself.

The Lowen of two weeks ago would have rolled her eyes and made little jabs, but this Lowen was serious, her eyes wide and focused on Taylor's face.

"I'm not really sure about the technicalities, but let's find out."

Taylor walked past the four-poster bed where Noah was sprawled and opened a massive oak armoire where she kept her stash of witchcraft materials, along with medals and trophies from tennis, spelling bees, cheerleading, and Speech and Debate. As she scrolled on her phone to peruse the list of ingredients, she plucked what she needed from the drawers reeking of incense and oils and placed them in a pile on the floor next to Lowen.

"Okay, this actually looks really simple," Taylor explained. "We just need to grab a strip of paper and each write the following intention: 'I wish that what this person thinks of me will be revealed in my dreams', fold the rosemary into the paper, and set fire to it with a white candle. Then we each rub a dab of the lavender oil on our temples before we go to sleep, and the person's thoughts should come to us in a dream tonight."

"This sounds like a whole lot more fun and less bloody than the whole Moon Water Death ritual," Lowen joked, popping a fry into her mouth.

"But which one of Taylor's man-whores will she choose?" Noah joked.

"Mmmmm, so many yummy choices," Taylor threw right back.

The three friends continued eating and laughing, cleaned up, and wrote on their strips of paper. Taylor noticed how much her two friends concentrated on the silly spell. It made her heart ache and swell simultaneously: she loved them both so much and wanted to give them anything they wished for, but knew they were now at the age where they couldn't be everything to each other.

They spent the rest of the day hanging out in Taylor's bedroom, just like the old days when Noah needed to get away from his home and his father, and when Lowen would tell them what was going on in her troubled mind. Tonight felt lighter than those times, with Lowen researching the Count of St. Germain while Taylor and Noah took turns applying each other's makeup.

When Taylor's parents came home after work, they insisted Lowen and Noah stay for dinner and ordered takeout from the most expensive restaurant in town. Stuffed full of pasta, Creme Brulé and warm, nostalgic feelings, Taylor hugged her friends goodbye and watched as Noah and Lowen stepped out into the cool autumn evening. The sun was already setting, but both friends only lived a less-than-ten-minute walk from her. She watched as Noah turned in the direction to walk Lowen home and smiled as they interlocked their fingers and swung their arms playfully, their sneakers scuffing against the pavement. Their voices chirped into the quiet night, probably chatting about the blissful nothingness of music, pop culture, and high school drama. Taylor closed her door and smiled at the thought of the little family she found that day in kindergarten, knowing in her heart she would kill for them.

Track 13 - "Moon Song" by Phoebe Bridgers

Wesley

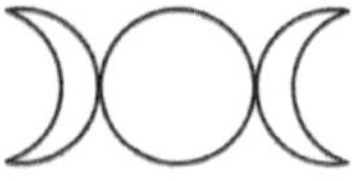

WESLEY DROVE BACK to his hotel, frustration simmering in his gut, after his first interaction with the girl—the girl the prophecy told him he would one day meet if the spell was ever broken. He tried to cut himself some slack; he didn't get out much. Still, there was no denying she didn't want anything to do with him, nor did she want his help. He was fine with not being well-liked, but he did need her to trust him.

Wesley knew without a doubt the stranger in the woods would have killed her if he hadn't been there. He knew it when the morning rays kissed his skin in his kitchen in New Orleans. Whoever she was, she would be in danger. What he had not expected was how quickly and ruthlessly they had come for her. A hitman in the middle of the day? It was bold, reckless. He knew now how serious their threats had been.

Using the old skeleton key the hotel clerk had given him to enter his room, Wesley sat down on a plush chair next to a small table and landline phone and exhaled the worry and disappointment he had been holding in his lungs. As his eyes adjusted from the bright sun, he ran his fingers through his sand-colored hair. Nothing else mattered but keeping her safe. He had to find her; it wouldn't be hard as Moon Creek wasn't large and she didn't even know she was in danger, so it wasn't like she'd be in hiding. Still, he found himself annoyed with a buzzing thought hovering like a pesky gnat: she hadn't seemed to like him. Why did he care? He knew it didn't really matter, but he couldn't help but let the fleeting human feeling of inadequacy haunt him for a moment.

With the single truth that nothing else mattered but keeping her safe, he pulled out his phone from his pocket and googled "Moon Creek Realtors", clicking on the first name to appear: Emily Lawrence. Silently and solemnly, he said goodbye to his life in New Orleans. He would give anything to be back in his beautifully renovated Greek revival style house, but instead he would have to stay here, Moon Creek, where the ghosts of his past would surely haunt him.

Track 14 - "Research" by Big Sean

Lowen

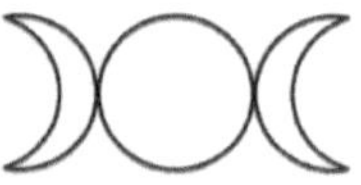

LOWEN WOKE UP feeling as if her eyelids were made of sandpaper. Despite falling asleep almost immediately after applying the lavender oil thanks to Taylor's reminder text, Lowen's mind hovered like a rain cloud above her bed. Her brain consciously worked above water, but her body lay just below the surface, unable to break through. She expected, or at least foolishly hoped, that Taylor's spell would work and she would dream about Sebastian. She was dying to know what was going on behind those emerald eyes. She knew they held a story, one in which Lowen felt she played a part. Instead, she only dreamt of her own haunted imaginings.

She lay paralyzed in the same spot on the soft brown trail in the Moon Creek woods. It was a cool night, and the leaves looked silver as they blew in the breeze. The scent of the earth rotting beneath her rooted her to reality, although her mind raced with irrational fear. The soft trickle of creek moving around the rocks steadied her ragged breaths. The quiet woods eased her panic, allowing her to blink and clear her blurred vision.

And then she saw him. His arm extended down, lifting her from the safety of her soft patch of earth. His eyes weren't their usual brilliant green but instead glowed a menacing black. Despite their darkness, they glittered with excitement. His signature smirk let her know he was there for her.

"Don't be frightened," Sebastian whispered, caressing her cheek with his long fingers. "I'll explain everything."

His voice sounded far away, as if she were listening to him from underwater. She reached her arm out to him, but when she glanced at it, she didn't recognize its skin or muscles, nor the hands, or fingers protruding from her body.

Lowen sat up, her sweat-soaked pajamas stuck to her clammy skin, and checked her phone: 7:17am. Her alarm wouldn't go off for another thirteen minutes, but the image of Sebastian's black eyes and the arm that couldn't belong to her shook her so badly she decided to shower and get ready for school a little early. With the extra time, Lowen decided to blow-dry her hair and wear something besides her standard sweatpants and T-shirt uniform. Attempting to distract herself from the dream, she picked out an outfit and applied a minimal amount of makeup.

"Wow, you look fantastic!" her mom said from the kitchen counter where she poured a cup of coffee.

"Thanks, Mom. What do they say? Dress how you feel... or in my case, the direct opposite of how you feel."

"That good, huh?"

Concern lined her mother's face, and for a moment Lowen regretted saying anything at all.

"Just a rough night of sleep," Lowen explained, taking the coffee pot from her mother's hand and pouring a mug for herself.

"Before I forget, I am showing a few properties to a new client this afternoon. If you want to, we could meet for an early dinner at the Daybreak Diner after you pick up Margot."

"That sounds really nice, Mom. I feel like I've barely seen you the past few weeks."

It hit Lowen then how much she needed her mom following the Moon Water ritual. She would normally tell her everything, but for some reason, a voice in the back of Lowen's mind whispered for her to keep her secrets. She couldn't take her mom's worry, especially after she had worked so hard to get back to a healthy mental state.

"It's a date then. I'll see you two after school. Don't forget to wake up Margot soon."

))●((

Forty minutes and one grumpy middle schooler dropped off later, Lowen sat in her Lit Classics class alone, enjoying the morning sun beaming through the windows as the school hallways began to crowd.

"Hey, Lowen. You're early today," Dr. Clarke said, dropping his leather bag in the corner behind his desk.

"Yeah, I'm just finishing up my research on the Count of Saint Germain."

"Fascinating stuff, huh?"

"Definitely," Lowen mumbled.

She found herself staring at an assortment of St. Germain drawings, portraits, and sculptures she had dug up online and dragged onto one single document. None seemed to really depict the same person, although all created a thin, tall man with dark hair. Something about a specific portrait made the hair on the back of her neck stand up. It felt... familiar. She shook away the feeling when the bell rang, once again bringing her back to reality. The classroom had filled with students without her even noticing. How long had she been staring at that portrait?

"Who wants to share their research first?" Dr. Clarke asked, as students shuffled uncomfortably in their seats.

Lowen raised her hand before she could chicken out. She hated public speaking, but she had learned that her anxiety got the best of her the longer she waited, so she always wanted to rip the Band-Aid off and get things like this over with first.

"This is how this is going to work. Give us your five best, most important facts about your alchemist of choice," Dr. Clarke explained, taking a sip of coffee from the same travel mug he used every single day.

Lowen stood, wiping her sweaty hands on her jeans as she made her way to the front of the classroom. On one notecard, she had squeezed all the information she needed to say. With her head bent to read the small letters, Lowen spoke.

"Okay, here goes. The alchemist I chose was the Count of St. Germain. He was supposedly born a prince of Transylvania in approximately 1691, but his identity was kept a secret to protect him from enemies after his older brother died."

She looked up at her quiet classmates. A few looked at her, but most were either looking at their cell phones or frantically searching on their own computers for last minute research. Lowen cleared her throat before continuing.

"St. Germain entertained King Louis XV and the French court with his skills in music, particularly the violin, his knowledge of history and languages, but mostly his wild tales of being 300 years old, turning tarnished gems into priceless gemstones, knowing the secret to eternal life, and being able to master nature. He always talked throughout dinners, and never ate himself, but asked for a specific chalice from which he drank during these parties.

"He went on secret missions for France and told King Louis XVI and Marie Antionette that they would one day see his people turn on him. This turned out to be true with the French Revolution, and St. Germain retreated to Russia. There, he helped place Catherine the Great on the throne.

"Finally, St Germain was said to have died in 1784, but has been seen since under various identities, even as recently as the 1970s. No one knows for sure, but even the philosopher Voltaire was quoted as saying that St. Germain is 'a man who never dies, and who knows everything.'"

The room was silent when Lowen finished reading from her notecard. She was fairly certain no one had heard a thing she said, as if she were a ghost hovering invisibly in front of a green chalkboard.

"Thanks, Lowen," Dr. Clarke said, his booming voice rousing some students from their morning naps. "So, how does this make you feel about alchemy?"

"I'm still skeptical but after this research, I'm willing to be a little more open-minded," Lowen admitted, wiping the sweat from her hands onto her pants.

"That's all we ask for here: an open mind."

Track 15 - "All the Pretty Girls" by KALEO

Lowen

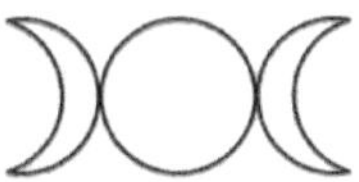

"DID YOU SKIP your last class?" Margot asked as her whole body, backpack, and lunchbox spilled into the passenger-side seat. "You're never here to pick me up this early."

"No, dummy. I was just so ready to get out of there and see your beautiful face," Lowen said, squeezing her sister's cheeks until they turned a vibrant shade of crimson.

"Sttttooooopppp!" Margot yelled, but her smile told Lowen she loved the attention.

"Off to an early dinner with Mom. You hungry?"

"Always!"

After surveying the parking lot in the Daybreak Diner's parking lot and not seeing their mother's car, Lowen gathered that she and Margot had arrived first.

"Three, please," she said to the hostess inside the restaurant lit with retro neon signs and chipper fifties songs pumping from the jukebox.

As the sisters perused their plastic menus, Lowen heard the bell attached to the door jingle and looked up. Her mom's voice floated over the noise of the restaurant, light and feminine and obnoxiously happy. Lowen noticed she walked in front of a man, with her head turned toward him so she could not see where she was going, all while her hands moved quickly and dramatically. It was just like her mother to invite her new client to dinner; she always trusted and gave so quickly, a flaw Lowen loved and hated. Unlike Lowen, she seemed to be innately wired to lead with an open heart, which allowed so much beauty and friendship to find her. But Lowen watched her mom get hurt time and time again by women who pretended to be her friends and by men who pretended to care for her.

As her mother and the man approached the booth, a wave of nervous sweat covered Lowen's body. Instead of a green hoodie and jeans, he wore a gray suit over a white button-up, but his disheveled sandy blond hair and liquid amber eyes were instantly recognizable. When their eyes met, Lowen couldn't help but notice the way his eyebrows pinched, revealing two creased lines between his eyes, forcing her to avert her eyes in embarrassment.

"Hi, girls," Lowen's mom said, her voice a little too chipper. "This is my new client, Wesley Edwards. We've spent the whole afternoon looking at properties so I figured he has worked up an appetite, too. Wesley, these are my girls: Lowen and Margot."

Lowen didn't know what to do, especially after the face he just made, so she did what any normal girl would do: she looked down at her phone and pretended to text.

Wesley

He had spent all day with her mother and had not even known it. So much for their magical connection, a spell binding them to one another. One would assume he would feel something, anything, being so close to her bloodline. But alas, it seemed to Wesley that nothing about the magic connecting him to Lowen was as remarkable as he had envisioned.

His mind rolled over what he had learned, albeit not knowing it was *her,* during his afternoon with Emily. Lowen was a senior in high school, and she planned to go to college on the West Coast. She was raised by a single mom, and was responsible, caring, and completely normal, according to her mother. And good. He could tell this much just based on the time he had spent with the person who had raised her. Although it relieved him on some level to know she was well-adjusted, he couldn't help the weight of a rain-soaked storm cloud resting on his shoulders. She had no idea what was ahead of her. He noticed he was looking directly at her as his mind wandered momentarily and caught her staring back, her mouth pinched as if she were holding back some very choice words. Had the sad frustration on his own face been noticeable?

"Nice to meet you, Wesley! How old are you? You look too young to buy a house. Are you a trust fund baby or something?" Margot blurted out.

"Margot! You can't just ask people those things!" Emily admonished before sitting next to her youngest daughter and smiling broadly at Lowen as she nodded for Wesley to sit next to her.

"It's no problem, really. I'm twenty-two years old. I just graduated from Tulane and got a tech job based out of Indiana," Wesley said, gently answering Margot's rapid firestorm of questions with a smile he couldn't help. She reminded him so much of his little sisters. "And yes, my parents are helping me buy this house."

His voice cracked at the mention of his family, and all at once, the all-too-familiar wave of grief knocked the air from his lungs. Clearing his throat, he attempted to regain his composure, searching everywhere in the diner for something to stop him from drowning.

He turned his head to catch Lowen's brown eyes studying him with concern.

"Do you have any old-man hobbies?" Lowen asked quietly, a small conspiratorial smile curling at the corners of her mouth.

The inside joke was a lifeline she threw to him, stopping the wave of grief from smothering him and bringing him back to the present.

"Why, yes," he said, exhaling a sigh of relief. "I know it may sound a little lame, but I am an avid birdwatcher." He watched Lowen almost imperceptibly nod her head before breaking their eye contact, as if she knew how close he had been to being washed away. As if she had been there a time or two herself.

"Lowen loves jogging in the Moon Creek woods, and I heard there are some amazing owls who have taken up residence. I'm sure Lowen would show you around there sometime," Emily said, her dazzling smile broadening.

"That would be nice," Wesley said with a genuine smile that felt foreign, but he was unable to hold it in any longer.

Lowen

Is she really trying to set me up right now? Lowen cringed.

Lowen's phone buzzed on the table loudly, breaking the

invisible tension at the table. She read the screen: NOAH MESSING.

"Excuse me, I need to take this. It's Noah, and we have a big test coming up," she lied.

"What do you want me to order for you?" Emily asked.

"My usual," she said, accidentally nudging Wesley with her thigh as she attempted to scoot out of the booth. A bolt of lightning rang through her nerves at the physical contact. "I'll be right back," she mumbled.

Lowen pushed the answer button as she made her way to the women's restroom.

"Are you busy?" Noah asked.

He sounded different, out of breath, maybe a little frantic. Worry bubbled in Lowen's stomach. Was it about his dad? Had he done something stupid while drinking? Her mind flashed with images of crashed cars and police mugshots.

"No. I mean, kind of, but what's up? Are you okay?" she asked.

"It's about that spell. You know, the one where you can tell what other people are thinking?"

She sighed, the worry receding as quickly as it came. It was just about Taylor's stupid spell.

"Yeah. Once again, another spell that doesn't work," Lowen said, rolling her eyes in the restroom's mirror before looking under the bubblegum pink stalls to make sure no one else heard her conversation.

"No, Lowen, I think it worked," Noah said, his voice low and quivering. "Well, in a different way. Not in the dream way. Can you come over tonight?"

Lowen's back straightened, the hairs on her arms standing up at her friend's seriousness. "Sure. I'm having dinner with my mom and Margot, but I can drop by afterwards," she said. "I have a story to share with you, too."

"Okay, I'll see you soon," Noah said.

Something nagged at her as she walked back to the table, like an itch she couldn't scratch. Noah's voice didn't sound right, as if fear had wrapped its fingers around his vocal cords. She didn't doubt her friend believed Taylor's spell had worked, but she was sure she could rationalize any magical coincidences that had occurred. But he hadn't even taken the bait when she told him she had her own story. Usually, he'd drill her impatiently until she caved and revealed every detail. Perhaps Taylor's spell had worked. Perhaps, Noah saw something he shouldn't have.

She shook away her unease, a habit she was becoming familiar with, as she studied the table where her cheeseburger and fries were awaiting her. Her mom and sister sat with their backs facing her, their familiar heads bobbing happily over the back of the booth. Across sat Wesley, his smile looser than before she left, as if its muscles finally worked without his brain commanding them. She noticed a dimple on his left cheek she hadn't noticed before as he laughed at something Margot had said, his eyes sparkling as he looked upon her as if she were the most important person in the room. That is, before he glanced up, his amber eyes meeting Lowen's under the glow of the pink and blue neon diner sign. Just as the jolt of electricity had radiated under her skin when their thighs touched under the table, their sudden eye contact threatened to melt her into a puddle of butter on the greasy diner floor. As if he, too, felt the electrical current, Wesley bit his bottom lip and clenched his fists resting next to his dinner plate.

Lowen walked slowly up to the table, her legs seemingly numb, as she and Wesley's eyes refused to break contact, the electricity gaining strength the closer in proximity their bodies became. Lowen found herself holding her breath as he stood up to let her back in the booth, the scent of his subtle citrus and sandalwood cologne knocking her completely from her foundation. Lowen stumbled, her toe stubbing the bottom of the red vinyl booth, but before she could fall forward, two hands wrapped around her waist, pulling her back to her feet with a gentle strength and speed that seemed unnatural.

Turning to face him, Lowen realized a moment too late that her face was uncomfortably close to Wesley's. She could feel his warm breath upon her cheek, so close they could have been mistaken for embracing. As she met his eyes once more, Lowen realized she could read every emotion he wore like pages of a book. First, hunger and desire flashed behind his amber eyes, almost blazing red in the diner's neon glow, but after a long blink, they shifted to reveal a sobering guilt, followed by a flash of grief she was sure would drown her. Lowen had to lower her eyes, unable to hold the weight of Wesley's shame and sadness.

"I should go," Wesley said, clearing his throat. "Thank you, Emily, for all of your help today."

"Anytime," Lowen's mom said, smiling brightly. "I'll be in touch soon to look at more properties."

"And Margot," Wesley said, "It was a pleasure to meet you."

"You as well," Margot said, straightening her spine as if she were royalty before breaking into a fit of giggles.

Wesley looked up from behind the curtain of his thick eyelashes to meet Lowen's gaze. She was sure she looked like a gaping fish, unable to form words for what she had just felt. For what she had just witnessed in his eyes. Now, they communicated nothing—just an empty coldness, as if he had erased every emotion he owned.

"Lowen," he said, as he gently tipped his head, her name choking from his lips like rough gravel and making a shiver rattle up her spine.

"Wesley," she said, unsure whether the electricity jolting through her nerves was from attraction or irritation. Before she could look up one final time to make heads or tails of the man who had saved her in the woods, he was gone. Quietly. Swiftly. As if he had never existed in the first place.

"I like him," her mom said, smiling into the coffee mug she held to her lips.

Lowen filled her lungs with grease-filled air from the diner, exhaling it slowly as she sat back down on the sticky vinyl booth cushion. Clearly, neither her mother nor her sister were privy to any of the strangely intense moments Lowen had just experienced with Wesley. She shook her head, attempting to parse what was real versus what her imagination had conjured. Sitting back at the dinner table, Lowen observed Wesley's plate sitting next to hers. She noticed he had ordered the exact same thing she did: a burger with pickles on the side and fries with a side of cheese sauce. She also noticed he hadn't touched one bite.

Sebastian

Outside of the Daybreak Diner, under the pink and blue neon glow of the restaurant's signage in the violet dusk, Sebastian sat in his car. He watched as Margot and Emily laughed easily as the man with sandy blond hair gestured animatedly, his blood boiling like a current of glowing lava. He watched as the man stood so Lowen could sit down at the booth next to him, but tore his eyes away when she tripped, and he put his hands on her waist to help her stand upright. As he turned the key into the ignition and tore down the dark, one-stoplight town, Sebastian's jaw tightened in disgust.

Track 16 - "Read My Mind" by The Killers

Lowen

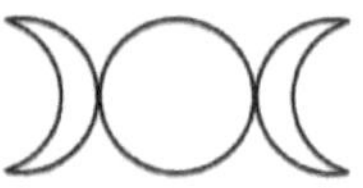

LOWEN'S MIND RACED as she drove to Noah's house, a light blue cottage-style home surrounded by tall trees and a real white picket fence. Images from dinner flooded her thoughts: Wesley's sad, amber eyes, his thigh grazing hers under the table, the strained pinch between his eyebrows as he stared at her, the annoying, yet alluring, buzz she felt hum through her body when she was close to him. Most of all, she remembered reading every fleeting emotion in his eyes; there was an exhilaration of understanding someone so innately, yet an intolerable nerve of such an intrusion. It was as if they were magnets, equally repelling and attracting one another. She smiled with familiar relief as Noah swung the door open the minute her tires began to crunch against his gravel driveway.

"Hurry up," Noah shouted from the front porch before she was able to close her car door.

To her dismay, he looked as frenzied as his voice sounded on the phone. His hair, usually perfectly styled, was disheveled, his eyes red-rimmed and glassy. As she passed him on the porch, she smelled the sweet odor of whiskey that seemed to ooze from his pores. Lowen shoved the ball of worry back down into the pit of her stomach; she knew an argument would ensue if she brought up his drinking now.

Despite the frenzied tension permeating the space, Lowen's shoulders relaxed slightly when she stepped into the house. She loved the feeling of Noah's home. It felt like *him*: warm and inviting, like a hug she didn't know she needed. But the house hadn't always been that way. Up until seventh grade, Noah never invited Lowen or Taylor over. They knew he felt ashamed of the place, and all three had an unspoken agreement not to speak about it. His mother had bought the house when she was pregnant with Noah, when life was simple and new beginnings seemed like genuine possibilities sprinkled like twinkling stars in the night sky, close enough to grab. The house was one of those brightly lit stars before everything happened. Before she died giving birth. Before his dad started drinking all the time. Before he had to raise himself.

Noah's father never sold the house, although he probably should have because the memories of his wife haunted him so much that he grew to resent the walls, the carpet, the cabinets, and stopped taking care of the place, and by extension Noah, altogether. Lowen remembered driving past the house one time on the way to school, weeds and tall grasses trying to smother the life from its frame.

"I swear the whole house has started to droop now that Kristen is gone," Lowen's mother had said, muttering softly to herself.

One spring, after returning home from a rare vacation to the beach with his dad and uncle, Noah went to work transforming the space into a sanctuary, as if the idea had wormed its way into his mind and he needed to exorcise it before it drove him mad. Months went by as the trio faded into a duo, Lowen and Taylor missing the glue that usually held them together. Noah had become a ghost, going through the motions of school to then rush home and work on his secret project.

Now, Noah stood in front of her, physically present, yet almost as much of a ghost as he had been back then. She wished his hands would once again reach for something to build, to make new, instead of a bottle that would only destroy, but she would save the conversation for another day. After all, the house was spotless, with fresh flowers blooming in a vase on the coffee table next to framed faded photographs of his mother. The comforting scent of fresh-baked cookies wafted from the kitchen.

"Were you baking again?" Lowen asked, lines of worry creasing her forehead, as she peeked her head into the kitchen.

"Three dozen," Noah said, his eyes widening.

"What happened?" Lowen asked, now understanding the severity of her friend's crisis.

Noah began stress-baking when he was eight years old, which just-so-happened to coincide with when he told his father he was gay.

"Yeah, so about that spell. Remember how we were supposed to think of a specific person and their thoughts would come to us in a dream?" Noah spoke rapidly but stared directly into Lowen's eyes.

Lowen nodded earnestly, walking slowly toward the couch.

"Well, I can see EVERYTHING now. I know what people are thinking." He almost whispered the last part but kept his stubborn chin high in the air.

Lowen frowned, studying her friend's face. Noah's eyes were bloodshot, with dark circles like bruises revealing a fatigue no one his age should be able to carry. His hair was in wild disarray, bleached blond spikes pointing everywhere, as if each strand had run in opposite directions to get away from the specters chasing them.

"There has to be a rational explanation for this," she said, although she felt a stab of traitorous pain in her gut for trying to explain away Noah's predicament when she herself harbored her own unexplainable secrets. She thought of the bent tree in the woods, haunting her with its magnetic pull. At least Noah was brave enough to say the truth out loud.

"How can you rationalize being able to hear what's going on in other people's minds, Lowen?" Noah asked, running his fingers through his hair with frustration.

"Okay, so try it on me," Lowen suggested as she sat down on the navy velvet couch, lowering her voice to a calming whisper. "Do you have to do anything or are you just able to hear my thoughts?"

"I have to concentrate, that's about it. And I don't hear them, I see them," Noah said, his voice lowering to match hers. "The thing is, it's not necessarily thoughts that make sense. Like, maybe it's not what you are thinking about right this minute, but I can see what you've seen."

"Well, let's give it a try," Lowen offered, patting the cushion next to her.

He sighed as he took a seat next to her, their knees touching as they turned their bodies toward one another. Lowen investigated the set of eyes she knew as well as her own, red and bleary from the contents of his hidden flask. A chill tickled her spine, as if glittering magic had cooled the temperature of the living room like quiet snowflakes. She swallowed the lump in her throat as Noah shut his eyes for what seemed like an endless stretch of time, before snapping them back open with bright white clarity she hadn't seen in so long, as if the flask had never existed.

"You were lying in the woods, looking up at a bent tree trunk that glowed against the backdrop of a starry night and full moon. A hand reached down to help you up from the ground. When you stood up, you were at the Daybreak eating a cheeseburger."

Lowen's mouth hung open like a door someone had forgotten to close. How could he have known about the woods and her trance-like habit of lying in that certain spot? How could he have known about the dream of the hand reaching down to help her up? Her cheeks burned, the room suddenly overheating from her embarrassment. She didn't recognize how much shame she carried until she realized Noah was able to see her body, uncontrollable and utterly useless, laying in the dirt.

"I was right, wasn't I?" Noah asked, miserably running his hands over his face.

"Yes," Lowen said, gently pulling his hands away from his face and holding onto them. "The weird thing is I didn't dream about anyone last night. I dreamt about what you just saw. I was lying in the woods, and someone extended an arm to help me up. You saw my dream."

The two friends sat quietly for a moment, staring into each other's eyes, trying to see if the other was as terrified as the other.

"Noah?"

"Yeah?"

"If I tell you something, will you promise not to tell anyone? Not even Taylor?"

"Of course," he said, squeezing her hand gently.

"I've been going out into the woods and lying in a certain spot for a few weeks now. It's like I don't have control over it. I feel like I'm in a trance, like I can't not do it. It feels so heavy, as if there's a giant brick on my chest. I feel utterly lost and terrified as I lie there, but I have to do it."

"Was it the place I just saw?"

"Yes, I've been dreaming about it, too. Sometimes, I see a bright light behind my eyes—like the sun or something, and then I wake up. It's the same bright light that flashed the night I cut my hand for that stupid moon water thing. I thought it was just a side effect of passing out, but it feels the exact same. Something happened out there, Noah. I know it."

Once she started talking, her secrets began to spill out, a

soothing rush of water breaking from the dam she had meticulously built.

"I went back the next day and found a rock in the creek," she said. "Noah, it had 'Thank You' etched into it. What the hell does that even mean?"

Lowen knew she was talking too fast and not making sense, but it still felt good. Noah's eyes glistened with tears, his brows lifting in incredulous worry.

"You've been holding all of this in? I knew something was off."

She nodded her head, gazing down at the couch in shame. Noah had called her immediately in his own unexplainable circumstance, knowing she would never judge him, yet she had been keeping so many secrets from him for weeks.

"It wasn't that I didn't trust you, Noah," she said, a wave of guilt washing over her.

"You don't have to—"

"Yes, I do. I trust you. More than anyone else in this world. I was just afraid. And ashamed," Lowen said, wiping away tears she didn't even realize had fallen from her eyes.

"Ashamed of what?" he asked, gently using his fingers to tip her chin up, searching her eyes for answers.

"Ashamed of losing control. Of falling back down the rabbit

hole of my dark thoughts," she said, her bottom lip trembling. "I've been so much better. The meds have really helped. This isn't in my head, right? I really feel like it's real. I need it to be real because if not—"

"It's real," Noah interrupted. "I don't know what any of it means, but it's real. And we can figure this out. Okay? We will figure this out."

Lowen sighed into her best friend's chest as he wrapped his arms around her and rested his chin on top of her head. She felt lighter than she had in weeks as she let her body melt into his.

After a therapy session that included devouring cookies and dissecting everything that had happened since the Moon Water ritual at Moon Creek, Noah told Lowen about seeing what was going on in the minds of their classmates and she told him about her unexpected family dinner with Wesley. As she climbed back into her car to head home, she thought about how she had only left out one detail to Noah: the part where the mysterious Sebastian said those two little words she knew in her gut connected him to this mess: THANK YOU. She wondered why she didn't include the tidbit in their very honest conversation. The only reason, she decided, was that what she wanted more than finding out what was going on was to see Sebastian again—and what fun would that be if her best friend was suspicious of him?

Track 17 - "Seven" by Taylor Swift

Noah

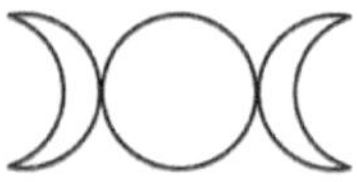

BORN IN MOON Creek, Noah Messing seemed cursed to die within its insulated borders. Besides an occasional trip to Ohio or Michigan, he hadn't seen even a speck of the world in seventeen years. He had only seen the ocean once, with his dad and uncle, on a four-day trip to Panama City Beach the spring before he turned twelve. The minute they arrived and dropped their luggage in their room, his dad and uncle belly-upped at the hotel bar, ordered Budweiser, and watched a football game on one of the flat screens. Noah wondered why they drove twelve hours to do exactly the same thing they could have done at home.

Normally, an eleven-year-old might feel an empty loneliness exploring a new place without a sibling, a parent, or a friend in tow, but Noah was so relieved to be away from his dad and uncle and their constant blabbering about sports and stock markets, he embraced his quiet solitude with a reverence usually bestowed upon someone far older and wiser.

Noah said goodbye to his father and uncle as they entered the bar (they didn't say it back) and wandered through the double doors to the outdoor hotel pool. His heart skipped a beat as he spotted sand from the pool deck: the white, sugary kind the Florida panhandle was known for. Abandoning his flip-flops with a pile of others, he walked past the billowing seagrass on an outdated boardwalk. The sun was brighter and hotter than at home, as if it hung lower in the sky here, and he wiped the sweat from his brow as he stepped off the hot wooden walkway into the equally hot sand. Digging his feet under the top layer, Noah smiled as cool sand ran through his toes, finer and smoother than the muddy, pebbly sand he and Lowen played in back at Moon Creek.

Noah whipped his head up from the white sand the minute she crashed like an avalanche in front of him. Her sound seemed to come from everywhere, washing over him like a baptism. Every minute or so, she sighed, her small emerald waves crashing onto the sand and leaving behind white foam as she slipped away once more. Her sighs beckoned him to rush toward her.

He inherently knew the ocean was a woman, and she felt like she was his mother, with each wave rolling in beckoning him to meet her for a welcoming embrace. He felt utterly insignificant as he dizzily stepped toward her, a tiny speck along her infinite shore. He yearned to see what was on the other side of her enormity, imagining a welcoming foreign land just past the horizon. His feet sank into the wet sand as a wave sucked its water away from him, letting him know she wasn't his to keep.

"Your mother is gone, and I'm not her," the ocean said.

Without his permission, salty tears fell down Noah's cheeks. Offended by them, he wiped at his face quickly and sat down. He wished his best friends were with him. Lowen would have understood the mixture of emotions he was feeling: the awe and connectedness intertwined with the earth-shattering enormity of how small his life really was. She would have let him sit with his thoughts, and she would have sat with him, holding his hand. Taylor would have told them both to grow a pair and then exclaimed what a crappy little beach town this was. She would have gone out of her way to make Noah feel like he deserved so much more than only this.

"You're made for the beaches of Capri. Nothing less," she would have told him.

Even at eleven, he felt lost when he wasn't with them. They were his strength, and acknowledging their importance ignited a fire of fear within him. What if he couldn't be with them forever? They had real families, unlike whatever debris was left over after his mother's catastrophic death. Eventually, they would all grow up and he would be left alone to suffer.

Noah did something on the beach that day he had never let himself do: he surrendered. Sitting where the sand met the ocean, he let himself feel all of the things he normally shoved deep inside: his mother's death while giving birth to him, the resentment his father had toward him for killing his wife and for not being the son he imagined, his loneliness as the only queer kid who was out of the closet in Moon Creek, and the fact that this was his first time at the beach and he was entirely alone. He promised himself he would never allow himself to feel this insignificant ever again. Instead of being swallowed up by the magnitude of the ocean, or anything else for that matter, he would emulate her. He would stand tall and not let the peons below affect him. His waves would crush them.

Instead of feeling sorry for himself for his mom's death and dad's lack of affection, he would create his own home and family with his friends. So, he didn't have a mom to bake cookies? He'd learn and bake them himself. So, he hated the old hand-me-down furniture and beer cans littering his shabby house? He'd transform it into a space in which he could be proud.

Noah saw two reflections of himself in the waves that day. The first wave showed him who he would become if he continued doing what he had been so far, a skinny kid with terrible posture who would sit and wait for someone to love and take care of him. The next wave showed him who he could be if he became that person for himself.

It's funny how standing at the ocean really does put things into perspective for you, he thought. *How cliché, but hey, clichés are there for a reason.*

"Thank you," he whispered to the ocean.

Even now, Noah still heard her voice in his dreams.

"You're welcome," she whispered as a wave curled and crashed gently, pushing its white foam over his feet.

Track 18 - "Somebody That I Used To Know" by Gotye

Sebastian

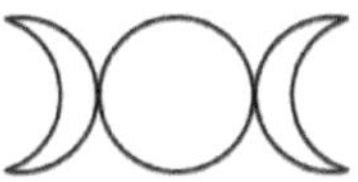

SEBASTIAN SAT FUMING in the dark, isolated driveway of his newly rented home on the outskirts of Moon Creek. The image of Wesley sitting with Lowen and her family at the diner wormed its way into his brain again, causing him to squeeze his steering wheel as if it were a neck to choke. He growled as he remembered Lowen's mother and sister smiling earnestly as Wesley gleefully chatted with them. And then Lowen came back to stare at him with those doe eyes. A vein on his forehead began to throb.

And Wesley. The man was actually smiling for the first time in his life. Their relationship had ended so many years ago, and like most other endings, Sebastian had moved on without much thought. He had a penchant for cutting people and things out of his life with little emotion, like annoying threads that must be snipped before they unravel everything. He knew Wesley was angry with him, but he wasn't sure how far he was willing to take it. Their relationship had been complicated, and they hadn't spoken once it abruptly ended. More than his irritation toward Wesley for possibly thwarting his plans was a gnawing feeling of something else. Jealousy? Maybe. Guilt? That would be a new one.

"Hey again, it's Sebastian," he texted, annoyance simmering in his gut as he remembered she had ignored his previous correspondence.

Three dots bounced on the screen. Patience wasn't his strong suit, and the small dots made the irritation in his gut more pronounced.

Lowen: Hi! Sorry I didn't respond lasttime; I didn't know the number

Sebastian: Not a problem. This is presumably forward, but I was hoping you would join me for a picnic.

Is that how people texted these things? He didn't know, but he didn't particularly care either. If anything, Sebastian could make up for his clumsy technology mishaps in person with his charm. It was one thing time could never take away from him.

Lowen: Sounds good. I'm free on Saturday if that works for u

Sebastian: Perfect. Text me your address and I'll pick you up at three o'clock.

He didn't need her address. Sitting in his car in his driveway, Sebastian smiled at the screen when the tiny dots stopped bouncing and Lowen gave him her address with a smile emoji. In most cases, an emoji and the overuse of exclamation points would annoy him, but tonight he found it endearing. The simmering feeling of irritation began to fade as he thought of plans for their date.

Sebastian: See you then.

Sebastian clicked off his phone as he closed his car door and walked up to his front door with a confidence that only came with immense time in a body. He paused, raising a thick eyebrow at the front door that stood slightly ajar. For a normal person, an open front door would be a cause for concern, but Sebastian smirked as he strolled in, like he was casually perusing the aisles of the grocery store. He turned the knob on a tableside lamp, allowing the soft golden glow to barely illuminate a portion of the massive great room. Taking his time, he walked to the fireplace along the far wall and pushed the button on the wall to ignite the flames. Lastly, he strolled to a small glass table holding an assortment of wines and liquors, along with long-stemmed wine glasses and thick crystal rocks glasses. He used a wine key to confidently stab the soft cork, dug deep inside its flesh with a twisting motion, and swiftly pulled the red-soaked cork out of the bottle with a soft pop. The action felt like a satisfying beheading. He allowed himself a heavy pour of the vintage blood-hued Malbec, swigging a generous gulp without so much as a swirl or sniff.

He smiled as the warm acidity travelled down his throat, freeing the cork from its instrument of demise, before turning his body without a sound. Not a drop from his wine glass spilled from his left hand. His right hand held the metal corkscrew at a ninety-degree angle to Wesley's throat.

"Is this how you greet your old friend?" Wesley asked, gasping as the tip of the corkscrew broke the fragile top layer of skin under his chin.

"Where is this friend you speak of? You can't possibly be talking of yourself," Sebastian countered.

Part of him seriously considered ripping off Wesley's head for a moment, but he couldn't. He was *his* Wesley. History overrode irrationality.

"Okay, maybe not a friend anymore. Maybe just somebody who you used to know," Wesley replied.

"Semantics. What are you doing here?" Sebastian looked Wesley up and down, softening a bit. It took him off guard how he was still quite affected by Wesley's square jawline and liquid amber eyes.

"Here, as in your house or here, as in Moon Creek? I guess I could ask you the same, but we already know, don't we?" Wesley asked, looking everywhere in the room but Sebastian's eyes.

Sebastian knew why, and a rush of sympathy threatened to crush his chest. Perhaps a tinge of regret. What was happening to him in this godforsaken town? He never felt these weak emotions anymore, but they had seemed to be spilling over from the moment he arrived back here.

"You knew it was only a matter of time before I came back. It worked. I finally broke the curse, Wesley," he said, fighting against the urge to hold Wesley by his arms and shake the possibilities into him.

"With patience not exactly being your strongest attribute, I'm shocked this plan of yours actually came together. You do know they will be coming for us now. And her." Wesley's brow furrowed. "She doesn't deserve this."

Sebastian sighed; only Wesley could take something as pivotal as this and turn it into a downer.

"Let them come for us. We've always been more powerful, and now we have daylight again. And as for the girl, I've got a plan," Sebastian smiled, and for the first time since seeing Wesley, it was genuine. The idea of strolling Moon Creek's streets during the day with Wesley had clouded his mind. Had made him too optimistic. "I've missed you, old friend. Will you at least stay for one drink?"

"Let's get two things straight. First, I'm not your friend. I never will be," Wesley said, anger rising in his voice.

"Noted," Sebastian said, his hope deflating like a ripped balloon. "And the second sentiment?"

"Your mess is mine when it comes to Lowen. I don't know what your plans are for her—or how any of this will continue to work—but I'm not going anywhere until I know she's safe. She's not one of us, and she never needs to be part of this world and its darkness. I know I would have never chosen it for myself."

Sebastian took a sip of his wine, wincing at Wesley's words. "Darkness? Always one for the melodrama, Wesley. Who knows what you would have chosen if you had known how fun *this world* could be? You have the chance now. You have a chance to know what it was like before the curse, so try to keep an open mind."

Sebastian hated thinking of what could have been with Wesley, but he knew his words would be in vain. Wesley was never going to embrace who he was. Not after what Sebastian had done to him. If he could do it all over again, he would have used restraint. He wouldn't have gone so far. Too far, he could now admit. Age and some distance from the intense feelings Sebastian once felt had granted him the gift of hindsight, although he would never admit so much to the bitter man standing in front of him.

"You never change, do you?" Wesley said, shaking his head before turning to leave, his black shirt helping him blend into the darkened shadows of Sebastian's lonely house.

Sebastian held his glass of Malbec as the door slammed, the stir of emotions mixing like a violent cyclone deep in his gut. He couldn't help but be surprised that Wesley was still so angry after all this time. He had deliberately deluded himself into thinking that being back here would stir old emotions of better times, and that his friend would once again want to set off on new adventures with him. It's what he would have done if roles were reversed. For all of his stubborn attributes, he wished someone would acknowledge he always was willing to forgive the ones he loved.

It's okay, he told himself. *Just give him time.*

Tilting back his wine glass and emptying its contents all at once, Sebastian realized with grim amusement that he was famished. He set down his glass, grabbed his car keys and headed out of the driveway and away from Moon Creek. He'd been on his best behavior since his arrival, but now with remorse, jealousy, and bitter nostalgia gnawing at his insides, Sebastian caved to two of his worst weaknesses: gluttony and the primal urge for uninhibited pleasure.

Track 19 - "It's Cool, We Can Still Be Friends" by Bright Eyes

Lowen

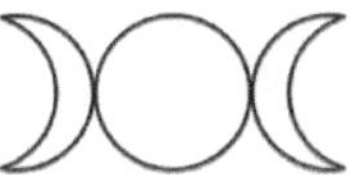

"I TOLD WESLEY you were available this morning to help him move," Emily said from across the kitchen counter.

Her mom hadn't stopped talking about Wesley since the night at the diner and had helped him find a penthouse apartment in an up-and-coming neighborhood that was home to quite a few new restaurants and bars that had been converted from old homes.

"Mom, I actually have plans today," Lowen said, a smile tugging at her lips at her mom's not-so-subtle matchmaking skills.

"Come on, Lowen. He knows absolutely no one here. You can lend a hand for a couple of hours before your big date."

"Why does Margot have to tell you everything?" Lowen whined, rolling her eyes. "Fine, an hour. That's all."

Lowen didn't quite understand her own attitude; Wesley was nice enough. At the diner, they had even had a moment. With anyone else, Lowen wouldn't have put up a fight to help, but there was just something about Wesley that triggered her. The teeth-grinding, fist-curling frustration that simmered in her gut whenever she was around him made her crazy.

"Are you going to tell me who you are going on a date with?" her mom asked, innocently fidgeting with her coffee cup.

"Just a guy I met at the bonfire a few weekends ago," Lowen said, refusing to look in her mother's prying eyes.

"Does he go to school with you?"

Lowen paused. "No, he graduated already."

She actually had no idea how old Sebastian was, where he went to school, or what he did for a job.

"Watch out with those older men. You don't want to end up like me," her mom joked.

"Says the woman trying to set me up with a twenty-two-year-old!"

"He's so sweet though!" her mom laughed, raising her arms up as if she were surrendering.

"Fine, I'll help Wesley move on my free Saturday morning," Lowen said, standing from her kitchen bar stool and pointing a finger playfully at her mom. "Just as long as you stop trying to set me up."

Wesley

On a clear, cold Saturday morning, Wesley walked out of the hotel room he had stayed in since he arrived in Moon Creek, dragging one measly suitcase behind him. He gently placed it in the trunk of his black Audi and drove a few blocks to his new home, where a rental truck was awaiting him with a fraction of the furniture, clothing, and miscellaneous home items he housed in New Orleans. The reality of living long-term in Moon Creek settled into Wesley's bones, cold and heavy, when he saw the truck. As he stood frowning, Lowen crossed the street toward him. When he saw her, he realized his face was distorted and attempted to conceal how he really felt and smiled casually.

"Your mom said you were coming to help me. I'm sure she put you up to it, but regardless, I appreciate it," Wesley said loudly over the cars driving by.

"She may have suggested it, but it's really no problem," Lowen said, shrugging her shoulders.

They stood awkwardly, both looking up at the brick building silently for a moment.

"So, I heard you got the penthouse," she said.

He smiled. "Well, I needed to make the act of moving as difficult as possible."

"I guess we better get started," Lowen said without acknowledging his joke, as she walked to the back of the truck and pulled up on the latch to release the large door, revealing neatly stacked moving boxes.

Wordlessly, Wesley grabbed a dolly from the corner of the truck and placed it on the street with ease, while Lowen climbed into the truck and began handing boxes down to Wesley. He stacked three on the dolly, while Lowen grabbed a smaller one to carry. Wesley noticed how seamlessly they worked as a team without any verbal communication, as if they had owned a moving company together in a previous life.

"It's a gorgeous day," he said, as they fell into a synchronized walk into the building.

Did I just talk about the weather? he cringed internally.

"It definitely is," Lowen said, a bored sigh escaping her lips.

Once inside the newly constructed apartment building, Wesley pushed the button to the elevator, which immediately opened to reveal the smallest elevator on the planet. Lowen stepped in first, squishing herself as far as she could on the back wall to allow enough space for Wesley and the dolly. Wesley backed in, and as he dragged the dolly into the elevator, the doors began to shut and automatically opened again.

"I'm sorry," Wesley said, his back pressing against the box Lowen held. They continued to adjust, but the front wheels of the dolly wouldn't fit.

"Here, let me see that one," Wesley said, as he held his arms up for Lowen to hand him the box in her arms.

Once she did, he set it on top of the other three on the dolly, giving him some extra inches to back up some more, thereby allowing the dolly to finally fit. The heat from Lowen's body radiated less than an inch from his back, creating a physical shockwave that ran through his body. He had never felt such electricity before. Her rhythmic breathing filled his ears, and the scent of her strawberry shampoo filled every square inch of the elevator. Her heartbeat vibrated through his ribs, causing hot saliva to fill his mouth.

Wesley attempted to focus on the buttons moving up each number until they hit PH. Overwhelming frustration washed over him, so much so that he clenched his fingers into a tight fist to keep himself from turning around to tangle them up into her soft hair.

The urge to pull her head back gently and run his fingers and nose and tongue down her soft neck made him shiver despite the stale heat inside the elevator. Before he could let his imagination turn into a gruesome reality, he closed his eyes, shutting out the cramped enclosure. The small, enclosed space spun as Wesley realized maybe he wasn't as strong as he anticipated he would be. The thought of hurting someone hadn't crossed his mind in such a long time, but clearly those inherent biological qualities were not completely dormant. His body tensed as the familiar thick, sludgy flow of self-hatred slowly pushed its way through his veins.

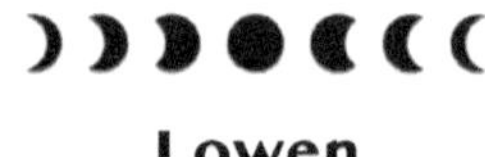

Lowen

Wesley's muscles tensed as he inched further back into the elevator. Even his hands seemed to clench into white-knuckled fists. Lowen didn't know much about body language, but she could only assume he was definitely not enjoying standing so close to her. Every single insecurity Lowen had felt from her early teen years bubbled to the surface: her scrawny legs, her awkward smile, her mousy brown hair.

She hadn't dated much, not since breaking up with Nate during their junior year. And Nate had been completely head over heels for her, making her believe that every one of those pesky insecurities had melted like snowflakes onto asphalt, disappearing forever. Only now did she realize they had just laid dormant, ready to crack wide open again the moment she made herself vulnerable.

I bet he wouldn't be so repulsed if he were in this tiny, stupid little elevator with someone like Taylor, she thought bitterly.

The opposite effect of her body being carried upwards while her self-esteem plummeted made her stomach flip. She didn't understand why it even bothered her that Wesley seemed somewhat repulsed by her. She wasn't exactly thrilled to be in his presence either, but still, it hurt. She tried to distract herself by thinking about her upcoming date with Sebastian.

Someone who doesn't seem completely disgusted by me, she thought.

Lowen sighed with relief as a final dainty ding signaled they had arrived at the penthouse. The door of the elevator opened directly into Wesley's new home: a massive, contemporary open-concept apartment. Everything was stark white, with a few walls of exposed brick and nearly black wood floors to add contrast. It smelled of fresh paint and sawdust. Floor-to-ceiling windows lined the largest wall of the living room, giving a spectacular view of the fiery red and bright yellow foliage decorating the town below.

"It's amazing," Lowen whispered, walking to the windows to take in the town she had lived in her entire life from a completely new point of view.

She momentarily forgot the awkward tension from the elevator as Wesley walked to where Lowen stood, matching her stance by standing shoulder to shoulder. He stood close enough that his arm brushed hers. A surge of invisible electricity ran through her entire body, as if someone had set fire to all her nerve endings. The sudden physical reaction to his close presence almost made her gasp.

Magnets, she thought.

It was just like the night at the diner, magnetic and forceful and it was more than just pheromones, more than his cedar and vanilla scent. This was cellular. Unavoidable. Uncontrollable. And maddening beyond belief. She clenched her jaw tightly, grinding her molars against one another to drown out the electrical current threatening to undo her.

Lowen was frozen, unable to adjust her footing or move an inch, so instead tried to conceal her state of blissful, yet extremely embarrassing, shock by keeping her face blank. They stayed like this for a few minutes, saying nothing, just looking at the town as if they were inside a snow globe made of red and yellow leaves. Finally, she turned and tilted her head up to look at Wesley and took a deep breath. Perhaps it was time to find out more about this man who had conveniently fallen into her life.

"I don't know if I sincerely thanked you for that day in the woods," she said, bringing up the subject they had yet to broach.

Why was that? It was as if he wanted to shove away the unpleasant encounter even more than she did.

"You did. It's bothered me that I didn't walk you to the park," Wesley admitted, pushing his fingers through his messy hair. "I should have insisted."

She wondered what his hair felt like as they crashed back into place, like small waves folding in the ocean.

"Well, I've been known to be stubborn," Lowen said. "So, I won't hold it against you."

"I appreciate that," he said with a sad smile. "I'm also sorry your sense of security was tarnished that day. You shouldn't need a guy who looks at birds for fun to deter another man from doing something to you. It's unfair."

"I refuse to let that one moment make me feel unsafe in my own town," Lowen said, shaking her head defiantly.

"I get that, but you do have to be careful," he said, pausing before opening his mouth to say something more.

"What?" she asked more defensively than she had intended. "What were you going to say?"

"Nothing," Wesley said, although his pinched eyebrows gave away that he had plenty more to say.

Lowen's blood ran ice-cold as she noticed him release an almost imperceptible sigh, as if she were foolish for not letting that man in the woods scare her. Did he want her to be afraid all the time? Did it make him feel tough to be the prince who saved her? Right when she was starting to think they could be friends. She almost unleashed her rage at him but instead decided to bottle it up. All she needed to do was help him unpack, for her mother's sake, and then he would be out of her life forever.

Wesley and Lowen spent the next two hours silently loading and unloading boxes into Wesley's beautiful new apartment. They worked in unison, as if they had done it their entire lives. No words were necessary, which was a good thing, considering Lowen was pissed and wanted nothing more than to get out of this loft apartment and get ready for her date with Sebastian, but irritatingly, she couldn't stay mad because she had the feeling Wesley knew exactly what she needed and stayed silent out of respect. She appreciated it, felt herself softening for a moment, and then remembered why she was mad in the first place.

"I guess that's it," Lowen said, breaking the silence as she wiped her hands on the back of her jeans.

"Thanks a lot for your help. I... um," Wesley stuttered. "I'm sorry if I did something wrong."

"Don't worry about it," she said with a small sigh of resignation. "I'm sure I'll see you around."

Lowen waved a small goodbye over her shoulder and left Wesley alone in his box-filled, vast apartment to get ready for her date with Sebastian.

Track 20 - "Mastermind" by Taylor Swift

Sebastian

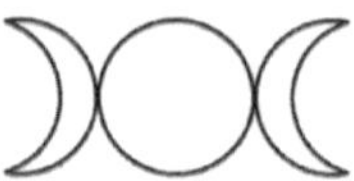

SEBASTIAN PULLED INTO Lowen's driveway at three o'clock precisely, checking his thick, black hair in the mirror before opening his door. Annoyance simmered in his gut when Lowen opened her front door and walked out onto the porch before he had a chance to knock and introduce himself properly to her mother and sister. Watching her walk down the steps toward him knocked him off balance in the most miniscule of ways. The average person probably wouldn't even notice such a small and fleeting sensation, but Sebastian found himself surprised by feeling, well, anything at all. He chalked the sentimentality up to Lowen's golden brown hair shimmering in the sun.

Remember, this is all a means to an end. Nothing more.

Immediately following Lowen's agreement to his invitation, Sebastian planned an itinerary that included a picnic in a secluded area of the local park. The date was low-stakes and would allow

Sebastian to gain some much-needed trust with Lowen before he could continue with his plan. The image of Wesley sitting at the diner with her family pooled like oil in the pit of his stomach, the slick weight causing him to worry he was moving too slow. He needed her to trust him. He needed her to need him. Not Wesley.

"Hi," Lowen said, approaching his car.

Her pulse pounded like a drum under her skin. Even from a football field away, he would have heard its quick, yet steady rhythm. Although she walked with gentle confidence, her eyes flashed with excitement when she looked at him. The scent of her skin, strawberry mixed with perspiration, reminded him of the moment a wild animal became caged.

"Skipping the introductions with your parents?" Sebastian asked as he got out of the car, nodding his head toward the front door.

"Just my mom, actually, but yes. I'd like to save myself the embarrassment for a while."

"Fine by me," he said, shrugging his shoulders before walking to the passenger side of the car and opening the door.

As she passed by him, he caught another scent mixed with her strawberry shampoo: cedar. He dug his fingernails into his palms, squeezing tightly against the urge to growl, to punch something, to murder the nearest bystander. A crushing wave of nostalgia pummeled Sebastian as he inhaled Wesley's familiar scent on Lowen's skin, and all he could do was let it pass over him as it mixed jealousy and desire and rage and sadness into a cyclone within his chest. He smiled as she innocently slid into the passenger seat, wondering if he would be able to hold back from every carnal urge threatening to undo him.

Lowen

Lowen tucked a strand of her hair behind her ear, quietly fidgeting as this near stranger drove her through town. What had she gotten herself into? As she glanced quickly at him, she couldn't help but feel equal parts intimidation and attraction. She was correct in trusting her gut when she slipped out of the house before her mother could meet him. He was trouble, that much was obvious. His sharp, stubbled jaw line whispered a quiet maturity lacking in the boys at school. His steady hands, covered with fine, dark hairs, easily maneuvered the steering wheel with a seasoned confidence. She looked away as his stunning green eyes darted over to her, playfully daring her to study him again.

"I know we hardly know each other," he said, returning his gaze back to the road. "So, feel free to ask me anything. I'm an open book."

She nodded as she watched the houses she knew so well on Main Street pass her by in a blur. Why did she feel as if it was going to be the last time she would ever see them again?

"Where are you from?" she asked, turning to look at his sharp profile.

"Hm, a little bit of everywhere, I suppose," he said, his eyes focused on the road ahead.

She raised an eyebrow. "So, what brings you to Moon Creek?"

"A little of this, a little of that," he said, a half-smile spreading across his lips.

Irritation began to burrow under Lowen's skin, tingling like tiny ants she wanted to squash.

"Okay, I've had enough. I think I'm ready to go home now," she said, her voice shaking at her sudden request.

Sebastian pressed slowly down on the break, his hands squeezing the steering wheel as they came to a stop. A bead of sweat trickled down Lowen's back, as the image of Sebastian kicking her out of his car to walk home crossed her mind.

"Are you kicking me out?" she asked, her voice shrill with her rising anger.

"What? No!" he said, looking over at her with wide eyes. "We just stopped at a light."

Lowen's eyes followed his hand as he pointed toward the red stop light in front of them.

"Oh my God," she muttered, slapping her hand over her eyes.

"What kind of monster do you think I am?" he asked, laughing with incredulity as he waited for an answer.

"I'm sorry," she said. "But you won't give me a straight answer about anything I ask. You do realize that, right?"

The car began to slowly accelerate as the light turned green, steering them toward the park where the two were supposed to enjoy a picnic. So much for her request to go back home. She watched as Sebastian relaxed his shoulders and loosened his grip on the steering wheel, as if he would begrudgingly tear down one brick in the massive wall he had clearly spent years building.

"I'm the one who owes you an apology," Sebastian said. "And answers. Can we start over?"

"I'd like that," Lowen said quietly.

The park was teeming with people, eager to soak in the last bits of October warmth before a long season of death and snow covered Moon Creek like a quiet blanket. Kids threw frisbees as couples held hands and meandered under blazing maples. It was the perfect place to plan a first date, she'd give him that. As Sebastian turned off the car, he turned to her, raising his pointer finger in between them.

"Stay right there," he commanded.

Lowen sat still as he quickly exited the car, then opened and closed the trunk before opening her door. Draped over his arm was a cream quilt.

"For sitting," he explained, noticing her eyebrows raise.

As they walked across the green lawn, Lowen studied Sebastian's mannerisms. His gait oozed arrogance, as if he claimed and conquered each square foot he traversed. He held his head high, much like Noah, but instead of skimming over the heads of people he didn't want to interact with, Sebastian stared at each individual as if he were ready to challenge them to a duel. Despite his hands casually tucked into his pockets, he instinctively puffed his chest to quietly announce his arrival.

Lowen didn't know what to make of him. His palpable arrogance made her clench her jaw but also sparked a small flame of curiosity. Why would someone so opposite to her find her appealing? The image of a moth flying directly into a sparkling, iridescent web, its velvet wings stuck in its fatal prison, flashed through her mind.

"You're quiet," he said, interrupting Lowen's dark thoughts.

"I'm waiting for you to answer my questions," she said defensively.

He raised an eyebrow as he glanced in her direction, a flash of some indecipherable emotion flaring behind his emerald eyes.

"Ah, yes," he said, pointing to a shaded area under a blazing red maple tree. "I'm from Europe, specifically Romania. My parents moved to the states when I was child, so more honestly, I consider Oregon my home."

Lowen stopped under the shade of the brilliant crimson tree as Sebastian spread out the quilt over the cool grass.

"What brings you so far from home, then?"

"Work," he said, gesturing for her to sit. "I'm a jeweler."

"Hence the necklace?" Lowen asked, pointing toward the obnoxious ruby hanging from a gold chain around his neck.

"A family heirloom," he explained, running the ruby along the links of the chain. "It's a family business. Anyway, I'm here to acquire raw quartz, and hopefully find some moonstones."

"It must be nice to work with your family," she said.

She must have said something wrong because Sebastian's eyes dropped to the blanket, a cold shadow crossing over his face.

"They're dead," he said, his voice flat.

"I'm so sorry," she said quickly. "I would have never—"

"No need to apologize," he said, looking up to meet her eyes once more. "It happened some time ago, but despite the years that continue to pass, the subject still stings like salt in a fresh wound."

Lowen nodded. "I know what you mean. My dad died when I was young."

She hadn't talked about her father in years. The words rolled off her tongue so easily, so different than how they usually lodged themselves like stones in her throat ever since the funeral. Sebastian's furrowed brows, as if she were a fragile puzzle piece he was trying to solve, surprised her almost as much as her own candor.

"How did he pass?" he asked, a voice barely a whisper being carried on the autumn breeze.

"He was murdered," she said, forcing herself to peel off the meaning from the words as they floated in the air around them.

She watched Sebastian's Adam's apple bob as he faltered momentarily, seemingly unable to come up with the right words. After a blink, he reached out his hand, a smile stretching across his face so charming that Lowen's lips couldn't help but turn upward despite the horrible timing.

"Well then, welcome to the Dead Parents Club," he said, taking her cold hand into his, the heat of his skin soothing much more than just her chilled fingers. "We meet on Tuesdays and have a Facebook group page."

No one in her life had ever been so candid, so morbidly flippant, when it came to conversing about her father.

"I'm not really a club kind of girl, but maybe I'll check it out some time," she joked back.

"We're a real blast on holidays," he said. "Standing room only on Christmas."

"I bet," she said, looking up as a gust of wind sprinkled gold and fiery red leaves from the maple's branches. "Sounds like a club I'd fit in with."

Memories of somber Christmas mornings, her mother's muffled sobs from the bathroom as Lowen distracted Margot with her new toys flooded her mind. Someone else understood.

They sat in silence for a few minutes, pretending to watch the other people in the park, but both kept glancing at each other. Each time their eyes made contact, Lowen felt her cheeks turn hot. She wondered if he would kiss her. She knew if he did, she would have a hard time closing her eyes when all she wanted to do was drown in the emerald sea of his. He was winning her over, minute by minute even as her gut screamed to take it slow. To be weary of the arrogant mask he wore to disguise himself that hid the skeletons rattling in his dark closet. But then he tucked a strand of her hair gently behind her ear and she drowned out any nonsense her gut tried to make her aware of.

"I like you," he said, his emerald eyes focused solely on her.

"I like you, too," she admitted.

Another gust of wind swept through the park, shaking the leaves as they whispered their secrets. They both looked up, watching as the leaves fell down silently and landed on the cream quilt. Lowen watched as Sebastian leaned forward, as if in slow motion, and placed his hands on the blanket so he was on all fours like a stealthy panther hunting its prey. She could only focus on his green eyes and thick black eyelashes as he leaned forward so their foreheads nearly touched in a quick, yet delicate, movement. His lips met hers, and without realizing she had been holding her breath, she released a soft sigh onto his lips. She had never before felt the sweet release of surrender, but as her heart beat loudly against her ribs, she knew she had. She would surrender her distrust of Sebastian if her lips could stay pressed against his forever.

Wesley

From across the park, Wesley watched as a tender kiss became more passionate. He had to look away when Lowen's fingers reached for Sebastian's black hair. He knew how easily Sebastian was able to spin his webs, and how quickly his prey could become trapped, their limbs stuck in his brilliant silk, squirming until they tired out, unable to fight as he drained them of all their blood.

Track 21 - "I Know the End" by Phoebe Bridgers

Lowen

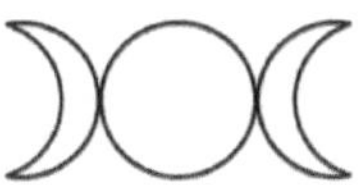

"SPILL EVERYTHING." TAYLOR'S eyes sparkled as she demanded the details.

It felt good to sit in Taylor's familiar bedroom with her two best friends. Lowen was bursting at the seams to tell them everything about her date with Sebastian, but she also had a strong urge to keep every tiny detail to herself. It was complicated. He was complicated. For every green flag he waved, a red one peeked from behind the shadows. Her friends were smart. And observant. And ferociously protective. An image of the black rock with those two simple words carved into it flashed in her mind. She didn't want to hide things from them, but she feared they wouldn't understand.

"I like him, you guys," she admitted.

That part was true.

"Of course you do. He's hot," Noah said, with a hint of jealousy. "So, tell us about this passionate kiss."

"Get out of my head!"

Lowen tried to hide her smile by avoiding eye contact, instead pulling at a thread on the blanket draped over her legs.

"Please don't pretend to be chaste with us. Give us the dirty details," Taylor demanded. "Or we will just have Noah go ahead and dig around in that little brain of yours."

Lowen thought it was funny how ever since Taylor's spell allowed Noah to see what people were thinking, the three of them had just gone along with it like it was a normal thing for them. They talked about it so casually that it had become just that: casual telepathy.

"The falling leaves were a nice touch," Noah teased, shoving a handful of popcorn in his mouth.

He looked so much better than the last time she had seen him, when his eyes were red-rimmed and wide with terror from the shocking arrival of psychic visions. Now, his eyes twinkled with humor as he wiggled his fingers, pretending his magic would unleash like tentacles pointed toward her brain.

"Seriously. Get out of my head!" Lowen exclaimed, ducking her head into Taylor's lap.

"I would like for us to take a moment to appreciate that my

spells actually work," Taylor said, while tapping Lowen's skull with her pointer finger, as if the acknowledgment was specifically directed at her.

"Well, what is going to be special about me when I have two friends with magical powers?" Lowen teased.

"I believe you have the magical ability to lure sexy strangers into your orbit. And if I could choose any magical power, it would be THAT one!" Taylor laughed, gently pushing Lowen off her lap.

The three spent the next hour dissecting Lowen's encounters with both Wesley and Sebastian. Lowen admitted how frustrated she was by Wesley's mixed signals. Was he a friend or did he actively hate her? And what about Sebastian? He was definitely more than a friend, but his charms seemed well-seasoned and rehearsed, as if he had done this type of courting many times before. But then, she remembered the sobering look he gave her as he welcomed her to the Dead Parents Club.

Some of it had to be real, she thought.

A comfortable silence blanketed the room for a moment, each of the friends in their own private thoughts.

Lowen watched as Noah gazed at Taylor before saying, "You're right, Taylor. We should definitely have a party so that we can meet these guys."

Taylor looked at Lowen and nodded her head in Noah's direction. "This man, Noah, has a GIFT!"

"This will never not be weird," Lowen said, laughing.

As the three friends ate popcorn and gossiped like old times, Taylor began planning what would be the most horrifying Halloween party the town of Moon Creek would ever see.

)) ● ((

Lowen quietly crept up the stairs to her bedroom after hanging with Noah and Taylor until way after sunset. She was grateful for a quiet night at home. Both her cozy bed and crappy reality television were calling her name. After changing into sweatpants and hoodie, she pulled her hair up into a loose ponytail high on her head and tossed her laptop onto her bed. Grabbing her phone off from her nightstand, she checked her messages: nothing. She hadn't heard from Sebastian since their date.

He has the mysterious vibes down pat, she thought, rolling her eyes.

She tossed her phone on the bed, sat cross-legged, and opened her computer.

Dr. Clarke had asked Lowen to help with some independent research he was doing about the folklore of Moon Creek. After seeing the amount of time she devoted to researching the Count of St. Germain, he said he could use some of that extra brain power. She was sold when he told her she would even receive a stipend and could use the experience on her college applications.

"I'd like to start researching the people who lived in Moon Creek in the mid-to-late 1800's," he had said. "Perhaps there are some stories published about the town residents at that time."

He didn't give Lowen any more information than that, so she figured she could at least start with Google and see where the search led her. She typed "Moon Creek, Indiana 1800s" into the search bar and clicked Enter.

Moon Creek Family Viciously Murdered,
Son Still Missing

It was dated September 1892.

Holy crap, Lowen thought.

She read on.

The Vincent family was found dead on the family farm in the small community of Moon Creek on Thursday morning after neighbors saw horses loose. Married couple, Gabriel and Emmaline Vincent, along with their two daughters, Gretchen (8) and Imogene (5), were found brutally murdered inside their home and in their accompanying barn. Their eldest son (22), is still missing, but not considered a suspect.

How had Lowen never heard of this story? Granted, no one was really telling tragic murder stories on a regular basis, but it was one of those tales she imagined would get passed down as a local urban legend. She clicked out of the article and returned to the Google search page to look up the Vincent family but was thrown off her task when her phone vibrated. She had a new text message.

Sebastian: Just wanted to let you know I had fun on our date

It's like he read my mind, Lowen thought.

Lowen: Same! We'll have to do it again soon

Sebastian: Of course

She looked back at her computer screen but lost her will to focus on anything aside from closing her heavy eyelids. With her phone and computer still sitting on her bed, she tucked her legs under the soft pink quilt her grandmother had made for her and turned off her lamp. Although she fell asleep as soon as she rested her head on her pillow, the night was full of tossing and turning through dreams and nightmares. Mixtures of images: Sebastian and Wesley, Noah and Taylor, the woods at night and the creek illuminated by the glow of the full moon, fires in an abandoned field and chanting voices, a clear starry sky and blood spilling onto the cold ground. So many images. All so very different, yet all part of a pattern she couldn't discern. Lowen awoke the next morning, feeling the heavy brick of anxiety resting just below her throat, invisibly and quietly strangling her.

Track 22 - "The Yawning Grave" by Lord Huron

Lowen

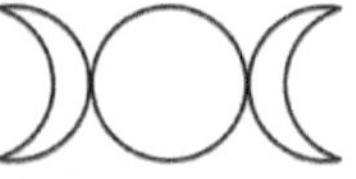

"HAVE YOU HEARD about the Vincent family? Apparently, they were murdered in Moon Creek in the late eighteen hundreds."

Lowen wouldn't have imagined she would be at school early on a Monday morning to go over murder mysteries with her English teacher, but here she was walking down the empty halls before the sun had even fully risen. She turned her laptop around to show him the screen.

"They believe the murderer was a serial killer who slaughtered over sixty people across the Midwest," Lowen explained. "I can't believe I've never heard this story before."

Dr. Clarke adjusted his glasses as he hunched over Lowen's computer screen. "Actually, I do remember hearing about the Vincent family before. The son escaped, didn't he?" he asked, grabbing his cup of coffee from behind his messy desk, littered with stacks of papers and various sticky notes with unintelligible one-word scribbles.

"Yes but does this have anything to do with whatever you are researching?" she asked, sitting in the chair across from his desk.

Dr. Clarke thought quietly for a moment. "I'm not sure, but sometimes you have to find a thread and start pulling. Would you want to check out where the farm used to be?"

"Haunted field trip? I'm game," she said, a spark of pride glowing in her chest at her discovery.

"Good. Meet me here after school and we'll drive out there," Dr. Clarke said, handing Lowen's laptop back to her. "I'm going to have to call your mother and make sure we have her permission, and I'd also like you to invite a friend so that we all feel comfortable."

Lowen pulled her phone from her backpack. "I actually have two perfect people to ask, if that's okay."

"The more, the merrier," Dr. Clarke responded with a smile.

Lowen: Hey! Are you two up for an adventure after school with me and Dr. Clark? It involves farmhouses where murders took place

Noah: Hell yes. Count me in

Taylor: Sorry, can't! I have tennis practice, but u 2 have fun

The school day dragged itself along as if each minute were tied to an

anchor, but finally the last bell rang, jolting Lowen from her seat in Calculus so she could meet Noah at her locker.

"Taylor is going to be pissed she's missing this," Noah said, leaning elegantly against the lockers as he watched kids walk down the hallway. "This is why we mustn't dedicate ourselves to sport life."

Lowen smiled as she reached into her back pocket to grab her cellphone. She winced as she admitted to herself that she had been checking for a text from Sebastian every three minutes for the past two days.

Pathetic, she thought.

"You're not pathetic. Also, you should probably go ahead and text him to extend the invite to Taylor's Halloween party," Noah said as he nonchalantly checked his immaculate pale blue nails.

"Quit getting in my head. Those thoughts are private!" Lowen said through gritted teeth.

Although Noah's new gift was exciting, she knew she was going to have an uncomfortable talk about boundaries and consent soon.

Dr. Clarke was already waiting for them outside of his classroom. "A friend. Hi, I'm Dr. Clarke. I don't think we've met."

"Hi! Noah Messing." Noah gave a small, perky wave. "I'm

taking lowly senior English, so I don't frequent this hallway much."

"Messing. Interesting," Dr. Clarke said, suddenly taking in Noah's face with more interest.

Noah cocked his head to the side momentarily but deflected with his overused joke. "As in, I'm always a mess."

The three made their way down a deserted dirt road on the outskirts of Moon Creek in Dr. Clarke's old Ford truck. All they saw for miles around them was farmland: flat, dry, and empty after the fall harvest. The familiar tree line of the Moon Creek woods was barely visible in the distance past the quilted fields. Despite feeling like they were so far away from their normal lives, the drive had only taken about twenty minutes from the school.

"I don't think I've ever been to this side of town," Noah said, staring out the window as if he were a tourist.

Dr. Clarke checked his rearview mirror, his steady, steel-gray eyes scanning the empty road behind them. "The farmland and woods surrounding the town are surprisingly expansive. Moon Creek is honestly the perfect spot to dive into nineteenth-century folklore."

"What kind of folklore are we talking about? Werewolves, dragons, ghosts?" Noah joked.

Dr. Clarke chuckled as he shook his head, his hair ruffling in the breeze his open window provided. "Nothing specific... yet. Let's just see what we come away with from this outing. We're on the lookout for any relics from the past. I read that the old Vincent farmhouse has been abandoned since the murders, so I'm hoping we can walk around the premises and possibly even peek inside."

"I didn't know we were going to be breaking the law and trespassing today, Lowen. I'm into it," Noah whispered, leaning in so close to Lowen's ear that she could feel his mischievous grin against her lobe.

"I didn't either. Honestly, I'm a little creeped out," Lowen admitted as she nodded toward a looming house in the distance, an invisible brick deciding to drop itself on her chest at the sight of the dilapidated building. "Thanks for coming with me."

After turning off the dirt road and onto a seemingly never-ending gravel driveway, Dr. Clarke parked his maroon truck in front of the abandoned farmhouse. Lowen's stomach twisted in response to the old white paint peeling from the wood on the front porch. As Dr. Clarke and Noah opened their doors to the dry, stale air surrounding the house, Lowen's arms felt as if they were made of cement while her legs bore the consistency of Jello. Taking a deep breath, she tried to shake off the overwhelming feeling of dread and climb from the middle seat of the truck.

"You okay?" Noah asked.

"Yeah, I think so," Lowen said. She knew the feeling well; it was the same heaviness she felt each time she lay down in the woods. The same, but even worse this time.

"Let's start by walking around the house to that barn over there," Dr. Clarke said, pushing his tortoise-shell glasses up higher on his nose as he pointed to a large white barn in the distance.

Like the main house, the white paint was peeling to expose the rotting wood underneath. The barn looked like a looming ghost frozen in time, like something that didn't belong in this modern world.

The three walked past the farmhouse, which was adorned with yellowed lace curtains still hanging on the windows. Lowen stared at the curtains, praying they wouldn't move involuntarily. She swore she felt eyes staring at her from inside the house, prickling the skin on the back of her neck. The feeling of heaviness did not lift, but as they got closer, it changed into a strong sense of sorrow.

Don't let your crazy imagination and anxiety run wild. None of this is real, she coached herself. *Noah is here. Dr. Clarke is here. You're safe. Just relax.*

The front door to the barn was unlocked and opened easily,

despite its age and massive size. Dr. Clarke and Noah began looking around, eager to find clues to what happened here all those years ago, but Lowen couldn't focus. She felt a familiar tug to walk out of the barn's back door, which was cracked slightly open. The tug felt the same as when she went to lay under the bent tree in the woods: involuntary, but also familiar, like she had been here before. She couldn't help herself as she quietly squeezed her body through the heavy door in the back before Dr. Clarke or Noah even noticed she had left.

As she walked out of the barn, she was able to reorient herself, realizing with surprise that the barn backed up directly to far edges of the Moon Creek woods. There was even a path, with the same fine brown dirt as the trails she usually walked from the barn's back door leading into the woods. As if in a trance, Lowen followed the trail deep into the cool shadows of the trees, the afternoon sun fading behind the canopy of fall leaves. The bone-chilling cold that had nothing to do with the temperature turned her fingers to ice, but her body would not stop and turn around, however much she tried to force it.

The further she walked, the more Lowen's mind screamed for her to turn around, but the magnetic pull to follow the trail a little bit further could not be beaten. She didn't know this part of the Moon Creek woods, but she could see up ahead the path opened a bit before splitting in two opposite directions. As she stepped closer to the fork in the path, she realized she knew where she was. The tall bent tree's branches waved a haunting hello as her body froze in shock. She was in the exact spot, the spot in her dreams, the spot in which she felt compelled to lay. How had she ended up back here, once again?

"Should you be out here alone?"

Lowen nearly jumped out of her skin when she saw a tall man with sandy hair standing as still as a ghost in front of her. Wesley stood on one of the paths branching out from the trail under the bent tree, his arms crossed as if bracing himself against the shadowed chill of the woods.

"You surprised me," Lowen whispered, hoping Wesley wouldn't notice her hands shaking by her sides.

"No seriously, you shouldn't be out here alone," Wesley said flatly, void of any emotion at all.

Lowen's brows furrowed as he seemed to send her a warning with no explanation. Did he know something she didn't?

"I know. I didn't mean to be. I just kind of... ended up here," she tried to explain.

"Where did you come from?" he asked, raw fear flashing in his eyes before he blinked it away.

She pointed to the trail behind her. "Back this way. I'm doing some research with my teacher, so we came out here to check out an old farmhouse that backs up to the woods."

Wesley's eyes glazed over before falling flat and dark again. His breathing seemed to come faster, shallower, as he looked past her toward the trail leading to the old farmhouse. Lowen's heart contracted as she felt the grief radiate from Wesley's body, as if the mention of the old farmhouse somehow threatened to shake an earthquake of heartbreaking secrets loose. But Wesley remained stoic, leaving the two to stare at each other in an awkward, heavy silence that quieted even the loudest birds in the woods.

"Well, I should head back," Lowen finally said, defeat weighing down her shoulders as she realized Wesley was a vault she would never be able to unlock.

"I'll walk you," he said, clearing his throat, yet still refusing to meet her eyes.

"Thanks," she sighed, before turning around to head back to the safety of Noah and Dr. Clarke. She didn't wait for him but was unsurprised to hear his footsteps lightly stepping over crunching leaves behind her.

"Why were you out here, anyway?" she asked, throwing the question over her shoulder to him without turning around.

"Birdwatching," he mumbled, finally speeding up to walk shoulder-to-shoulder with her on the path.

As Wesley kept his intense amber eyes on the ground, Lowen heard him exhale an apprehensive sigh when the barn came into view. There was something about this place that made him even more on edge than usual, the intensity of his emotions crushing Lowen like a roaring wave. Perhaps this place really was haunted.

The large back door creaked, startling Noah and Dr. Clarke, as the two stepped into the barn. Both looked up to see Lowen now standing with a tall, sandy-haired stranger.

"Um, this is Wesley," Lowen said, awkwardly gesturing toward the man with a storm cloud hovering over his shoulders.

Noah looked Wesley up and down before slowly smiling indiscreetly at Lowen. "I'm Noah, Lowen's best friend. And this is Lowen's English teacher, Dr. Clarke."

Dr. Clarke quickly set down a large book he was holding and walked over the barn's dry straw and mounds of dirt to shake Wesley's hand, frantic guilt flashing in his eyes as they darted back and forth from Lowen to Wesley.

"I'm sorry to say we didn't even notice you left, Lowen," Dr. Clarke said, his cheeks turning a deep shade of crimson. "Some chaperone I am."

Lowen watched as Wesley lightly shook Dr. Clarke's hand with a gentle formality, as if he didn't want to scare the professor away. "It's a pleasure to meet you both. I just happened to run into Lowen in the woods and wanted to make sure she was safe getting back."

"No worries, Dr. Clarke," Lowen said, feeling a stab of guilt in her gut. "I was only gone for a few minutes."

She smiled at her teacher, hoping he wouldn't be too hard on himself or her for wandering into potential danger. Her curious trances were not only impacting her sanity but also beginning to complicate other people's lives. She hated it. Hated she had no control over it.

"Wesley, are you from around here?" Dr. Clarke asked.

"I'm from New Orleans. Here for work," Wesley explained, glancing around the barn with wide eyes, as if he were an animal trapped.

Lowen could see how hard Wesley attempted to be normal, calm, when he was anything but. From his soft, yet steady eye contact to the pleasantly glued smile stretching across his lips, no one besides Lowen could discern the inner turmoil raging just below the surface. It was so recognizable because she was trying to do the same thing. This place was haunting them. Shuffling her feet, she waited for the awkward small talk to finish so they could get the hell out of this barn and far away from the horrific heaviness that soaked into the wet soil of the farm.

"Well, I should be going," Wesley finally said, glancing at Lowen for a moment too long. "Nice meeting you both. Bye, Lowen."

"Bye," she said quietly, wondering if he, too, felt the strange magnetic push and pull when their bodies inevitably ended up in the same time and space.

The barn door closed behind Wesley, his absence allowing Lowen to feel like she could finally breathe for the first time since stepping out of the car. Noah and Dr. Clarke were so engrossed in the folklore project, they didn't even notice or question her little exploration of the woods. She shook off the peculiar dread, the intense pull from moments ago evaporating like morning fog after Wesley left and unsteadily joined them in looking for anything of importance in the old barn. To Dr. Clarke's surprise, they found some treasures: old horseshoes, a few farm tools, and, most interestingly, a very old and very fragile photo album.

"Don't open this yet," Dr. Clarke said, putting on gloves to carry the album back to the truck. "It's very fragile. We've done enough for today and it looks like the sun is beginning to set. We'd better head back to school."

Relieved by the revelation that they wouldn't be exploring the main house, Lowen settled into her seat as they drove back toward town. Her mind oscillated between thinking about the pull leading her exactly back to the bent tree and the fact that Wesley had been there. They had to be connected. How had she never taken the path leading to the old barn in all of her years of exploring the woods? It seemed that it had appeared out of a storybook. How did she keep ending up back in front of the bent tree? Why was Wesley acting so strange? She couldn't make sense of any of it, so she pulled out her phone for the millionth time that day for a much-needed distraction.

Sebastian: Hey.

She thought about what to type for way too long before rolling her eyes and pressing on the three letters:

Lowen: Hey

At least one thing in my life is going right, she thought to herself as she leaned back in the old truck and smiled wearily.

Dr. Clarke

When they got back to the empty school building, still smelling of pencil shavings and dirty gym shoes, Dr. Clarke thanked Noah and Lowen for helping and hurried them out of his classroom. They were good kids, and he was glad to have their company on the adventure into the old barn, but now he needed to do some investigating alone.

Excitedly, he slid a new pair of plastic gloves over his hands and picked up the old photo album, afraid the oils from his fingers had already damaged the delicate artifact back at the farm.

What a fantastic discovery, he thought, turning the book over like an archeologist holding a dinosaur bone, allowing his gloved finger to trace over the beautiful front calligraphy that read "The Vincent Family".

Dusting off the old, yellowing cover, he gently opened the first page to a black and white family photograph. The ghosts staring back disarmed him for a moment. The husband and wife sat at the center, unsmiling, yet the warm expressions in their eyes jumped off the page. Flanked on both sides of the parents were two young girls, unsmiling as well, who wore matching floral dresses. Behind the parents stood a tall, sandy-haired young man with a small grin on his face. Every fine hair on Dr. Clarke's forearms stood up as the classroom began to spin around him. It couldn't possibly be.

Staring at him in black and white was the young man he had just met in the barn with Lowen: the man in the photograph was undoubtedly Wesley Vincent.

Track 23 - "Closer" by Kings of Leon

Wesley

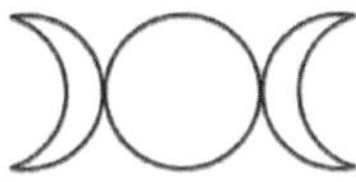

WESLEY'S HANDS SHOOK as he poured a glass of whiskey and paced back and forth in his expansive living room. He hated how modern the apartment was and longed for his familiar historical home in New Orleans. He missed being a short distance from the roaring nightlife that made him feel less alone as he lay awake until the early hours. He missed the warm, humid air and the friendly anonymous faces of the never-ending cycle of tourists. He had left a life behind, albeit a lonely one, but a life nonetheless, all to come back to this godforsaken town and its wretched memories.

And for what? To stop the inevitable? And why were they at the farmhouse? What was that teacher researching? The questions rattling in his head kept him from sitting down. What if they found out about him? He forced himself to remember something that he only now dreamed about when his conscience was no longer in control. Pulling a worn black and white photograph from his wallet,

Wesley sunk into the corner of his leather couch, gently rubbing his thumb over the four faces staring back at him.

It was the summer of 1892, and the small Vincent farm was in full swing. Wesley's parents had inherited the land from his grandfather when he passed, and Wesley's father spent one hour every Sunday in the small family cemetery by the woods to visit and pay his respects. Wesley's father was a gentle, quiet soul with the same liquid amber eyes who worked hard and loved his wife. His mother gave birth to Wesley as soon as they were married and tried for many years to give him siblings to no avail, so Wesley grew up mostly alone on the small farm.

He spent his boyhood days exploring the woods, making friends with the deer and the birds, and dreaming of heroic adventures across the seas, all while his parents focused as co-conspirators of their own love affair. He was already a boy of twelve when his mother finally gave birth to a healthy baby girl, Gretchen. Imogene was born three years later to complete the Vincent family. Wesley was happy to be joined by his little sisters, but the age gap proved to highlight the already gaping wound of loneliness, as his sisters became each other's best friends. Wesley was once again left on the outside, alone.

Wesley was eighteen the summer when the vagabond appeared. Seemingly out of nowhere, the stranger walked from the dirt road to the doorstep of the Vincent farmhouse. The traveler, who was making his way to the west coast in search of gold, was in need of money to continue his journey. Wesley's father could use the help on the farm to prepare for the harvest, so he offered the young man a job and a place to sleep for a few months.

"Where do you plan to travel out west?" Wesley asked timidly as the two spent a grueling afternoon baling hay, a lightweight flutter of hope beating against his chest for the first time in eighteen years.

"Everywhere," the stranger said, his green eyes flashing wide with mischief. "Everywhere one can find women and gold and unspoken treasures."

Wesley chuckled, wiping the sweat from the scorching midday sun from his brow. "Tell me more about these women."

In the months of the traveler being on the farm, Wesley opened up himself in ways he had never been able to before. He had a friend—one who he could talk with about his hopes and dreams, who taught him about the world outside of Moon Creek. Those days were simple, surrounded by his family and familiar farm life, but they were some of Wesley's most cherished because for the first and last time, he didn't feel alone.

"I'd like you to come with me," the stranger said one day in early September, as the two men walked along the babbling creek in the woods adjacent to the James property. "I've grown fond of you, and think a grand adventure is just what your soul craves."

With those few words, Wesley's life had purpose beyond his family's farm. The two men made maps, made lists of stops, and made dreams they wished to fulfill when they arrived in California. And although Wesley's parents were sad to see their son go, they supported his dreams and even gifted him with funds and two horses for the adventure.

The night before they were set to leave, Wesley sat at his bedside table, writing a letter of goodbye to his dear family. He wanted to leave the letter where it would not be forgotten, so after it was written and folded in half, he walked down the hallway, past the traveler's room, to the staircase leading directly to the kitchen below. The traveler had a few idiosyncrasies, one of which was that he firmly requested no one disrupt him when his door was closed.

Wesley softly stepped past the door and down the stairs. He looked out of the window from the kitchen, contemplating his life on the farm and his many isolated adventures in the woods. The light was on in the barn, with the shadows of his mother and father walking back and forth. It wasn't odd for them to work, or otherwise enjoy each other's company, in the barn so late, and Wesley smiled sadly knowing he would be leaving them behind. He could only hope for a love affair one day that matched his parents' fairytale romance.

Wesley was startled from his thoughts by the sound of a blood-curdling scream coming from upstairs. He couldn't tell which sister it was, but he knew one of them was hurt, and badly. He ran up the stairs three at a time. The flickering glow of candlelight coming from the traveler's room, telling him the door was now open. Saliva welled up in Wesley's mouth as the copper scent of blood became tangible. Sweat-soaked fear lingered like a skunk's spray in the room.

When he glimpsed inside, Wesley recognized his two sisters lying still, side by side and face up, on the wooden floor. Their eyes were wide open, with blank expressions that almost mimicked confusion, frozen eternally on their small faces. Their flower-printed dresses that their mother had sewn for them were covered in deep red. As Wesley got closer, he saw the blood dripping from their necks, collecting into sticky pools beneath their heads. He stumbled back as he realized Gretchen's head was fully detached.

Wesley turned and ran down the stairs, acidic bile rising in his throat. The front door was already wide open, and a light was shining in the barn. He sprinted toward the light, his eyes wildly searching for danger, hoping his parents were safe. As he entered the barn, he yelled out for his mother and father but couldn't hear the sound of his own voice over the blood pumping in and out of his ears.

His stomach dropped as something caught his eye across the barn. He knew it was them before he reached them. On a pile of straw, his mother and father lay together. From afar, they looked like peaceful lovebirds tangled up as one, but as he inched closer, he could see they were carelessly discarded like ragdolls onto the bed of hay. There was so much blood Wesley couldn't even tell where it came from. What he could tell was they were dead, their limp limbs dangling in inhuman ways. Whatever had done this had the strength of ten men and the violent temperament of something wicked and predatory.

Instinct kicked in, screaming in raw truth for Wesley to run. So, he did. He ran from the back door of the barn down the dirt trail of the woods. He pumped his arms and legs until he couldn't breathe anymore, the shock overtaking his system.

In the middle of the woods, where a peculiar tree with an

unnatural bend in its trunk slumped sadly, Wesley stopped to catch his breath. He listened. Nothing but the breeze rustled the leaves overhead. He looked around, his eyes darting from tree to tree. But there was nothing but the moonlight flickering playfully through the trees. He leaned over, resting his hands on his knees, attempting to catch his breath and make sense of what he just witnessed. Hearing a twig snap on the path behind him, he swiveled around. Still, nothing but darkness.

When Wesley died that night by the same beast who had murdered his family, his body rested under the bent tree in the Moon Creek woods, as if it had leaned over in an attempt to shield him. He would dream of this spot for days, months, years, and decades. He would try to put it behind him, but it would forever haunt him, not just because it was where he died, but also because it was where he begged his murderer to let him live—and let him live, he did.

Track 24 - "Little Dark Age" by MGMT

Lowen

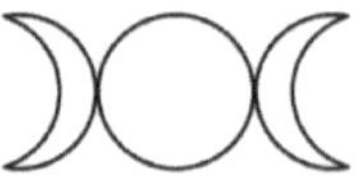

LOWEN TYPED ON her phone, both thumbs moving in rhythm, as she walked into Dr. Clark's first period class.

Lowen: My friends are throwing a Halloween party on Friday. Wanna come?

Sebastian: Of course. Details?

Lowen took a picture of the neon orange paper invitation she held and texted it to Sebastian.

Sebastian: What costume are you wearing?

Lowen: It's not appropriate to ask a lady what she is wearing :)

Sebastian: My apologies. I'll see you there. Until then.

Lowen: K bye

Sebastian: K bye

Lowen grinned as she stuffed her phone into the side pocket of her backpack and took a seat at her desk in front of Dr. Clarke's desk. The teacher and student had fallen into an easy routine of both arriving early and going over research and artifacts from the old farmhouse. She was excited to hear what he had found in the photo album but quickly noticed that Dr. Clarke seemed troubled. His hair was even more disheveled and his clothes even more crumpled than usual, but the lines of worry that creased at his downturned mouth revealed the severity of whatever situation he might reveal.

"Lowen, how do you know that young man, Wesley?" he asked, taking off his glasses to look at her, his gaze holding a sharp alertness uncommon for this time of morning.

"Just randomly. I was jogging, and he was birdwatching. But then my mom helped him find an apartment here. She's a realtor," Lowen explained. "Why?"

"Just wondering." His brow furrowed, creating two deep parallel lines on his forehead, before the look evaporated and he waved his hand dismissively.

"Okay," Lowen said slowly, as she attempted away the gnawing hole that could devour her whole if she let it. "Any news on the photo album?"

"Not much, just photographs of the family," Dr. Clarke said half-heartedly, swiveling absentmindedly in his chair. "They looked nice."

"Does their murder have to do with the town's folklore? Like werewolves or something? I guess I just don't understand the connection," Lowen half-joked, frustrated that she was trying to pry information from the man who usually never stopped talking.

Dr. Clarke perked up as he stopped moving his chair and looked directly at her. "Nope, I'm pretty sure this is just a homicide. But there is the possibility that alchemy was somehow involved and led to their demise."

"Alchemy? On a farm? I guess I always imagined alchemists lived in Europe and wined and dined with kings," Lowen said. "Why would the Vincent murders have anything to do with alchemy?"

Dr. Clarke stood up and paced in front of the classroom, as if the green chalkboard were a necessary component to the act of teaching, even if she was the only student. "Do you remember what alchemists can do?"

"Extend their lives," Lowen said, clenching her jaw in frustration by the didactic nature of the conversation.

"And..." Dr. Clarke prompted, irritatingly extending the 'A' sound.

"They turn lead into gold. Or say they can, at least."

Lowen hated not knowing, but hated it even more that Dr. Clarke did know, but wasn't going to make this puzzle easy for her to solve. What would gold have to do with a small family farm in the middle of nowhere?

"Even if alchemy isn't real, many men would kill for the chance to get their hands on gold," Dr. Clarke said, as if he could read her thoughts.

Lowen's eyebrows raised as the puzzle pieces began to fall into place.

"So, you think someone in the Vincent family was an alchemist? Or pretended to be one?"

"Perhaps. Or perhaps an alchemist was teaching someone in the family his craft," Dr. Clarke said, pausing from his rapid pacing to let the idea settle in Lowen's mind.

But, Dr. Clarke's hypothesis felt like a stretch... unless he knew something she didn't.

Lowen stood up and walked to the window, suddenly restless. "Well, how do you know alchemy is involved? Are there records of an alchemist living in Moon Creek?"

"He didn't reside here, no, but archives show he was said to have visited," he said, a small smirk pulling up the corners of his mouth.

"He? You know who it is?" Lowen asked, her eyes widening as she turned around to face him.

"The Count of St. Germain. Why else would I have chosen you to help me? Your extensive research of the man could really be valuable," Dr. Clarke finally admitted.

"St. Germain. Here? In Moon Creek?" Lowen's mind reeled with this information. "So, that's why you came here to do your doctoral research. You knew the Count of St. Germain was said to have visited here and you wanted to find out more? I wondered why you were teaching high schoolers with a doctorate."

Quietly piecing together all of the new information Dr. Clarke had just divulged, Lowen wondered why her teacher had been so dodgy about the real reason he came to Moon Creek. Perhaps, everyone would have thought he was crazy. Maybe he was.

Slowly, as the first bell rang and her classmates shuffled into the classroom, Lowen's mind faded from alchemy and murders to Halloween costume ideas and her flirty text exchange with Sebastian. Despite all the strange happenings going on in her life, she felt hopeful for the first time in a long time. She had found someone who made her feel alive, and she was willing to surrender herself to the idea of happiness.

The week crept by as Lowen anticipated seeing Sebastian again. She kept herself busy by going through the motions at school, helping her mom with Margot, and being Taylor's go-to for party planning. It was nice to feel connected to Taylor again, like when they were younger, and life was less complicated. The whole school was talking about the party, and as the days of the week passed, the energy began to ramp up. Taylor had used her parents' credit card to have the massive house professionally decorated and the party catered by a local restaurant with Halloween-themed appetizers handed out on silver trays.

"How did you get your parents to agree to leave for the party?" Noah asked, as the three friends rode home from school in Taylor's Jeep on a rainy Thursday.

"I didn't have to do anything. They already had plans to go out of town with another couple," she said as she sped through a red light.

"Taylor," Lowen said, gesturing to the streetlight fading in the distance behind them.

"What? It was pink," Taylor insisted.

"I can't believe they trust you that much. My dad would never," Noah said.

"It's because I'm a perfect angel," Taylor said, batting her lashes in an exaggerated manner. "Speaking of angels, Lowen will you make your famous Jello shots?"

"It's my honor and duty to supply her majesty with sustenance," Lowen said, placing her hand on Taylor's shoulder from the backseat.

It had been a long time since the two girls had really connected. Lowen noted she needed to schedule some one-on-one time with Taylor after the party. She missed her friend. When Lowen looked up again, Taylor had pulled into her driveway and put the car in park as the windshield wipers skidded across the wet glass.

"I'll be at your house early tomorrow to help you set up," Lowen said, scooting out from her seat and grabbing her backpack. "Love you."

"Love you!" her friends shouted back in unison.

Things felt good.

Really good.

Too good.

But then again, Lowen thought, what could possibly go wrong?

Track 25 - "Heads Will Roll" by the Yeah Yeah Yeahs

Lowen

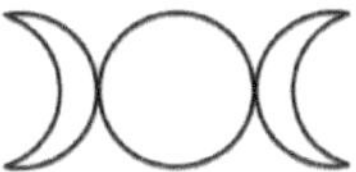

"HERE, TAKE A shot to calm those nerves, girl. I can feel your chaotic vibes from across the room." Taylor handed Lowen a shot glass filled with warm, clear tequila.

The two girls stood in front of the bulb-framed mirror in Taylor's spacious marble bathroom. Lowen felt like she was getting ready for prom instead of a Halloween party. Taylor already looked like a goddess in a strapless white dress. The short hem was lined with white fur, as were the white and silver angel wings attached to her back. After clinking their glasses and gulping down the strong liquor, Taylor went back to the tedious application of silver glitter to her eyelids.

"Okay, that helped," Lowen said, exhaling the fiery aftertaste of the tequila into the mirror.

She studied her reflection. The dress she ordered was perfect: it was a full-length black Victorian dress with buttons all the way up to the neck and intricately detailed with black lace. She wore her hair up, with only two strands draping down in loose curls, like mysterious curtains covering her face. Her eyelids were smudged with smokey eyeshadow, with long fake lashes that were offset by pale, barely-there lips. Spreading her lips into a wide smile, she flashed white fangs that were molded to her actual teeth.

"You're creepy and beautiful all at the same time," Taylor said, assessing Lowen's reflection in the mirror.

"Thank you," Lowen said earnestly.

If Taylor handed out a compliment, she meant it. The warmth of the tequila smoothed all the rough edges surrounding Lowen, and as she turned and straightened Taylor's silver halo, she smiled at her friend. For a moment, they stood in silence, enjoying the moment of quiet before the party started. Breaking the momentary spell, Taylor grabbed a glass bottle from her counter and sprayed perfume into the air. They twirled through the fragrant mist before making their way down the winding grand staircase.

Taylor's house was already filled with excited teenagers as the girls descended the stairs. Phones recorded the graveyard set up in the front lawn, complete with fog, strobe lights, and *Thriller* pumping on repeat through huge, hidden speakers. Groups, tightly packed together, crammed into the entryway, admiring the giant crystal chandelier opening to the winding staircase. Fake glow-in-the-dark cobwebs lined the staircase railing, while countless battery-operated candles flickered on each stair. When the two girls, their arms interlocked, reached the bottom step, Noah strolled up while taking a swig from his not-so-secret flask.

"You both look gorgeous," he said, kissing each of their cheeks.

The smell of whiskey hovered around him like a gloomy cloud.

"And what are you supposed to be?" Taylor asked, pulling at the familiar fabric shrouding his slim frame.

"A psychic," he said, pulling a crystal ball out from under a dark green velvet cape. "I might set up a spot and charge twenty dollars for a reading. Thoughts? Concerns—ethical or otherwise?"

"I think it's amazing," Lowen said, looking away from Noah to scan the crowd.

"Looking for someone?" Noah searched above the heads obstructing Lowen's view and then shrugged. "Okay, look for me in the dining room later, loves."

Lowen rolled her eyes playfully but smiled at Noah as he sauntered away. With their arms still linked, the girls walked through the party with the knowledge that everyone was looking at them. She secretly relished the power she was able to wield when she and Taylor became a combined force. The fun, yet intimidating, energy they exuded as they made their way to the kitchen where the keg and punch bowls were located seemed to be an impenetrable force field. As Taylor glanced at her with sparkling eyes, she knew she felt it, too.

A group of football players, including Nate, were gathered around the keg laughing rambunctiously. Of course, they wore their football jerseys as their costumes. As if on command, they looked up in unison as Lowen and Taylor entered.

"Sweet setup, Taylor," Nick said.

As a junior running back, Nick was short and small, but quick. By the way he stared at Taylor in wide-eyed awe, it was obvious he was into her. Lowen smiled at the frivolity of it all, as if she were floating above herself, observing each detail with nostalgia as if it had already happened ages ago.

"Yeah, thanks for the invite, Taylor," Nate said, his eyes focused on Lowen for a moment too long. After years of knowing him, she recognized that he seemed a little sad.

"No problem, boys. Just don't act like neanderthals and get the cops called on us," Taylor warned, her killer smile simultaneously startling and entrancing them.

The girls scooped the neon green spiked punch—Swamp Water—into three special gold goblets Taylor had purchased just for the trio, and passed couples standing closely together in darkened shadows, before heading back to the living room. Hip hop music blared from the speakers, the bass rumbling in everyone's bones, as some kids danced, while others lounged on couches, talking and laughing and feeling invincible.

"Um, is that your man?" Taylor asked, pointing her long finger toward the front door.

A figure stood in the doorway, wearing a dark hoodie and jeans. Lowen could see his amber eyes staring at her from across the room.

"Wesley," she whispered.

Why is he here?

An unsettling chill crept up her spine as she remembered Dr. Clark's worried expression when he asked her about him.

Taylor left her side, which was for the best because all of a sudden Lowen felt very much frozen in place and walked up to Wesley at the front door. She watched as he took Taylor's hand, shaking it gently before walking inside. His eyes did not look up from the floor until he stood in front of her.

"Nice costume," Lowen said loudly over the music as he approached. "Going as a birdwatcher?"

She couldn't help but feel familiar with him, like she had known him her whole life. She felt compelled to touch him, which was odd as she wasn't an affectionate person usually. She wanted to take his arm reassuringly, to comfort him maybe. Instead, she crossed her arms across her chest and gripped her fingers tightly against her ribs.

Wesley shrugged his shoulders slightly, rolling his eyes to indicate he didn't take himself too seriously. Lowen smiled, revealing her white fangs. Wesley winced, as if he touched a hot stove.

Here we go again, she thought.

"You don't like my costume," she said flatly.

"No, it's not that. It's—you look good," he said, looking down at the floor again.

Lowen felt the anger rise through her arms and rest like flames atop her tense shoulders. She couldn't understand why every encounter had to be so difficult with him. Like magnets, sometimes the attraction was undeniable, but more likely than not, they repelled one another. Before she could open her mouth to confront him, Taylor's mischievous grin flashed from behind his shoulder.

"Somebody was waiting for you," Taylor said, stepping aside to reveal the guest. "And you're right, he's hot," she whispered with a wink exaggerated by her fake eyelashes.

Lowen's cheeks burned red as she took in the sight of Sebastian. His green eyes pierced through her, his charming smirk immediately disarming her. Every tense muscle in her body melted as electricity jolted like a current through her body. The heat of her cheeks radiated, and she prayed no one noticed what Sebastian was able to do to her by merely being in the same room. Everyone else in the room disappeared, even Wesley. Especially Wesley.

Sebastian

Sebastian cut through the crowd, making the split-second decision to skip with pleasantries. He saw Lowen talking to a young man whose back was facing him, the sudden jolt of jealousy moving him to action. Without stopping to look at anyone else, he stepped inches from Lowen's body, dressed in her black Victorian dress, and paused just millimeters away from her lips.

"Hi," he whispered, pressing his lips against hers as if they had done this exact thing countless times. He didn't let his green eyes look anywhere but the target of her mouth.

"Hi."

Lowen's lips moved against his as he wrapped his arms around her waist. The Victorian dress, made of a stiff black lace corset that accentuated her narrow waist, prompted a wave of nostalgia, throwing off his balance momentarily. Her mouth felt unusually clumsy, so he used his thumb to press down on her bottom lip to reveal two large, white fangs protruding from her upper canines. He felt the urge to lick them but was interrupted.

"Ahem."

Lowen hesitantly dropped her chin, disconnecting herself from Sebastian. Annoyed, he turned around slowly to take in the sight of the young man who had rudely disturbed them. He would have known those sad, amber eyes anywhere. He was surprised he didn't take in the clues sooner; he usually knew when he was near. His citrus and sandalwood scent, his stiff mannerisms, his miserable holier-than-thou vibe—usually filled the room like an overpowering cologne for Sebastian. His preoccupation, if that's what one would call it, for Lowen was possibly clouding his ability to utilize his extraordinary senses. He noted such with irritation before staring directly into Wesley's eyes.

"Sebastian, this is Wesley," Lowen said, her fangs flashing as she spoke. "He's a... friend of the family."

Sebastian confidently extended his arm to forcefully shake

Wesley's hand. Wesley glanced over Sebastian's shoulder to make eye contact with Lowen, sadness seeping from his liquid amber eyes. Sebastian remembered how those eyes had bewitched him so long ago and wondered if Lowen would fall prey to them as he had. He would never forget the day he arrived at the James farm to be greeted by the doe-eyed, young man with an easy smile and paralyzing dimple.

"Can I help you?" Wesley had asked, as he opened the squeaky door to the old farmhouse.

"I was wondering if you would have some work for me on your farm?" Sebastian had said before adding, "Only for the summer months. I'll be out of your hair before harvest and am much stronger than I look."

Wesley had smiled broadly with rosy cheeks, eyeing Sebastian up and down before wiping his dirty hands on the pants of his gray overalls before responding. "Well, we will have to ask my father, the owner of this farm, but it sure would be nice to have an extra pair of hands."

Wesley had extended his hand out to Sebastian, taking it in a firm grip. "I'm Wesley," he said, his amber eyes sparkling in the afternoon sun.

"I'm Sebastian," he had said, letting his real name escape his lips like a foreign language he had almost forgotten to be able to speak. The man had unknowingly put a spell on Sebastian, a feat most would consider impossible.

Sebastian shook away the memory as he was jolted back to the present moment: a darkened, opulent house lit with black lights highlighting neon gravestones and bone-rattling thumping beats coming from speakers larger than cars.

"Nice to meet you, Wesley," Sebastian said.

"You look familiar," Wesley said, smiling slightly. "Have we met before?"

Sebastian furrowed his brow and pursed his lips in a small frown. "I don't think so, but then again, my memory can be spotty. Lowen, would you like a refresher on your beverage?"

"Sure. Wesley, are you good on your own?" Lowen asked.

Despite all his nerves itching with irritation, Sebastian had to admit a small part of him appreciated that Lowen felt a sense of responsibility in regard to Wesley. After all, he used to feel the same way.

"Don't worry about me," Wesley said, his voice almost too quiet to hear over the thumping music.

"Okay, well, we will be back in a few," she said, reaching for

Wesley's forearm before turning to face Sebastian.

Guiding her by the small of her back through the crowd, Sebastian and Lowen drifted away from the sad man who stood like a statue, staring at them with a look of profound sadness as they left. Lowen didn't turn around to glance at him. Neither did Sebastian, but he knew. He could feel the grief ooze from Wesley a neighborhood away.

"You look beautiful," Sebastian whispered, pressing his soft lips on her ear as he spoke. He could feel goosebumps on her arm as her heart beat like a hammer against her sternum.

I've won this round, Sebastian thought, a smirk stretching across his lips.

))) ● (((

Wesley

Frustrated by the sight of Sebastian's hands on Lowen's lower back, Wesley tried to refocus on why he was really at a high school Halloween party. He walked through rooms and hallways, on the lookout for anyone who may want to harm Lowen. He knew they would know where she was and the dark hallways, teens in costumes, and liquor consumption would make it much easier for them to target her.

Wesley walked through a dark hallway where two kids were

pressed up passionately against a wall before ducking into a grand formal dining room. The lights in the crystal chandelier had been replaced with battery-operated, flickering candlesticks, creating a haunting shadow effect on the light blue paisley lined walls. Sitting at the long oval dining room table was a young man with bleach-blond hair smoking a cigarette with a deck of tarot cards, a tip jar with some single bills, and a glowing purple crystal ball sitting in front of him. Wesley could smell the whiskey from across the room. The young man looked up regally, yet sadly, as Wesley walked in.

"Sorry, I didn't mean to interrupt," Wesley said, instantly sensing the pure angst radiating from the boy.

"Not at all," Noah said. "We met at the old Vincent farmhouse. Wesley, right?"

Noah crushed his cigarette in the half-full ashtray next to him and exhaled a plume of smoke.

"Oh, sorry. Yes, we did," Wesley said, stepping further into the dining room. "Noah, correct?"

"Yeah, Noah Messing, Lowen's friend. Did you see her yet?"

"I did. Now I'm just... wandering," Wesley said.

"Well, wanderer, are you interested in a psychic reading?" Noah asked, a mischievous smile stretching across his face.

"That's okay," Wesley said, eyeing the plastic crystal ball glowing purple in the dark room.

"No really, have a seat. Free of charge."

Noah patted the seat next to him.

"I was just..."

"Come on, it's just for fun," Noah said, rolling his eyes playfully at Wesley.

His face lit up as he saw Wesley consider his proposition.

"Palm, crystal ball, or tarot?"

"Palm, I suppose," Wesley said, sitting down in the seat next to Noah.

He hadn't sat so close to a person or interacted this much with anyone except Lowen. It felt so natural and human that he almost forgot why he was there.

Pulling Wesley's arm over toward him, Noah gently flipped his hand so his palm was upright. After experiencing real mind-readers in New Orleans, Wesley knew to shut out his thoughts as Noah sat quietly with his eyes closed. He couldn't help but play it overly safe, even if a sad, yet friendly high school boy was just trying to have a good time at a party. Both sat quietly for a long moment. With an unnatural jerk as if lightning had suddenly struck him, Noah dropped his hands away from Wesley's and pushed his seat back with force. Wesley frowned, thinking the boy was simply being theatrical, until he noticed Noah's body trembling like an autumn leaf.

How does he know? Unless he truly does have the gift?

"Um, I have to go," Noah said, standing up from the dining room table and leaving Wesley alone yet again.

Another mess to clean up.

Mess.

Messing.

How could he have missed it?

Lowen

In the stuffy kitchen crowded with bodies waiting in line for the keg, Lowen watched as Sebastian casually walked over to the pack of football players who filled red solo cups as if it were their civic duty. They inched away as a group as he came closer, like a school of fish darting from a shark.

"Good evening, gentlemen," Sebastian said, tipping his red solo cup slightly and pressing down on the lever that connected a hose to the keg.

The boys stayed silent, staring intently into Sebastian's green eyes. Everything about him, from his clothes to his mannerisms to how he talked, felt so much older than these boys she had known for her entire life. But that couldn't be right, could it? He couldn't be much older than twenty-two or twenty-three. His skin was still smooth, with hardly a wrinkle around his eyes or forehead. His black hair was youthful and plentiful. She felt like her mind was playing tricks on her as she observed him intently.

I guess a lot of maturing happens in those three to five years, she thought.

"Hey man. Good to see you again." Nate walked inside the kitchen's back door, where a group of kids were congregating outside. His cheeks were ruddy from the cold, making his eyes shine an even brighter shade of blue.

"Remember me from the bonfire? I'm Nate."

"Nice to see you again," Sebastian said, extending his arm for a formal handshake. Nate grasped his hand and shook it firmly with a smile.

Lowen couldn't help but study the blatant dichotomy of the two men in front of her. Nate was so honest, an open book of innocence; sweat and sweetness and shades of blue. Sebastian, on the other hand, was darkness and mystery; sharp edges and secrets.

"I won't ever forget what you did for Lowen," Nate said

sheepishly, flashing his blue eyes at Lowen before lowering them back to the kitchen floor.

"Accidents happen. I'd have to say it was a happy accident for me," Sebastian said.

He stepped away from the keg, wrapping his arms around Lowen's waist from behind. He rested his chin on her shoulder and shot Nate his signature mischievous grin. Lowen noticed Nate's eyebrows arch for a moment as his eyes darted from Lowen's face to Sebastian's.

"Oh. Good for you guys," Nate said with surprise before recovering and smiling his dazzling, schoolboy smile that melted everything in its path.

Lowen stepped away from Sebastian's suffocating bear hug, turning instead to face him. She knew the game Sebastian was playing, but she couldn't stand to hurt Nate, nor did she want to feel like a claim to be staked.

"Let's see if we can find Noah," she said, leading Sebastian from the cramped kitchen where it felt like all eyes were on her.

She could feel the group of football players' eyes burning holes in their backs as they walked out of the kitchen together.

"That was weird, right?" she asked, once they were out of

everyone's earshot in the kitchen.

"What's that?" Sebastian asked, smiling as if nothing odd had just happened.

"None of those boys talked to you. They seemed terrified of you."

"An older guy at what they perceive as their territory? It's natural. No offense taken though," he said, shrugging his shoulders.

"At least Nate made an effort," she said, with a weary smile. "He's actually a really nice guy."

"I love your fangs," Sebastian said as he changed the subject. He used the tip of his pointer finger to touch the bottom of one of the fake teeth. "You look absolutely exquisite."

"I almost went for a little fake blood but figured it might be too gory."

"I would have loved to see some blood," he said, stopping to look at her, his pupils dilating, almost completely obstructing his dazzling emerald irises.

"Really?" she asked, nodding her head over toward Taylor's dining room where Noah said he was setting up his tarot station.

"Oh yeah," he said, interlocking their fingers as she led him down a long, dark hallway.

Lowen turned around to look into his darkened eyes, seemingly glowing against the black light bulbs scattered throughout the house. An electric shock coursed through her veins just by holding hands with him. The hallway seemed to lean, as if the Earth had tilted on its axis.

What is this, she thought?

Her body never behaved this way with Nate. Every nerve seemed to stand on edge and the slightest touch threatened to push her over. When they passed the restroom, Lowen excused herself and told Sebastian to find Noah. She needed a breather. Knocking on the closed door and leaning in to hear no sounds on the other side, Lowen jiggled the handle to find that it was locked.

I've had more to drink than I thought, she thought.

The hallway spun as she tried to focus. She pulled her phone out of a hidden pocket in her dress to try to distract herself while she waited. She felt slow and clumsy, and as she looked at the screen; she realized everything looked slightly fuzzy.

The next round has to be water.

She had three texts from Noah.

Noah: Where are you?

Noah: Hello?

Noah: Meet me in the downstairs bathroom

Lowen looked up at the closed door and pressed her lips to the crack. "Noah, is that you?"

The door swung open with violent force as a hand grabbed her wrist, pulling the door closed quickly. The owner of the hand made sure it was locked before he turned and looked at her with eyes full of fear.

"Noah, what is going on? Are you okay?"

His skin was pale, as if he'd seen a ghost; his eyes darted around the small bathroom wildly as if he'd see it again. Lowen sat him down on the toilet seat, instinctively reaching for the expensive hand towel and soaking it with cold water. As she wrung it out in the small pedestal sink and placed it on the back of his neck, she wondered if maybe he had taken something he shouldn't have.

"Can you tell me what's going on now?" she asked, gently tipping his chin so their eyes met.

"It's about Wesley," Noah said, looking up and staring directly into her eyes. "He sat down for a reading."

"Okay, and?"

Lowen's heart dropped to the floor as she thought back to Dr. Clarke's questions regarding the boy her blood seemed to recognize.

"Lowen, it was bad. Unlike anything I've ever seen," Noah said, closing his eyes tight as if he were trying to erase the terrifying images from his mind. "All I saw was darkness and death."

Lowen crouched down on the black and white-tiled bathroom floor so she was eye level with her friend.

"How do you see death?" she asked, her voice gentle.

"I mean, that's the thing, I don't. All I feel is deathly cold skin, damp soil, and dark, rotting death."

Rotting death. What am I supposed to do with that, she wondered.

"He's dangerous, Low. I think he might be—"

Noah shook his head, unwilling or unable to finish the sentence.

"Might be what?" Lowen asked, pulling her hair off of her damp neck.

"This sounds crazy, but I think he might be dead," Noah said, his voice almost a whisper. "I can't explain it, but I felt it."

Lowen glanced at her own expression in the ornate gold mirror hanging on the glossy black bathroom wall. Usually, she loved Taylor's parents' decor, but now the dramatic color scheme in the cramped bathroom made her dizzy. Her pale skin, black eye makeup, pointed teeth, and black lace dress seemed all wrong now, as if they were a cruel joke to taunt Noah.

Perhaps he had gotten it wrong. Had drank too much whiskey. Had gotten too caught up in the Halloween decorations. No one could actually be walking around town, breathing and eating and smiling and birdwatching and be dead. After all, they weren't living in a horror movie.

"I'm in no way judging you, but did you drink too much tonight? Or take a little party favor in the pill variety?"

As she watched Noah's face fall, guilt washed over her like a tidal wave. He confided in her because he trusted her, and instead of hearing him out, she had just thrown his greatest weakness in his face.

"I'm sorry, Noah. I didn't mean—"

"I'm not drunk. I'm not high. I know what I saw," he interrupted, his eyes clear and laser-focused on her.

Lowen nodded, breathing a heavy sigh from her mouth. She had seen and felt strange things, too. Why wouldn't she suspend her disbelief for her closest friend? Because she was terrified, she finally admitted to herself.

"I believe you. I just don't know what to do about it at this moment," she said, absentmindedly fixing pieces of Noah's disheveled hair. "But, you know who else is about to be dangerous if we don't get back to the party? Taylor. Let's just go back out there and deal with this tomorrow. I promise we'll keep our distance from Wesley, okay?"

"Okay," Noah said, reluctantly. "No more readings tonight."

"Good, more quality time with your best friend in all the world," Lowen said, pulling him to his feet and kissing his cheek clumsily.

"And you're questioning me about my alcohol intake?" he said, finally smiling weakly.

The two friends linked arms and left the bathroom, walking past a growing line of impatient teenagers.

Wesley

"We have a problem," Wesley whispered in Sebastian's ear in the crowded living room, despite the party music thumping so loudly he could have yelled the words and no one would have heard.

The thought of having to speak to Sebastian caused acidic bile to rise from his stomach into his throat, but the situation with Noah was bigger than them.

"*We* don't have anything," Sebastian said, rolling his eyes with irritating indifference as he scanned the crowd as if he were perusing the snack aisle at the grocery store.

"The kid is a Messing," Wesley said. "He saw who I was. What I am."

"And this is my problem, how?"

Despite the callousness of his words, Wesley noticed the lines crease between Sebastian's brow with worry.

"He will put it all together, and Lowen will find out. And when she does, I'll explain *everything*. Everything you did. Everything you plan to do."

A flash of anger darted through Sebastian's eyes before softening once again.

"Let's discuss this in private," he said, turning down a dark hallway as if he owned the house.

Sebastian walked slightly ahead of Wesley as they began to ascend the wide, winding staircase to ensure no one would see them together. Wesley kept his chin down, watching each step he took with self-loathing. The last thing he wanted to do was work with Sebastian—it always led to trouble. And usually it was the bloody, violent kind.

Lowen

Walking into the empty foyer with arms linked, Noah and Lowen scanned the crowd for Taylor. Empty solo cups littered the sticky floor and the scent of stale beer and Red Bull wafted through the air. The noise—the thumping bass and shouts from the crowd—had amplified in the last half hour, and Lowen wondered if the Moon Creek police would make a visit soon.

Tilting her head up to the winding staircase, she noticed Wesley's sandy blond hair at the last step before arriving on the second floor. His head was bent, as if he were studying his shoes as he walked.

What is he doing up there? she wondered, deciding not to point out his whereabouts to Noah, who was finally beginning to calm after looking into Wesley's mind.

"There you guys are," Taylor said, prancing up to them with twinkling eyes and a broad smile. "It's getting a little insane, right?"

Lowen and Noah glanced at each other, both noting Taylor's words were slurred ever so slightly. Noah smiled weakly, while Lowen playfully rolled her eyes as they watched their friend teeter slightly on her usually steady feet.

"This is going to be a party that goes down in the—"

A blood-curdling scream interrupted Taylor's sentence, piercing through the air and ripping away all other noises, as if someone had pushed the mute button on the entire house. The party seemed to pause; a collective breath was held. Muscles tense, everyone seemingly frozen as the scream echoed through the air of Taylor's high ceilings. Everyone looked at one another with wide eyes, each wondering if the scream was just someone playing a prank but knowing in the deep primordial parts of their bones that this kind of guttural noise came from fear. Or violence. Or pain.

"Which direction did it come from?" Taylor asked, whispering with wide, clear eyes, as if the scream had wiped away any evidence of the party.

"It felt like it came from everywhere all at once," Noah whispered back.

"Upstairs," Lowen said, as a brick fell from her throat and landed deep in her stomach while she pictured Wesley ascending the last step.

Taylor was the first to budge from the spot gluing them to the living room floor and bounded up the steps two at a time. Noah and Lowen followed behind, both timidly holding on to one another.

As they stepped onto the second floor, Lowen could see the glow of a lamp from Taylor's bedroom. She remembered Taylor had locked her door to make sure no one wandered into it from the party. How was it open now?

As she stepped into the bedroom, a man with thick black hair was crouched down in the center of the room, looking at a pile of clothing. It was only when she gasped that Sebastian lifted his head and looked past Taylor to connect his gaze to Lowen's. He didn't wear his signature grin; rather his face now looked pale and gaunt, as if he had seen a ghost.

Before the maroon pool was visible, the smell of copper hit Lowen's nose, landing thick like peanut butter in the back of her throat. Déjà vu ran through Lowen's veins, overwhelming her senses for a moment. She was certain she had walked into this scenario before, but before she could reach into the recesses of her mind for a memory, a frantic stream of words cut through the silent air.

"No. No, no no no," Taylor said, her rapid, breathless voice unrecognizable. "How is this happening?"

Lowen watched as Taylor's white angel wings and halo began to tremble, as if she may take off and fly away.

"Is she... Is she dead?" Noah asked, unconsciously wrapping his velvet cape tight around his body.

Sebastian stayed in his kneeling position, looking up at the three as he nodded his head yes. Lowen forced herself to look at the pile of clothes beneath him. A girl dressed in a yellow plaid skirt and matching jacket laid crumpled on Taylor's white-fur rug. Blood had stained her brown hair, turning it a deep burgundy, and Lowen could see that it was still draining slowly like quiet lava down her neck into a black puddle beneath her. Her familiar blue eyes stared at Taylor's ceiling fan with a wide, surprised expression. It was Blair, the cheerleader who they had known their whole lives, who decorated lockers for special events, and who Lowen had spoken to last at the Moon Water Ritual.

"How? Who?" Lowen uttered, her legs trembling under her black lace dress.

"Why don't you guys go downstairs and clear out the party? I'll call the police and make sure no one comes up here," Sebastian said, surprisingly calm, despite being huddled over a dead girl.

Lowen's shoulders relaxed slightly as Sebastian's commands fell from his lips. Someone had a plan, and thank God, because her brain seemed to be malfunctioning. As the three ran in a single-file line, with Taylor leading and Lowen coming down the stairs last, Lowen decided she needed to tell someone what she saw and tugged Noah's arm in front of her.

"I saw Wesley walking up the stairs a few minutes ago," she whispered, their knowing eyes locking with one another.

"Where is he now?" he whispered.

"No idea," Lowen whispered back.

She nodded slightly in Taylor's direction, holding a finger to her lips. Noah nodded in silent understanding.

"Guys, I don't even know what the hell to do right now," Taylor said, turning to face them when she reached the bottom step.

Taylor's eyes were wider than Lowen had ever seen them, her pupils dilated, and as she stepped off the final step and grabbed her hands, her gut twisted by how cold and clammy they were. She realized Taylor was experiencing shock—they all were—but much more than Lowen was herself. With a deep inhale, she knew she needed to clear out the party. Their classmates were standing around, clumped into tiny groups, whispering behind shielded hands with wide eyes, trying to make sense of the terrifying scream they had just heard. Blaire's scream. Lowen shook the memory of her blue eyes staring blankly at the ceiling. If Sebastian could keep his wits about him, she could, too.

Lowen walked over to where the music was blaring and

unplugged the speakers from the wall socket. The sudden quiet made everyone's ears ring. She then grabbed the microphone she and Taylor used for karaoke sing-alongs in middle school and held it close to her mouth.

"Sorry, guys. The cops have been called. It looks like we're going to have to clear out now."

Her voice shook, but she got it out. As if cops with paddy wagons carrying breathalyzers had already burst into the room, the partygoers pushed past each other, bolting out of the house. In less than ten minutes, Noah, Lowen, and Taylor were left alone on the first floor. They each stood perfectly still, taking in the stacks of red solo cups, fallen streamers, and neon spiderwebs surrounding them. Lowen glanced at the ceiling above, making sure Blair's blood wasn't seeping through the floorboards, waiting to drip on their foreheads.

"What do you think happened to her?" Taylor finally asked, staring at a glowing jack o' lantern, its toothless smile mocking them.

She lifted a visibly shaky hand to her head and took off her halo, dropping it onto the sticky ground.

"She was murdered," Noah said quietly, before glancing at Lowen with a knowing expression.

There is no way Wesley did this, she thought. *Sure, he is a little odd, but no. No way.*

"The cops are on their way," Sebastian said, walking down the stairs with his hands tucked into his pockets.

"Thank you," Lowen said, watching him as he closed the space between them and pulled her into a protective embrace, his body warming the cold chill working its way through her bones.

"It's going to be okay," he whispered above her head.

Lowen let herself melt into his chest. The sudden exhaustion after the adrenaline rush almost brought her to her knees. Sebastian must have sensed her heaviness because his arms wrapped around her body more tightly. Protectively.

"Yes, thank you," Taylor said, finally peeling her gaze from the jack o' lantern to meet Sebastian's eyes for a mere second before walking away from them. When she came back, she held a box of trash bags, pulling one out and handing it to each person.

"Help me," she said, as she began gathering cups and tattered decorations. The trio, along with Sebastian, quietly picked up empty bottles and smashed cookies and orange napkins until the flashing blue and red lights reflected off the living room walls.

After the police questioned them and the ambulance brought

down Blair's body, covered in black plastic on a stretcher, Sebastian instructed the three friends to get into his car. Lowen called her mom to tell her they were on their way home. Noah and Taylor sat closely in the back with Noah stroking Taylor's head as she rested it on his shoulder. Lowen sat quietly in the front seat with her head resting against the cold window, thinking about how she would explain this to her mom. She would not be allowed out of the house ever again. If she even wanted to leave the safety of her home again. Sebastian glanced at her a few times, but she couldn't muster the strength to look back. She kept drowning in the image of Blair's blank blue eyes. The black pool of blood. The nauseating scent of copper. Six words repeated themselves over and over in her head, like a mantra, before Sebastian arrived at Lowen's house:

Nothing will ever be the same.

"Get some rest," Sebastian said, parking the car in Lowen's driveway.

She looked into his eyes, full of worry, and smiled sadly.

Nothing will ever be the same.

"Thanks for everything tonight, Sebastian," Noah said, placing his hand on Sebastian's shoulder before pulling Taylor's weary body from the backseat.

The two walked into Lowen's house like defeated soldiers after a long and bloody battle.

Nothing will ever be the same.

Lowen, sitting alone in the car with Sebastian for a moment, summoned the strength to finally speak.

"You really kept your head on straight, you know? Thanks for that."

Her eyelids felt like they each weighed one hundred pounds as her voice floated a million miles away from her body.

"I'm just glad I was there. I can't imagine if..."

His voice trailed off, so she turned her head to face him. He leaned over and kissed her forehead, lightly but affectionately, before clearing his throat. "I'm not going to finish that sentence. Get some rest, and I'll call you first thing in the morning."

Lowen knew how he was going to end the sentence: "I can't imagine if *that would have been you up there.*" She had the exact same thought when she saw the girl's blank eyes staring at Taylor's ceiling. She and Blair were the same age, the same size, had the same color hair. It was too easy to imagine her body lying crumpled on the white fur rug. The familiar clawing at her gut brought Lowen back to the present moment, as her anxiety manifested into what would surely become a terrible stomachache.

Hunching over to lean into an awkward hug, Lowen sighed. "Goodnight, Sebastian."

Despite everything that had happened tonight, she was grateful for Sebastian's steady calm steering her and her friends' frantic ship. She didn't know how she would have made it through the ordeal without him, and the trauma had instantly brought them into a swift dynamic of intimacy.

"Goodnight, Lowen," Sebastian said gently as she climbed from the front seat of the car into the chilly October night air.

As his headlights receded from the driveway, Lowen turned around to wave, but stopped in her tracks as she saw Sebastian focused intently on his glowing phone screen, a look of anger she had never seen before taking over his face.

Track 26 - "This Place Is A Prison" by The Postal Service

Lowen

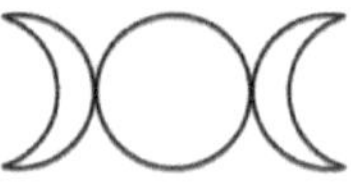

THE SOUND OF droplets, thick and sticky, roused her to consciousness. Her neck was on fire, throbbing relentlessly as she willed herself to open her eyes, looking up to see the trees gently swaying in the midnight breeze above her. As she reached her arm, heavy and slow, to her neck, a shadow descended upon her from a tall, naked branch. Lowen awoke as the demon's face plunged mere inches from her own, glaring into her soul with liquid amber eyes, its subhuman legs and arms grotesquely outstretched to grab her.

Lowen jumped from her bed to stand in her cold, sweat-soaked pajamas trying to catch her breath. The nightmare had left her disoriented, piecing together the fragments as if they were actually real. At once, the memory of the previous night descended upon her, erasing the terror from yet another odd dream to the very real truth that Blair was dead. Every minute after seeing Sebastian crouched over her body had an ephemeral quality, as if all of life's solidity, police lights and car rides home and warm blankets, had become impalpable. She willed herself to remember the night before, the blur of what happened after leaving Taylor's house when the police arrived.

Sebastian dropped off Noah, Taylor, and herself at her house where her mother slept, unaware of the nightmare her daughter had just endured. Luckily, Margot was at a sleepover and couldn't hear the three talking in hushed whispers for over an hour before Taylor's parents called, saying they had arrived home after receiving the worst call parents could ever imagine from the police.

"Apparently, my house is still an active crime scene, so my mom and dad are picking me up to go to a hotel for the night. They want us all to be together," she said, gathering her purse. "Wish me luck."

"Text us right when you get to the hotel," Lowen said, pulling Taylor into a tight embrace.

She could still feel Taylor's body shaking, as if she'd spent the night in a freezer.

"You're going to be okay," she whispered in her ear.

As Noah hugged Taylor goodbye, Lowen wrapped an oversized sweatshirt around Taylor's shoulders. As the front door closed and a pair of headlights pulled away from Lowen's driveway, Noah made a bed on Lowen's floor, the two friends turning out the lights and settling in to find some rest in the early hours of the morning. Staring at her ceiling, she heard Noah toss and turn, with sighs of frustration floating from his lips every few minutes.

"I'm sorry, Low," he finally whispered. "I can't sleep. Do you mind if I just head home? I don't want to keep you up."

"I'll drive you," she said.

"No, I don't want Emily to wake up," he insisted. "It's only a five-minute walk, and I could really use the time to clear my head."

"I don't know if it's safe, Noah," she whispered, images of the shadowy demon swooping down from the trees replaying in her mind."

"Look," he said, gesturing toward her bedroom window. "The sun is already rising. I'll be fine."

After another hug and a promise to call as soon as he arrived, Lowen was left alone, the eerie silence ringing in her ears like a tornado siren. She didn't want to be alone with her thoughts, so she texted Sebastian twice.

Lowen: Did you make it home okay?
Delivered.

Lowen: Just wanted to check in

Delivered.

She feared the cold loneliness seeping into her bones might be permanent, wrapping her lavender comforter around her shoulders as she scrolled the social media tributes to Blair that were already popping up.

Word must have gotten out, she thought as a lump formed in her throat.

Before now, it had all still seemed like a dream from which she could still wake. Now, with the evidence, pictures of Blair's smiling face, accompanied with "Fly high" and "RIH", it was real.

Lowen didn't remember when she finally drifted into a fitful sleep, but the sky had already turned from a deep gray to cotton candy pink. She was jolted awake by a scent trapped in the back of her throat, gagging her until her lungs coughed in protest.

The smell of coppery blood is still in my nose, she thought as she sat up in bed, clutching her throat.

She thought she might be sick as she forced her mind to go to the one place she didn't want to visit. Did Wesley have something to do with Blair's death?

He was upstairs when it happened, she acknowledged, a wave of guilt washing over her as she remembered seeing him on the stairs. Would she have to talk to the police? She promised herself she would tell them everything she saw, even if it meant they would question Wesley. Her gut screamed he was innocent, but what if she was wrong? She and Noah had not discussed his whereabouts in front of Taylor, but she would put money on the fact that Noah believed he had done it. After what he had seen. What had tormented him unlike any other vision. Death and decay. She ran to the bathroom as the demon's amber eyes descended upon her, its grotesque arms and legs reaching to take her away.

After retching into the toilet bowl, Lowen stared at her reflection in the bathroom mirror until her face didn't look like it belonged to her anymore. Black mascara smeared under her eyes, highlighting her exhaustion and lingering hangover. The paleness of her cheeks almost made her look gray.

You honestly look deader than Blair, she thought. *Also, you're going to hell for even thinking that.*

Lowen turned on the shower, determined to wash away any lingering trace of the Halloween party. After scrubbing at her skin with a loofah until it turned pink, she wrapped herself in a deep maroon robe her mom had gifted her last Christmas and walked with wobbly knees downstairs.

The house was empty, a rare occurrence for a Sunday morning. Emily had left a note that she was showing homes to a client and that Margot would be home around noon from her sleepover. The silence itched under Lowen's skin, the empty house reminding her how alone she truly was. Grabbing the remote and aiming it at the television, Lowen forced the living room to light up with the comforting voices of local news reporters chattering in upbeat voices.

Must be nice to be blissfully unaware, she thought, although she knew it was only a matter of time before the news stations reported Blair's death. She wished she could be them though, communicating the sanitized version of events, rather than the bloody horror she lived through. She was irrevocably changed by the darkness of last night, and wondered if the stain would ever fade, even if it was permanent. The voice on the television interrupted Lowen's spiraling thoughts.

"We have breaking news from the Moon Creek Sheriff's Office. A Moon Creek High School student was found dead at a party last night. Let's go to Jeremy Stewart, who is live at the press conference. Jeremy."

The screen switched from the local news station to outside of the police headquarters where the young male news anchor stood facing the camera, his back facing a small crowd and podium where the press conference would begin.

There is already a crowd? she thought, her stomach twisting.

"Thanks, Angela. We are outside of police headquarters where Sheriff Jones will speak in a moment," the news anchor, Jeremy, said, his brows furrowed in the morning sunlight. "What we know so far is that a female minor was found dead at a Halloween party in the early hours of Sunday morning." Jeremy paused, holding his earpiece for a moment. "All right, Angela, I just got word the sheriff is about to speak."

Lowen sat on her couch, her muscles shaking involuntarily inside her skin. With her eyes glued to the television, she reached for the remote to turn up the volume, drowning out the violent pounding of her heartbeat against her ribs as a pudgy man with graying hair and brown uniform stepped up to the podium.

"Good morning, Moon County residents. In today's very early hours, we received a call to our emergency response team that a young woman was found unconscious at a local residence. When we arrived, we were prepared to perform life-saving measures, but the victim was already deceased. We will not be giving out her name, as she is a minor. There were no other injuries or incidents. Based on the nature of the victim's gruesome wounds, we are treating this case as an active homicide. If anyone has any information about what happened last night, please contact the local police station. We will also be enacting a town-wide curfew starting this evening, November first, at nine pm for all residents."

Lowen sat frozen on her couch as the screen flashed and went back to the newscaster in the studio. Each word of the news report conjured visceral images of last night's gore to Lowen's mind, details she had shoved into dark corners of her brain where she hoped she would never relive them. Now, they all began flooding her senses: the sights, the scents, the noises, all swirling in her mind as if she were back in that bloody room all over again. Taylor's room. Where she had once felt the safest. Now, that security was shattered.

The ringing in her ears made it impossible for her to hear what the newscaster was saying. Gray started to form around the corners of her eyes as each inhale she took grew shallow. Laying in the fetal position on the couch, Lowen closed her eyes and waited for the sweet release of unconsciousness before a buzz in her robe pocket brought her back to reality. With numb fingers, she reached for her phone, squinting to see Noah's name on the screen.

"Hey," Lowen answered weakly, setting the phone next to her

while using the speaker feature.

"Hey. Are you watching the news?"

"Yeah," she mumbled, closing her eyes.

"Are you okay? I mean, I know you're not okay, but you sound terrible," Noah said, his voice softer than before.

"I felt like I was going to pass out. I just think I need to eat," she said as her voice trailed off.

"I'll be right there."

He had already hung up before she could answer.

Ever since they were little, Noah always looked out for Lowen in a way she never felt she deserved. He always made sure she was physically and emotionally well and never made her feel like she was a chore, or even worse, fragile. But perhaps she was fragile, she started to think. How else could he call her, put on clothes, walk to her house, and make her a meal? She knew she couldn't do the same for him. As she lay in a fetal position on her couch with wet hair, she felt utterly empty and helpless.

When the doorbell rang, Lowen dragged herself off the couch to open the door for Noah. As he walked in, she realized he looked pale, too.

"You look like dog shit," he joked, before wrapping his arm

around her waist and guiding her back to the living room. "Scrambled or poached eggs?"

"Thanks a lot. And poached, please," she muttered.

From the living room couch, Lowen could hear Noah rattling around in the open kitchen. He knew his way around, and before long, water was boiling for the eggs and the scent of toast wafted through the air. With effort, Lowen stood up and wandered over to the coffee maker to brew a fresh pot before sitting on a stool and watching it drip.

"Did you hear what they said at the end of the newscast?" Noah asked as he cracked an egg into the pot.

"I stopped watching after the sheriff spoke," she said, resting her head on the kitchen island, the cold granite soothing her hot cheek.

"They brought up the 'gruesome nature of the wounds,'" he said, using his finger as air quotes. "They said that when they arrived, she had been decapitated."

Lowen swallowed the acidic bile in her throat. "There's no way. We saw her. It was... attached."

"I know. Maybe it's just a rumor," he said, opening a few drawers before finding a butter knife. "How is Taylor?"

She studied her friend as he buttered the toast and cut it diagonally before placing the pieces on two paper plates. She wished she could help him, but her legs stopped working after the mention of decapitation.

"I can't get ahold of her. But I'm sure her parents are freaking out," she said. "This looks really bad for them—out of town while their teenage daughter throws a massive party ending with a murder."

"I hope she's okay," he said, turning to pull two coffee mugs down from their shelf above the toaster. "Have you talked to Sebastian?"

"No, I texted him last night, but nothing," she said, automatically reaching for her phone in the pocket of her robe to check her text messages again.

"He was really calm, considering," Noah said.

The image of his eyes glaring into his glowing phone screen while the corners of lips narrowed into a tight line came crawling back into her memory.

"Lowen, are we going to talk about the elephant in the room?" Noah asked, gently pushing the mug full of steaming coffee across the island to her.

"The elephant being Wesley?" she asked, swallowing hard.

"We have to go to the police," he said firmly. "Who else could have done this? We know everyone else who was there. We've grown up with them. There is only one person who YOU saw walk up those stairs right before."

Lowen sighed and rubbed her eyes. "I just want to talk to Sebastian first. He probably remembers details we don't. And then I'll talk to the police."

"I know it's not tangible, but what I saw when I read him was bone-chilling. In my gut, I know he's capable of this," Noah said, ripping off a corner of his toast with his teeth.

Lowen watched with envy as Noah ate the breakfast he had prepared while she pushed the pieces around on her plate until her phone buzzed on the countertop. Her heart jumped at the possibility of a text from Sebastian, but instead it was from Dr. Clarke.

Dr. Clarke: Would you be up for some research today? There is something from the Vincent farm I'd like you to see ASAP.

Lowen wordlessly pushed her phone over to Noah to read the text.

"You might as well. Maybe it will help distract you from this insanity," Noah said.

Lowen: I'll meet you at school at noon if that's okay.

Dr. Clarke: Perfect. I'll prop the door open for you.

Lowen inhaled deeply, feeling like she had just found a small lifeline to grab onto to keep from sinking into an infinite darkness. The mysterious murders on the Vincent farm and the news that the Count of St. Germain had visited Moon Creek sounded like a welcome distraction from the very real murder she had just witnessed.

Track 27 - "Photograph" by the Verve Pipe

Lowen

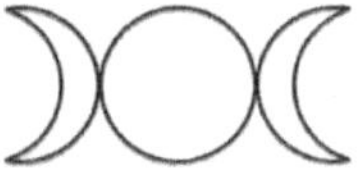

LOWEN WALKED UP the steps to the front entrance of Moon Creek High and noticed the middle door stood ajar just a few inches. Wedged between the door and the frame was a copy of *The Alchemist*. She smiled wearily as she grabbed the book from the ground and walked into the empty building.

Maybe things can go back to normal, she thought.

Walking through the dark, quiet halls of what was usually an obnoxiously loud cacophony of voices and lockers slamming felt fitting—like someone had just died.

"Lowen, I'm so glad you could meet. I wouldn't bother you on a Sunday, but this is... well, important."

Dr. Clarke looked like he hadn't slept last night either. His messy blond hair looked unwashed, and the bags under his eyes could have carried a week's worth of travel necessities.

"No problem. Is everything okay?" she asked.

He hadn't turned on the fluorescent overhead lights but instead used only his small desk lamp. The local newspaper lay open on the desk, illuminating Blair's senior picture already printed on the front page. Seeing her photograph smiling up at the tiled ceiling reminded Lowen of when their teachers used to confuse the two of them because of their straight brunette hair and similar build. She used to hate it. Now, it made her stomach tie itself into knots.

"Not entirely. I don't even know where to begin, so let me just start by showing you," Dr. Clarke said, dragging his fingers through his hair.

He gestured for her to sit at the desk that belonged to her during first period. As she sat, he placed the Vincent family photo album in front of her. The smell of time and dust and mold trapped inside her nostrils instantly. Her eyes fell closed for a moment, as if magically forced shut by the overpowering grief. A flash of the full moon behind the leaves of the Moon Creek trees popped into her mind.

"Just look through it," Dr. Clarke said, unknowingly pulling her from the vision.

To her relief, he hadn't even noticed Lowen's peculiar behavior, as he was too taken by whatever was within the pages of this photo album. The sigh escaping his nostrils was quiet but told Lowen that whatever she was about to see was not going to be good.

The very first page held a yellowed oval frame with a vintage family portrait in the center. The unsmiling faces staring back at her made the hairs on her arms stand up straight. The husband and wife were centered in the photograph and despite their serious expressions, they held each other's hands lovingly in the wife's lap. Flanked on both sides of the parents were two young girls, their expressions serious as well, with dark-haired curls and lace-trimmed dresses. Behind the parents stood a tall, light-haired young man, staring directly back at her. If the photograph had been in color, Lowen could have drowned in the rich amber of his eyes.

"Wesley," she whispered.

"Keep going," Dr. Clarke said ominously as he paced in front of the chalkboard with his arms crossed in front of his chest.

Lowen gently turned the page of the album to see a letter was tucked gently into the frame.

"May I?" she whispered, her hands shaking as she reached for the fragile paper.

"Yes, just be gentle."

Lowen unfolded the one crease of the yellowed paper to see elegant handwriting in black ink covering the page.

Dear Mother and Father,

Tomorrow, my traveling companion and I will take leave to head out West. We have spent months while helping you with the farm, planning for our great adventure. He tells me of the gold and treasure we are sure to find, and I believe him wholeheartedly. He travels with rare gemstones, and even rarer stories from across the seas. The point is, I suppose, I am in good hands. I know you have found him to be peculiar during his time with us, as have I admittedly, but you mustn't worry. I will return with glorious stories of adventures at the very least, and hopefully riches to allow you to finally rest from your relentless labor here on our family farm. I feel nothing but gratitude and admiration for you, mother and father, and I intend to make you proud.

Your loving son,
Wesley

Lowen lowered the letter and looked up at Dr. Clark, unsure of whether to laugh or cry at the absurdity of it all.

"What does this mean? Is this a distant relative of the Wesley I know? A namesake?" she asked, her voice an octave higher than usual. "That could be possible, right?"

"I suppose, but there are no records of Wesley Vincent after the murder on the farm. No records of returning. No record of death. No records of a family. So it seems the family lineage would not have continued," he said, finally looking up to meet Lowen's eyes as he stopped pacing and returned to his desk. "Lowen, there is no one else in the Vincent family to keep these genes going."

"What are you trying to say?" Lowen said, aware of the growing frustration and panic in her voice as she gripped the sides of her desk to keep from floating away.

"Turn the page," he said gently, as he sat back down behind his desk in front of her.

Lowen did as she was told and stared at another set of yellowed photographs. The first was the family standing in front of the barn, but this time all were smiling candidly. The men wore trousers held up with suspenders and light shirts, dirty and worn. The young girls wore long, light skirts, with one holding a kitten and the other smiling with her hand atop its head. The elder Vincents stood closely to each other, with the husband's arm around his wife's waist. In the center, Wesley stood smiling brightly with his arm wrapped around another man's shoulders, about his same height. The man stared back at Lowen from the photograph with jet black hair, light eyes, and a mischievous smirk. She closed her eyes for a moment, allowing her brain to catch up, and then reopened them.

Sebastian was still smiling at her, as if he knew she was looking at him.

When the room stopped spinning, Lowen looked up silently at Dr. Clarke.

"I think the other man in the photo is the Count of St. Germain," Dr. Clarke said quietly, as he resumed pacing in front of the chalkboard.

"What?" The ringing in Lowen's ears warned her another wave was coming, the gray appearing hazily around the corners of the classroom, fuzzy and all-consuming.

"Let's look at what we know: his physical attributes line up: the dark hair, the light eyes, the olive skin," he said, walking over to her desk and pointing to the photograph. "The letter acknowledges this stranger carried rare gemstones and knew how to 'find' gold. It sounds like Wesley thought he was going on a trip west to dig for gold, but what the Count wanted was actually an apprentice."

"Why would he want an apprentice?" Lowen asked, her voice sounding a million miles away as she fought the sweet escape of unconsciousness.

"Companionship, I suppose," Dr. Clarke said as he casually shrugged his shoulders, oblivious to Lowen's impending panic. "If he could really extend his own life for that long, the Count was probably very lonely. He hit the jackpot finding Wesley; he was lonely as well, came from modest means, and also wanted adventure. It was a match made in heaven."

Lowen rested her head, heavy and spinning, in her hands, and closed her eyes. Every conversation with Sebastian since she met him replayed in her mind like a movie montage. Could this be real? Despite the rational side of her brain telling her it was insanity to even consider the possibility of Sebastian being the Count of St. Germain, so many things added up in a weird way. His nondescript age and mannerisms. His jewelry business and gaudy gems.

"So, you think this man is the Count of St. Germain?" Lowen asked slowly, raising her head to point at the picture.

"Yes, I believe so. Has Wesley ever hinted to be incredibly old, even if by accident?" Dr. Clarke asked.

"Not directly, but his whole demeanor is… odd. I guess lurking in the woods behind the Vincent farm makes sense if it was his home," she said, her mind bouncing in frustration from Sebastian back to Wesley. "But it still doesn't make sense as to why his family was murdered."

Lowen thought about the heartache always hovering so tangibly over Wesley like a permanent rain cloud smothering out any light in its path.

"No, it doesn't," Dr. Clarke agreed. "But there were also many documented murders in the area—and across the Midwest at that time. The archives reveal that most folks thought there was a serial killer or an uptick in wild animal attacks."

He rotated his computer screen so it faced Lowen.

Squinting, she read the archived headlines on the screen: **THIRD MURDER IN MOON CREEK THIS MONTH.**

"You think they're all connected?" she asked, looking up at Dr. Clarke.

"People's throats were torn out, and there were gaping wounds. Sometimes the heads would be detached," he said, shaking his head as he turned the computer screen back around.

Detached. She thought back to what Noah had heard on the news this morning about Blair. Lowen attempted to take a deep breath through her nostrils, but only shallow air scraped her lungs as the room spun like a maniacal merry-go-round. Murders, decapitations, alchemists, Wesley, Sebastian. Blaire's murder couldn't be a coincidence.

"I don't feel very well," Lowen said abruptly. "I think I'm going to head home if that's okay." She had the urgency to run. Run away from all of it.

"Sure, sure. Do you need me to drive you?" Dr. Clarke asked, his face pinched with a look of worry.

"No, I'll be okay. I just need to go."

Her legs shook as she rose from the desk and walked to the door without making eye contact. She had to get out of there and into the fresh air.

"Lowen, be careful around Wesley until we find out more," Dr. Clarke warned.

"You got it," Lowen mumbled as she stumbled into the hallway.

Finding out more about Wesley *and* Sebastian was exactly what she intended to do.

Track 28 - "Bury a Friend" by Billie Eilish

Sebastian

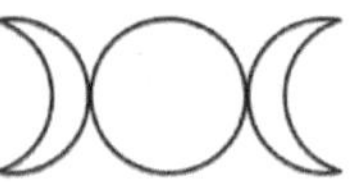

SEBASTIAN PACED IMPATIENTLY in the small, claustrophobic elevator until the metal doors opened to the penthouse level of the trendy apartment building where Wesley lived. His muscles hadn't felt quite so tense in decades. Not only did they come so close to taking Lowen's life and ruining his plan, but the whole event stirred something inside of him he assumed was dead and buried long ago. Panic. Worry. About her.

He gritted his teeth and clenched his fists as he entered the home of the last person he truly cared about. The irony of it all made him want to throw himself from the beautiful windows of Wesley's penthouse. Not that it would kill him.

"Much more modern than your usual taste, yes?" Sebastian asked, as he stood within the threshold of the elevator, holding the door ajar. "From my memory, you have always had an affinity for historic homes."

"Is now the appropriate time to make small talk about architecture?" Wesley asked, a scowl washing over his face as he took in the sight of his guest. "Especially when you need my permission to come inside?"

"You're not going to let your old friend inside?" Sebastian questioned, his eyebrows raising in feigned innocence before a wicked smile stretched across his lips. "Always a whining loner, aren't we?"

He knew now was not the time to bait Wesley, but he couldn't help himself. Wesley's melancholy was the main reason for Sebastian's varying degrees of unhappiness, and he couldn't help but torment him with it.

"Stop with the banter," Wesley said through gritted teeth. "There is a dead girl with a pretty damning wound on her neck. They are after us. They are after *her*."

Sebastian noticed as Wesley ever so slightly choked on the last word.

"I must admit, I was even surprised they went so far as to harm an innocent, especially in a crowded house," he said. "But as for the wound, I fixed that specific problem. Let me in, and I'll tell you all about it."

Wesley sighed, considering his choices, before finally muttering,

"Come inside."

"You are too kind," Sebastian said, slowly stepping over the threshold with his hands casually tucked in his pockets.

He strode directly into the kitchen as if he were the one who owned the place and opened the wine fridge that was hidden in a lower cabinet. Withdrawing a dark bottle of Cabernet, he began opening and shutting all of the drawers in search of a wine key.

"They did it to show us it could have been Lowen," Wesley said before stepping beside him and opening a drawer. "They could have done it right under our noses."

Wesley handed a wine key to Sebastian, their fingers briefly touching before Wesley jerked his arm back to his side.

"Which *they* are you referring to?" Sebastian asked as if nothing had happened, while plunging the key into the cork and pulling up until they both heard the sound of a small pop.

"Does it matter? Because of you, we have too many enemies to name," Wesley said. "But from the looks of it, the witches are our first concern."

Wesley turned his back to Sebastian and reached for two large red wine glasses in an upper cabinet. He brought them over and set them on the counter.

"You know and have always known I won't cower and I won't apologize. The witches cursed us and have wanted us to play by their rules for far too long," he said, hissing anger rising from his tone as he poured generous amounts of red liquid, too thick to be wine, into the two glasses. "Who are they to decide? To judge and condemn?"

Sebastian felt the scorching heat of rage burn under his skin. He allowed himself a moment to settle, hating the weakness tied to any emotion, and tempered his fury swiftly.

It's like blowing out a candle, he thought.

"As difficult as this is for me to say, I agree with some of your points," Wesley conceded, taking a small sip from his wine glass, allowing the coppery taste to coat his tongue. "But this is your fault, so I hope you will negotiate with them. We can fix this without anyone getting hurt. Especially Lowen."

"Now things get interesting," Sebastian grinned, images of blood and chaos flooding his thoughts. "What negotiations do you have in mind?"

"I'll help you," Wesley said quietly. "We can work together against our common enemies, with negotiations and explanations. I will even attempt to forgive the past. In return, you help keep her safe. And alive."

"I don't know if I can agree to that. You know deep down there is only one way for us to win. And negotiations and explanations are not part of that process," he said, shrugging his shoulders as he studied the burgundy liquid in his glass.

"Don't do this, Sebastian."

Wesley turned to face Sebastian, willing him to meet his eyes. It was the first time Sebastian had been granted access to Wesley's gaze since that horrible night. He missed the adventurous sparkle they once held, but now that twinkle had been replaced with a plea. The unspoken request almost weakened Sebastian enough to give Wesley anything he wanted.

Almost.

Because he knew what Wesley wanted. Lowen.

"I'm surprised, but I shouldn't be," Sebastian said, breaking their silent conversation with a smile that didn't quite meet his eyes. "The curse always did hint to this."

"What are you talking about?" Wesley asked.

"You care for her," he said, walking from the kitchen into Wesley's dreadful mid-century modern living room. "I've never seen you so desperately care for someone this way. The devil knows you never did for me. But then again, it was always there, written in the curse. The witches made sure to intertwine your life with hers, to make the two of your twin flames, soulmates spanning against time and space who would be harder to bring together than needles in a haystack."

Wesley looked down at the ground. Sebastian sighed, deciding to change the subject.

"Don't you want to know how I fixed the problem of the girl's gruesome, two-pronged wound?" he asked, circling the leather couch as if he were marking his territory.

Wesley looked up from his wineglass as the color disappeared from his cheeks.

"How?"

"I ripped off her head," Sebastian said, throwing back the thick red liquid in one long gulp. "You're welcome."

Setting down his glass on Wesley's coffee table, Sebastian stepped into the elevator, disappearing into the dark night without looking back.

Track 29 - "My Beloved Monster" by Eels

Lowen

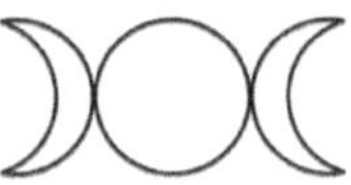

OUTSIDE, IN THE fresh air and warm sun, Lowen hoped she would feel better. Instead, the panic seeping into her veins flooded her nervous system. With shaking hands, she pulled out her phone.

Lowen: We need to meet up. Now.

Noah: K. I'm with Taylor getting coffee rn. Want her to come?

Lowen: No just u. Meet me at my house when ur done.

As she put her car in reverse, Lowen's phone buzzed. After hoping for a call or text from Sebastian, her stomach plummeted as his name appeared on her screen. An hour ago, she would have been relieved and maybe even giddy to hear his voice. Now, all she wanted to do was press down on the accelerator and drive far away from this place.

Who was Sebastian, really? In her gut, she knew he had to be the man who appeared in the photograph from the Vincent farm in 1894. Every single detail that made her fall for him jumped off the yellowing piece of paper: the smirk, the jet-black hair, the piercing eyes, even the necklace he wore. In her head though, Lowen had a hard time reconciling that magic was real—that men could create elixirs of life to cheat death, that they could turn lead to gold, and that they lived right here in Moon Creek. It all seemed too much for her rational brain to handle. Despite what she now knew, she needed to know more, so she did what she promised herself to never do: she played dumb. With a knot in her stomach, she connected the call to the Bluetooth in her car.

"Hi!" she said into the stale air of her empty vehicle.

A little too excited, Low. Calm it down.

"Hey," Sebastian said. "Are you doing okay?"

She didn't know how she expected an ancient alchemist to sound, but certainly not as casual and normal as Sebastian did in this moment. All at once, she began to doubt the photograph. Perhaps her mind was playing tricks on her.

"I'm okay," she said. "Last night was... a lot. I'm processing. How are you?"

"Same, that was a lot of blood. I'm not used to that," he said. "Anyway, enough about me. How are your friends doing today?

They didn't seem to be holding up so well last night."

Lowen paused at Sebastian's odd admittance about blood. Could she hear his smile through the Bluetooth? A chill involuntarily ran up her spine.

"They're doing as well as can be expected," Lowen said, forcing her vocal cords to act casually. "Actually, Noah is stopping by my house in a few. Wanna hang with us for a bit?"

A half-formed plan, stupid and reckless, brewed in her mind as she drove home.

"Sure. I'll be there in twenty," he said, coolly. "Want me to pick up some food? You have to be starving."

"Cheeseburgers would be great," she said.

She needed to stall him until Noah arrived.

"Okay, I'll see you soon," he said.

"Can't wait to see you," she lied, as she clutched the steering wheel tightly to keep her hands from shaking.

Lowen paced in her living room as she waited for Noah and Sebastian to arrive, willing her nerves to calm themselves. When had she last taken her anti-anxiety meds?

Maybe I can get a higher dose, she thought as her brain manically jumped from thought to thought.

She tried her hardest to piece everything together: the ritual at Moon Creek, the rock that said *thank you*, Sebastian helping her at the bonfire, Wesley's presence coinciding with Sebastian's appearance in town, the recurring haunting dreams, Blaire's murder. As much as she tried, none of the pieces fit together. What was it Dr. Clarke had said?

Sometimes you find a thread and keep pulling.

There had to be some mysterious thread tying all of these incidents together; she just needed more information. The door knob turned, interrupting her thoughts and causing her heart to pound in her chest.

"Hello? Lowen?" a familiar voice called out.

"Noah, I'm in here," Lowen said, relieved the voice at the front door was her best friend's and not the supposed alchemist's.

Noah walked into the living room and dropped his body dramatically on the couch, kicking up his bare feet on the ottoman.

"That good, huh?" she asked, unable to hide a genuine smirk.

Despite it all, Noah was still Noah, which meant perhaps she could still manage to salvage some part of herself when this was all over.

"Witnessing a murder will do that to you," he sighed as he

casually took out a flask from his jacket pocket and unscrewed the lid.

Usually, Lowen would frown and make a comment about the early time of day, but today she understood. Hell, she had the urge to share Noah's flask, but she knew she needed a clear mind.

"Well, I have some good news. Sebastian is coming by with burgers to go with that bourbon."

"Good, I'm starving. Apparently dead girls don't affect my appetite," Noah said dryly.

Lowen winced at his flippant words.

"How's Taylor?" she asked, still pacing back and forth across the living room floor.

"Can you please sit down? Your anxiety is killing me," Noah said, pinching the bridge of his nose and squeezing his eyes shut. "And she's... good. Like normal. It was weird."

"Maybe she's in shock."

Lowen thought back to the night of the party and Taylor's blank, yet terrified, expression; her angel wings shaking like brittle leaves.

"Yeah, I don't think so," he said. "She seemed good—and, like, happy. Her mom is taking her out of town for a few days to some fancy spa in Phoenix to unwind. I guess money does buy something—maybe not happiness, but at least the ability to run away."

He snorted, a hint of jealousy and misery mixed with his apparent exhaustion, as he tipped back his flask and sunk further into the corduroy couch Emily had saved an entire commission check to purchase.

"Must be nice," Lowen said, biting her lip as she finally sat in the wooden rocking chair across from him. "I tried to text her this morning, but she didn't respond."

"Yeah, that's the other thing. She was quick to change any subject involving you," Noah said gently, avoiding eye contact with Lowen at all costs.

You two will have a falling out, Noah had said the night he told Lowen of psychic abilities.

Noah warned her this was going to happen, but it didn't make the apparent rift any easier for Lowen. She and Taylor were so happy, so in sync yesterday. Their friendship had been like the old days. She hadn't realized how much she had missed her friend. How much she needed her. What had she done to make her mad?

"Did she say anything in particular about me?" Lowen asked, rocking too hard and too fast in the antique chair.

"No, she was pretty busy hauling ass to get out of the house where a murder just occurred, remember?" Noah snorted.

"I guess we all have a lot more to worry about than petty arguments," Lowen said, trying to swat away this particular problem like a gnat. "I'll fix it as soon as she gets home."

"Like murderers on the loose killing teens in Moon Creek?" Noah said while cracking a smile.

"Sounds like a perfect horror movie," Lowen whispered conspiratorially, finally easing her rocking into a gentle rhythm.

The two friends discussed who would play themselves in the movie version of the previous night with the morbid humor one could only openly embrace with those closest to them until they were startled from their dark, cathartic imaginations when a light knock tapped on the door. Lowen jumped, but tried to recover before Noah sensed her fear.

"It's unlocked!" she yelled from the living room, her legs unable to move underneath her.

"My hands are full," a muffled voice from behind the door said.

"Okay, give me a minute," she said.

Lowen's legs felt like Jello as she hurried to open the door, wondering if she could act like a reasonably normal human. How could she face the man she suspected of being an ancient alchemist? After taking a moment to compose herself and steady her breathing, she turned the knob and faced him.

Even after everything she learned earlier in Dr. Clarke's classroom, the sight of him took her breath away. A man with his hands full of cheeseburgers, fries, and Cokes was a thing of beauty for even the most ordinary male specimen, but as he looked up through his thick black lashes, her heart was pierced by his emerald eyes. The juxtaposition of the moment almost made Lowen laugh out loud: was the Count of St. Germain standing in all his ancient beauty with bags of greasy fast food at her request?

Take that, Catherine the Great, she thought to herself.

"Come in," she said, breathless while he let his arm brush hers, winking and walking past.

"Hello, Noah," Sebastian said, placing the fast food on the coffee table.

"Hey," Noah said, opening his eyes as the scent of grease wafted under his nose. "Thanks for the food. Also, thanks for everything last night. You really kept yourself together like a real adult."

Noah reached across the table, grabbing a container of fries.

"Like a real adult," Sebastian repeated with a grin. "I feel eternally young, but I appreciate that you found me to be responsible."

A chill ran down Lowen's spine. Had she missed other innuendos along the way? She was certain she had; he seemed to revel in playing this game. His eyes darted toward her, catching her staring at him. She blushed and grabbed a cheeseburger as she looked down at her mother's blue rug.

"Aren't you going to eat?" she asked as she took her seat back in the rocking chair.

Lowen's research included multiple sources stating that the Count of St. Germain never ate but instead insisted on drinking a red liquid—believed at the time to be wine and then later the elixir of life—in a special chalice.

"I just ate, actually," Sebastian said, as he stood awkwardly in the center of the living room.

"At least eat some fries," Noah said, extending an arm with a full container to Sebastian.

Lowen watched the interaction with intensity. Sebastian hesitated but accepted the French fries after a strained moment. Leaning over the coffee table, he reached out to Noah's extended hand, and for a brief moment, their hands touched. Noah's eyes changed ever-so-slightly. If Lowen had not been watching so closely, she easily would have missed the small moment, but it was exactly why she had brought them both together today. She hated using her friend, but she needed more information.

"Thanks. They do smell delicious, although I usually try to eat a little cleaner," Sebastian said, elegantly sitting in her mom's favorite blue armchair, popping a fry into his mouth with a smile.

Lowen knew Noah had seen something the moment he made contact with Sebastian. His eyes had gone wide, a flash of surprise lighting up his pupils before returning them back to normal. She watched as both men silently ate their fries, time and conversation seemingly frozen.

))) ● (((

Sebastian

I know you just read my mind, Noah, Sebastian whispered into Noah's mind.

How are you in my head right now? Noah asked, his face stoic as he sat across from him in Lowen's living room.

Because you let me in, Sebastian said, popping a fry into his mouth. *What did you see?*

Noah squirmed uncomfortably. *I saw a fragment of the future,* he said. *Although I don't really see things; they are more like a feeling about the future that involves you.*

A feeling? Sebastian pressed.

Multiple feelings, actually. Fear, chaos, the quiet stillness when someone is on the brink of death.

Interesting, Sebastian said, leaning back and smirking subtly. *Be sure to investigate your history, Mr. Messing. Throw yourselves at the wolves, or one Wolf in particular.*

Sebastian watched as Noah stood up abruptly, making Lowen jump on the cushion next to him.

"Um, I forgot—I promised my dad I would help him with something," he stuttered. "Thanks for lunch, Sebastian. Lowen, I'll call you later."

"Um, okay. Don't forget to call me," Lowen said, lines of worry creasing her forehead.

They both listened as the front door closed, the cozy, cottage house silent without Noah's boisterous presence.

"You're quiet," Sebastian said, turning his focus to Lowen. "Are you sure you're okay?"

He watched as she fidgeted with a thread coming loose from the couch cushion.

"Yeah, I am," she said, finally looking up to meet his eyes. "I keep thinking about something from last night though. Do you remember that guy, Wesley, who I introduced you to?"

Sebastian clenched his jaw at the sound of his name dropping like a whisper from her lips.

"Yes, the blond, quiet guy. A little dorky, right?" he said, setting the fries on the coffee table between them and wiping his fingers with a napkin.

"That's the one. Well, he went upstairs right before the murder," she said. "It's been bothering me that I saw him go up there and haven't said anything. What if he did it? What if he killed Blaire?"

This isn't good, Sebastian thought. Despite his complicated relationship with Wesley, he couldn't have Lowen suggest that Wesley murdered the girl.

"Are you sure it was him you saw? He wasn't anywhere upstairs when I went up there after I heard the scream," Sebastian lied. "I believe we both saw him downstairs not long before."

"Perhaps you're right," Lowen said, chewing on her bottom lip as a frustrated sigh escaped. Sebastian didn't understand why he felt the urge to bottle up the sound to keep forever, like a shell endlessly whispering the sounds of crashing waves.

"You can't be too hard on yourself," Sebastian said, searching her eyes to make sure she no longer questioned Wesley.

He had to admit a surge of joy jolted in his veins at the idea that she could imagine lonely, timid Wesley as a brutal murderer. Perhaps the witches' twin-flame curse wasn't entirely accurate. Perhaps, Wesley and Lowen weren't souls destined to be bound eternally in a romantic way.

"I should go," he said after a long moment of the two staring at each other in the quiet of Lowen's living room. "I just wanted to make sure that you were okay."

"Thanks for the cheeseburgers," she said, still studying him with an intensity that seemed to strip him bare. "I'll walk you out."

When they stopped at the front door, Sebastian turned to face Lowen and was surprised when his hand involuntarily reached out to gently touch her face. None of it felt like an act anymore.

"I want to make sure you're safe," he finally said, frightened by how blurred the lines had become.

"I'm okay, really," she said softly, stepping back slightly with wide eyes.

Is she afraid of me, he wondered, a pit gnawing at his stomach.

"Do you mind if I keep you close to me?" he asked. "Just until the police find out who is capable of such a heinous act."

Lowen inadvertently placed her hand on her collarbone and

cocked her head to the side as if she were trying to figure him out again.

"How close?" she asked.

"You might start referring to me as your shadow," Sebastian whispered, his instincts urging him to stop her from staring at him so directly. So inquisitive. She couldn't know, could she?

Bending his head down, he pressed his mouth against Lowen's. In unison, both of their lips separated slightly. Lowen sighed as he took her bottom lip into his mouth and lightly bit down. He drew away, still tugging lightly until he finally let go, allowing it to gently flip back to where it belonged. With that, Sebastian turned on his heel and walked out of the house, a grin stretched wide across his face for her to never see. He still had it.

Lowen

I'm in trouble, Lowen thought to herself, closing the door and locking it.

Her head became fuzzy, a light dizziness washing over her, as if she had drunk too much bubbling champagne too quickly. As she leaned her back against the front door, she realized that despite everything she knew, she was falling for Sebastian.

Would it be that bad to fall for an ancient alchemist who was capable of doing God knows what? She knew the answer when she reached her fingers to her lips and noticed the faintest trace of blood left over from their kiss.

Track 30 - "Sisters of the Moon" by Fleetwood Mac

Taylor

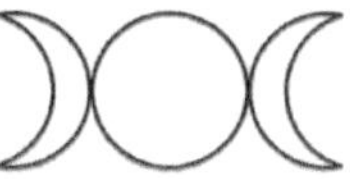

TAYLOR HAD NO idea where her mother was taking her, but she only felt relief as they pulled into the airport parking garage. The night before, she and her friends found Blair, their classmate murdered. At a party. At *her* house. In *her* bedroom. Her parents had been out of town, but very quickly and discreetly swooped in like her own personal crisis intervention team. Her father took care of the police/active investigation part of the dilemma, while her mother acted as her own public relations manager and whisked her away on the earliest flight to Phoenix, Arizona.

"Why Phoenix?" Taylor asked, although she was almost too exhausted to listen to the answer.

"I figured a small trip somewhere warm for rest and relaxation might be just what you need," her mom said as she patted her arm gently, but Taylor was already being lulled to sleep by the hum of the plane's engine. She fell into a fitful rest before the plane even took off, dreaming of soup and teeth.

She faded back to the same repetitive dream about the second day of kindergarten. The image of mucked up soup flashed before her. Too Many Babas. Too many cooks in the kitchen when they made the girl who was too much for everyone.

After pretending to be sick, but failing to will a fever into existence, little Taylor reluctantly walked into her kindergarten classroom and sat down stiffly at her desk with her chin high, unable to look anyone in the eye. Taylor watched as her classmates laughed and screamed and ran around the room, completely oblivious to her unfolding identity crisis. A boy with white-blond hair and a crusty nose that seemed to constantly drip ran toward her and stopped at her desk, looking at her before wiping his nose with his sticky fingers that looked like they hadn't been washed in weeks.

"Ewwww," he screamed as he ran away, completely oblivious to the irony of his statement.

Rage and humiliation simultaneously coursed through Taylor's veins, two feelings her little body had never experienced. She felt like her skin was on fire as ice-cold blood coursed through her veins. She turned around to stare at him, hoping he would trip and hurt himself. Bad. Hurt as bad as she did. It would serve him right.

Suddenly, the boy tripped over his untied shoelace, launching into the air. He landed face first into a desk. Everyone in the room could hear his teeth shatter as his mouth made uninterrupted contact. A wave of unnerving power and sickening horror simultaneously overcame Taylor. She watched as her teacher ushered the boy to the nurse's office with a handful of broken teeth floating like pieces of cereal in a mixture of blood and saliva in the palm of her hand. He howled like a wounded animal all the way down the hall. The class sat in silence waiting for the teacher to return, watching as the janitor sprayed bleach on the desk and attempted to scrub the bloodstains out of the carpet.

Taylor stood up quickly to go to the restroom, but didn't make it that far and vomited in the hallway, where fate would have her two best friends step into her life.

"That kid was an asshole," Noah said.

"An asshole," Lowen repeated, looking up at Taylor solemnly.

Taylor cracked a smile and remembered how to breathe again.

"An asshole," she said, letting the forbidden word roll off her tongue, forcing it from her gut where it lived.

She watched it float into the air like a hummingbird, wondering if there were other thoughts and words deep in her gut she could make materialize into the physical world. Taylor had a sneaking suspicion she was the reason for that kid's missing teeth but pushed back the momentary wave of guilt because something else was rising to the surface: happiness. She'd found her power.

Taylor was startled from her sleep by the drink cart jostling past her right shoulder. She sat up to see her mom looking at her, her eyebrows pinched with concern.

"They never got the soup wrong," her mom said, smiling as tears welled up in her eyes.

"What?"

How did she know what I just dreamt? Taylor thought.

"All of the ingredients were and still are absolutely perfect, but it's time you started making sense of all of the components," her mother said, wiping away the tears running from her almond eyes and down her perfectly high cheekbones.

"Okay, the soup metaphor is confusing me, Mom. How did you know about the babas? I've never told a soul," Taylor said, scanning her mother's eyes for some level of truth.

"That dream you just had?" she said. "It unlocks the thing I've kept from you your whole life.

Her mother took a deep breath before continuing. "What you did to that boy... I had to make sure you were old enough to responsibly wield that type of power. I had to shut it down so you couldn't use it for a while, but I think you're ready now."

She grabbed Taylor's hand, holding it between both of her own on the armrest separating their two seats, while gently rubbing her fingers over her daughter's skin.

"Shut what down?" Taylor asked. "Ready for what?"

Suddenly, the plane felt too hot. Too claustrophobic. She needed to get up. To pace. Was the altitude making her hallucinate? How was it she just now remembered the kid had smashed his teeth into the desk? Her memory of that day never included him losing his teeth. Or rather, it never included how she had knocked his teeth from his gums with her mind.

"I had to shut down your magic," her mother explained, gently guiding Taylor's chin toward her face so she would look at her. "Many witches do it for their children when they are young. They're too little to understand the consequences, while their emotions are too big to control it. Hence, the teeth floating in that poor teacher's palms."

"Mom," Taylor pleaded. "Mom, are you serious? I'm a witch? You're a witch? Please provide context... like right now."

"Do you remember what I told you about my family?" her mother asked, her voice low so the other passengers wouldn't overhear.

"Only that you grew up in the foster care system and that when you turned eighteen, you focused on your future instead of reconciling a past that didn't include you," Taylor said, the heartbreaking words catching in her throat.

"Well, there's a bit more to it than that," her mom said. "Please don't be mad at me."

"You know about your family?" Taylor asked, the familiar heat of anger coursing through her veins knowing her mother had lied to her.

"Let me try the simple version of the story," she said, her voice irritatingly calm.

"You trapped me on an airplane to tell this story, didn't you?" Taylor asked, staring at the woman who was a mirror image of herself with thick black hair and slim, long limbs.

She looked so much like her, yet at this moment, Taylor could hardly recognize her at all.

"Perhaps," she said, with a sad smile. "My maternal side of the family comes from a long history of magic. We are one of the several witch families in the world, and the only real coven in North America, but all the families are descendants from one: Hecate."

"Hecate? Like the Greek Goddess?"

Taylor would have thought her mom was losing her ever-loving mind if she hadn't been so calm.

"Yes, that Hecate," her mother said, nodding. "You know, Greek mythology isn't a myth at all. Much of it is absolute real history, just as true and factual as what you have been taught in your American History books. And just like American History, it's all about whose perspective you have access to. We'll have some time to delve into Hecate—who she was and what she gave us—but before all that, I want you to meet my family. Your family."

Taylor could hardly speak. "Do you know them?"

Taylor's mom looked down at her lap in shame. "I'm so sorry, honey. We saw how powerful you were at such a young age, and felt like the only way to protect you was to eliminate all magic from your life until you were ready. Unfortunately, that included access to your family. With your innate powers, you would have found out. We did it to shield you."

Her mom looked out the plane window, wiping the tears that had fallen from her eyes as she spoke.

"So, how did you do it?" Taylor asked, her voice harsher than she really wanted it to be. "You just, like, flipped off my magic switch? Are you able to turn it back on? Does Dad know?"

"Of course, he knows and he was in agreement with everything I chose," her mom said, squeezing Taylor's hand once again. "And no, it's not that simple. We have to perform a spell. I turned mine off, too."

Taylor's eyebrows raised at the admission; it was one thing to learn she had magic, but it was another to imagine her mother, so strait-laced and rule-abiding, wielding the same powers.

"My mother begged me not to, but I didn't feel right taking your magic from you and keeping mine. So now we have to go to Phoenix to visit our family and perform the spell for both of us," she said. "I'm so sorry, honey. I'm rambling now. Can you forgive me?"

Taylor watched as her usually even-keeled mom held her trembling hands to her mouth, looking as though she could burst out sobbing at any moment.

Taylor always knew there was a piece of herself missing but could never quite find it. It was like a gaping hole deep in her chest. No matter how many straight As or clubs or sports or scholarships she earned, she couldn't fill the void. It all made sense now. She could only begin to imagine how deep her mom's emptiness must have felt knowing what she once possessed and then having it taken away. Or giving it away as a sacrifice.

"You surrendered a part of you for me," Taylor said, her own tears welling up in her eyes. "Mom, I love you. Of course I forgive you, but I'm still a little pissed."

Her mom sighed in relief, a small laugh escaping her lips. "I've been waiting so long to tell you."

"So, we aren't going to a spa? Your lies are really piling up," Taylor joked, wiping away her tears with her hoodie's sleeve.

"Just wait until you meet them, honey. They are going to love you," her mother said as she brushed a piece of hair out of Taylor's face.

"One thing though, Mom. Why now?" Taylor asked. "With Blair and the police, this seems like interesting timing to unload a deep, dark family secret."

Her mother paused, thinking of how she was going to explain herself as Taylor felt her irritation rumble like fire under her skin again.

"It's complicated," her mom finally said. "Let's get to your grandmother's house, and we will fill you in on everything, I promise."

Taylor's mind raced at the idea that there was another story even more complicated than the one she just heard, but realizing she had a grandmother who she was about to meet created a whole new anxiety upon which she could fixate for the time being.

The plane would land in twenty minutes, and Taylor was on her way to meet her family of witches.

Track 31 - "Blood Bank" by Bon Iver

Wesley

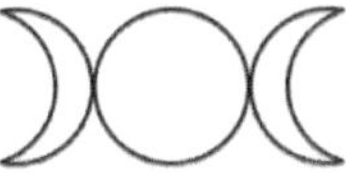

WESLEY SWUNG HIS fist down in frustration, watching his granite countertop crack as if an earthquake had just split it down the middle. He inhaled deeply.

Don't let your anger in, he coached himself.

It was the warning he repeated over and over throughout the tedious decades. His phone call with Sebastian hadn't gone well. Not only was it evident that Sebastian was earning too much trust with Lowen, but also Lowen had seen Wesley go upstairs the night of the party and seriously suspected him of being the murderer.

How bad had their interactions been for her to think he could do something so terrible? Sebastian had all but promised he would keep Lowen close, which should have been enough for Wesley, but the fact that he could practically hear Sebastian's slimy grin through the phone didn't set his mind at ease. At all. He knew exactly who Sebastian was—and exactly what he could do. Most of all though, he knew the kind of beings who were after Sebastian, and by extension, also after Lowen and himself. As powerful as Sebastian was, he wasn't powerful enough to keep himself and Lowen safe.

Sitting down on his chestnut leather couch, Wesley ran his fingers through his messy hair and closed his eyes for a moment. How he longed for the quiet nights under a soothing blanket of humidity in New Orleans. The curtains ruffled, despite the fact that the windows had all been shut earlier in the day. As Wesley snapped his eyes open, a man with dark, curly hair falling to his shoulders stood in front of him. Wesley shot off the couch in a sudden burst of movement, landing mere inches from the man's face. In return, the man put up his hands, as if surrendering. They stood, staring into each other's eyes, not knowing what the other would do. Then, the man smiled, his light brown irises glistening under thick-framed black glasses that Wesley knew he didn't need anymore.

"Wesley, it's been too long," he said, his voice soft.

He noticed a large, intricate tattoo peeking from the man's shirt sleeve against his tan skin. That was new. How long had it been since he had seen him last?

"Nadeem," he exhaled, his body relaxing.

The two men embraced, and for a moment, Wesley felt as close to being a human as possible under the circumstances. When he pulled away, he tried to hide the tears that had traitorously formed in his eyes.

"It's been too long since you've shown your humanity, yes?" Nadeem asked, reading Wesley's emotions as if they were a novel.

"It's easier to be alone," Wesley admitted, sitting back down on the leather couch and gesturing for Nadeem to do the same.

Nadeem nodded quietly, acknowledging the price they paid for their bargain with eternity.

"I can't stay here long; it's too dangerous," he continued, "but I needed to let you know what you're up against."

Nadeem's urgency erased any hope that Wesley would be able to spend time with his old, and only, friend.

"Sebastian has really gotten us into a mess, hasn't he?" Wesley asked.

"Honestly, I'm surprised he was able to break the witches' curse. He's been trying for over a century. I thought our kind would have killed him by now, for no other reason than he has never played by the rules. With this stunt though, he's proven himself to be back in their good graces," Nadeem informed him.

"He did it for himself, no one else. He doesn't care who loves him or hates him," Wesley said, sighing as he settled back onto his couch.

"I can't lie though, as much as I detest the man, I'm glad he broke the curse too and I hope it remains broken," Nadeem said. "That's why I came to tell you your most immediate threat comes from the witches. Word around town is they're looking for you and Lowen. You two are the keys to repair the curse and set things back the way they were. You both need to go into hiding immediately."

Wesley pinched the bridge of his nose and closed his eyes. He knew this message would be coming but hearing it out loud didn't make it any easier.

"What about Sebastian?" he asked.

"Do you actually care?" Nadeem asked, an incredulous laugh bubbling in his throat. "He's put you in danger time and time again for his own gain. Let his magical alchemy save him now."

Nadeem let the bitterness simmer in each word he spoke. "He may have broken the curse, but it doesn't mean I don't loathe him any less."

Wesley understood Nadeem's paradox; it was a knot he was trying to untangle, as well. Sebastian's selfishness had gotten them all into this mess to begin with, but it also fixed it and gave all of their species a common goal: to keep Lowen and Wesley safe. If not, the witches would use the twin flames to rebuild the spell and their whole species would go back to the darkness they loathed.

"Nadeem?" he asked, looking up at his friend who seemed so much more suited to live in this modern apartment.

"Yes?"

"How do I tell her?" he whispered.

Nadeem paused, carefully considering the advice he would bestow.

"Don't you wish you would have known the truth?" Nadeem asked. "I wish I would have been given the opportunity."

He looked away to gaze out of the window with a sadness Wesley knew deep in his bones. "I have to go now," he said. "Wesley, stay safe. I mean it; the witches are no joke."

With a soft whoosh, Nadeem transformed into a majestic brown and white owl. Stretching his wings, he flew out of the open window, leaving Wesley alone again. He let the emptiness, like a gnawing hole in his chest, linger for a brief moment before shoving clothes into a duffel bag.

Wesley knew what he had to do, and he knew for a fact Lowen wasn't going to like it.

Track 32 - "The Night We Met" by Lord Huron

Lowen

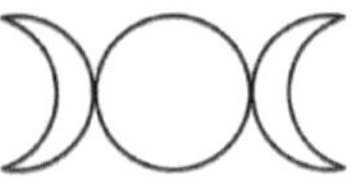

"SO, YOU'RE TELLING me Sebastian and Wesley are both old AF *and* they're alchemists?" Noah asked, his voice screaming incredulously through Lowen's phone.

"I know it sounds crazy," Lowen said, sighing with overwhelming exhaustion.

She felt the one-thousand-pound elephant lift off her shoulders as she unloaded a secret she had carried alone all morning. Leaning back against the pillow on her bed, she lifted her MacBook onto her lap.

"Honestly, it kind of makes sense," Noah said, a laugh escaping his lips as voice softened.

"How so?" she asked, confused by how easily he could believe what she had divulged.

As Noah spoke, Lowen searched Google images of the Count of St. Germain, zooming in on portraits of a man she didn't recognize. She searched into acrylic eyes, looking for his mischievous stare, and studied sketches of his lips, comparing the shape of his Cupid's bow to the one she just touched, but no details gave her the affirmation she craved. She wanted to know for certain. Needed to know.

"I guess the visions I had of Wesley at the Halloween party were accurate," Noah said. "If Wesley truly is a son of the Vincent family, he witnessed his family get slaughtered. It would make sense that all I saw—or felt—from him was death and darkness. I mean, unless he was the one who killed them. Then, death and darkness really is coming from him."

"And what about Sebastian? What exactly did you see?" Lowen asked, tossing her computer on her lavender comforter before standing up to pace the room.

"Well, your boyfriend didn't really show me anything about his past, just some feelings in the future, but..." He hesitated.

Lowen stopped in the middle of her bedroom floor, dread pooling like thick oil in her stomach.

"But what?" she asked. "No secrets, Noah. We're surrounded by craziness, and you are my only lifeline to staying sane, so no holding back on anything, promise?"

"Promise," Noah said through the phone. "Okay, as I was

reading him, he was reading me."

He paused, waiting for Lowen to comprehend what he was telling her.

"What? Like he could read your mind?" she asked.

"Exactly like that," he said. "We were able to have a conversation without speaking. Straight up telepathically."

The pool of oil in Lowen's gut began to churn. "Oh my God. What if he can read *my* mind?"

Lowen heard a breath of air escape Noah's lips.

"What was that, Noah?" she asked. "Are you laughing right now?"

"I don't think he needs to do any mind-reading to know how you feel," Noah giggled before stopping suddenly. "The thing is, he could read my mind without me letting him inside, but I have this feeling he could keep thoughts from me. Like he could control what he wanted me to see."

"What makes you think he has that kind of power?" Lowen asked, trying to focus on anything besides her own mortification.

"Because when I saw what he felt in the future, he knew it. And he turned it off right away," Noah said, his voice quieter, deeper than before.

"What did you see, Noah?" she asked, sitting down at the end of her bed.

"I think I felt him die," Noah said. "And he felt himself die through me."

The line went silent for a long moment, both weighing the enormity of what Noah had just admitted. Lowen's ears rang as the gray fuzziness obscured the corners of her vision. Before she could lay back onto her bed, a man's voice coming from downstairs pulled her from the darkness threatening to swallow her whole.

"I'm going to have to call you back," she whispered, her phone dropping from her shaky hands as she strained to hear her mother's conversation with the stranger downstairs.

"Lowen, someone is here for you," her mom yelled.

The house was silent for a moment before Lowen heard her mom speak again in a gentler tone.

"Come on inside. It's getting cold out there," she said, the front door gently closing behind her.

As Lowen left her room, she double-checked her appearance in the mirror in case Sebastian was making a surprise visit. She hated that she cared, but as she thought back to their shared kiss earlier, she couldn't deny her feelings for him.

Even if he was an ancient alchemist.

Perhaps, even because he was one.

She had always been drawn to the darkness, so maybe he had always been her destiny. As she descended the stairs, she had to blink a few times before registering a man's sandy brown hair instead of Sebastian's midnight black.

"Hi Lowen," Wesley said, not quite meeting her eyes.

"Hey," she said flatly. "This is unexpected."

What is he doing here? she thought to herself.

She hadn't seen him since Taylor's Halloween party. Since watching him walk up the stairs toward the room where Blair was murdered. Even though Sebastian had assured her he hadn't seen Wesley when he found her dead, Lowen couldn't shake the idea that Wesley was somehow involved.

"Lowen, be kind," her mom admonished.

"It's okay," Wesley said, smiling respectfully. "I deserve it for showing up unannounced. Um, I was hoping you and I could talk. Maybe over ice cream?"

"I have homework," Lowen said, forcing the lie from her lips. "I'm sorry," she added to soften her delivery. "Plus, Mom has had me basically on lockdown since the Halloween party."

"Lowen, grab some ice cream. I trust that you'll be safe with

Wesley," Emily said.

Her mother's ability to instantly trust was going to get her killed one of these days, she thought. It had only taken one day of showing Wesley some places to live and she was ready to plan their wedding. Lowen understood her mother's perspective, though. Without all of the very strange coincidences, she may have seen him through the same filter: handsome, kind, respectful. She shoved the thoughts from her mind, as if she let them linger, she would be betraying Sebastian.

You sure know how to pick them, she thought to herself as she rolled her eyes. *One an alchemist Casanova, and the other a possible murderer.*

"I'll have you back before curfew," Wesley insisted, his eyes pleading for her to join him.

"Go," her mother prodded firmly, her eyes locked on Lowen's communicating that her bratty behavior wouldn't be tolerated much longer.

"Fine," Lowen said, walking down the remaining steps. There was no way she was going to get out of this without blurting out to her mother and Wesley that she suspected him of murder. The more her mind mulled over this hypothesis, the more her gut screamed that it was absurd. Looking at Wesley from the last step of the staircase, she couldn't imagine him hurting anyone. His movements were slow and gentle, as if he were afraid he would break something if he even breathed too forcefully.

Besides, Lowen's curiosity was getting the best of her. She had so many questions screaming inside her mind about both strangers who had shown up in her life at the exact same time. Perhaps Wesley could unknowingly shed some light on who he and Sebastian were if she played her cards right. A bundle of nerves traitorously dropped like dead weights in Lowen's belly as a vision of Blair's blue eyes staring blankly at the ceiling flashed through her mind. What if Wesley was dangerous? She still wasn't entirely convinced he wasn't the one who decapitated Blaire or if he murdered his entire family.

Learn to trust me, her gut whispered. *He's not a murderer.*

Lowen tucked away the words in her pocket, holding onto them for safekeeping.

After saying goodbye to her mother and promising to return within an hour, Lowen and Wesley walked into the crisp November night to Wesley's black Audi. He didn't attempt to open her door, and she appreciated that he didn't.

Stay on your side, she thought to herself.

"Your seat heater button is on the door," Wesley muttered. "It's getting cold out here—do you not wear a coat?"

"Usually, but we won't be gone long," Lowen explained, irritated by his judgment on her wardrobe.

Lowen's irritation melted ever so slightly as she heard Lord Huron playing lightly through the car's speakers. "I love this song."

"I do, too."

She looked over to study him. His fingers lightly tapped on the steering wheel as he drove. Everything he did was gentle, from flipping on the turn signal to how he lightly turned up the volume so they could hear the song better. Even his golden eyelashes blinked so slowly, she wondered if they held the weight of invisible tears as they closed. The more she observed, the more she couldn't believe he would hurt anyone. As the car slowed in the ice cream shop's parking lot, Wesley turned down the music.

"I'll go in and grab the ice cream," he said, unbuckling his seat belt. "We can eat it in the car in case we break curfew. Plus, I don't want to hold up the workers being able to close up in time," Wesley explained, turning to finally meet her eyes.

"Good plan, Captain," she said, unable to take the sarcasm out of her tone.

"Can I ask you something?" he said, pausing before opening his door.

"I'm sure you will anyway," she said, hating herself for how rude she was being.

It was as if she couldn't help herself. Wesley brought out the absolute worst in her.

"Are you always this hostile?" he asked, his eyebrows pinching together.

"Only with the right people," she said, choking on the words when she saw his face fall.

He nodded silently for a moment before opening the car door and climbing out. Leaning down so his eyes met hers through the open door, he asked, "What flavor do you like?"

A crushing wave of guilt pummeled Lowen's chest.

"Mint chocolate chip," she said softly. "In a cup, please."

Wesley looked at Lowen and smiled for some reason. "Okay, I'll be back in a second. Keep the doors locked."

She watched him shove his hands into his jean pockets as he walked up to the door of the ice cream shop. As she observed him running fingers through his hair, she thought back to the first time she had seen him in the woods, a beacon of safety looking through his binoculars as she was chased down by that strange man. He had run his fingers through his hair nervously then, too. She had to admit it was an endearing habit. She studied his movements as he paid: how he reached into his back pocket to smoothly grab his wallet, how a dimple appeared on his left cheek when he smiled at the cashier and dropped multiple bills into the tip jar, how he easily held two cups of ice cream in one large hand as he casually walked back to the car. Suddenly, the seat heater felt too warm.

Lowen didn't realize she was holding her breath until she unlocked the doors to let him in, feeling the icy cold air enter the warmth of the suddenly too-hot car. Grabbing the two cups from his outstretched hand so he could settle into the car, she noticed they held both scoops of mint chocolate chip.

"Your favorite, too?"

"We might have more in common than you think," he said, resting his head against the seat.

Lowen felt a smile tug at the corner of her lips, taken aback by the ebbs and flows of her emotions. Wesley brought out a frustration in Lowen, but also a sense of connectedness, as if a piece of her had known him forever.

Magnets.

She couldn't discern whether her irritation toward him was brought on by his gratingly niceness or because she wanted more of it. His hand brushed against hers as he took his cup of ice cream, causing a jolt of electricity to surge through her entire body. Lowen jumped, her cheeks heating as she looked down at the floorboards.

What the hell was that? she thought.

Squirming in her seat, she fidgeted with her spoon before taking a bite of her ice cream. "What did you want to talk about?" she asked with her mouth full.

He looked over at her, his sad, amber eyes piercing into her soul, opening his mouth to speak but stopping short of uttering any words.

Oh no, she thought. She couldn't let him put himself out there. Especially when she knew she would reject him.

"Wesley, you know I am seeing someone, right?" Lowen blurted out.

He winced and then smiled at the remark, as if it was silly for her to assume he could have romantic feelings for her, the sad smile making her feel like an idiot.

"Well then, what do you want from me?" Lowen asked, the skin on her cheeks blazing with heat.

"I'm sorry. I'm so, so sorry," he said, setting down his cup of ice cream on the center console. "I've been lying to you."

Lowen's hands began to tremble as she thought of the burgundy pool of blood seeping through Taylor's floorboards.

"Lying to me? About what?" she asked, her voice cracking.

"About who I am," he said, running his fingers through his hair in frustration. "I don't even know how to explain this."

The night sky began to spin as Lowen attempted to focus on the twinkling stars against the velvet black backdrop. The car felt too small. Too hot. She cracked her window, attempting to breathe in fresh air. Was he going to admit what she and Dr. Clarke had uncovered? Could it really be possible? She turned to meet Wesley's eyes as the cool November air covered her arms with goosebumps.

"I think I know, Wesley," Lowen whispered.

Wesley whipped his head around to stare at her, his usually sad eyes now blazing with intensity.

"What? What do you mean you know?"

"I know you're an alchemist, or, at least, you were trying to be one," she said, the insane words rolling awkwardly off her tongue as if she were speaking a new language. "I know you're old, like really old, probably from the elixir of life. And I know your last name is Vincent."

She whispered the last part breathlessly, unsure if he even heard it. Wesley's hands went from his hair to cover his face.

"How do you know this?" he asked, his voice muffled from

behind his hands.

"I've been working with Dr. Clarke," she explained. "Helping him do research on the Count of St. Germain. He had a hunch that the Count had come to Moon Creek and stayed at the Vincent farm for some time. We found your family's photo album that day I ran into you out in the woods behind the barn. You were in it—you looked the exact same as you do now."

"So, you believe I am the same age as I was in 1894 because of *alchemy*?" he asked.

"Well, when you say it that way," she said, her cheeks burning hotter than ever as she distracted herself from his stare by swirling her ice cream with her spoon.

"There is only one elixir of life, Lowen," Wesley said quietly.

Although she wasn't looking at him, she could feel his eyes laser-focused on her.

"I know," she muttered. "And Sebastian gave it to you. He's the Count of St. Germain."

She listened as a frustrated sigh escaped his lips. Surprisingly though, she didn't feel afraid. If anything, overwhelming sadness washed over her as she sat next to the man admitting he wasn't entirely human.

"Lowen, how long have you known this?" he whispered, his voice thick with guilt.

"For about twelve hours," she confessed.

They sat silently for a few minutes, both lost in their own thoughts and admissions.

"Lowen?" Wesley asked finally.

"Yeah?"

"You're in danger."

"What? Why?" she asked, attempting to pull her eyes from the stars and look at him.

Her mind screamed to her to be afraid, to jump into action, but her body commanded her to rest. Her arms and legs tingled like they were being poked by hundreds of tiny needles, a curious weight washing over them.

"You are in close proximity to me and Sebastian, and trouble follows us," he said, as if he had recited these lines many times in advance. "Also, you know the truth, which makes you a liability in some circles."

"What circles? Are there other alchemists?" she asked, her words slurring as she tried to speak. "Are they the ones who killed your family?"

She suddenly felt so tired she had trouble holding her eyes open.

Seconds felt like an eternity as Wesley sat silently before answering.

"The witches," he said. "They don't like us, nor what we are able to do."

"Witches?" Lowen asked as she leaned her head back against the headrest. "Like the broomstick and cauldron types?"

Alchemy was one thing—a sort of scientific magic she could almost rationalize, but real witches? Not like Taylor, who looked up spells on Pinterest, but real witches? As her brain began its hazy descent into unconsciousness along with her body, she wondered if she was hallucinating.

"Well, no pointy hats, but yes, spells and grimoires and magnificent powers," Wesley said, pausing to look at Lowen's limp body with sad eyes. "They see us as abominations, as threats to their survival. Now that you know about us, they will come for you."

Lowen raised a heavy hand to her numb face and rubbed her eyes.

"Who is 'us'? Alchemistsss? And why are you abominationsss?"

Her words slurred so badly she was sure that Wesley had to have noticed. Why wasn't he concerned? Instead, he sighed and continued answering her questions as if the answers were as important as life or death.

"Yes, alchemists are abominations to real witches," he said, his jaw clenching each time he paused to consider his next words. "They see themselves as naturally inclined to perform magic because they are born into it, while believing we have forced our way into their world. Too much magic is dangerous, and they want to shut us down. They've been chasing us, Sebastian and me, for a long time. They are ruthless when it comes to getting what they want. You wouldn't stand a chance against them, and they won't let you live knowing what you know."

"So, what am I s-supposed to do?" she mumbled, her heavy eyelids closing.

"Hide," he said, definitively. "That's why I've asked you to come with me tonight. We've got to go somewhere safe. Now."

Lowen forced her eyes to open again, Wesley's face merely a blurred watercolor painting without defining details.

"N-n-no, Wesssley, I need to go home," she slurred, trying to move her heavy limbs from the seat.

"Listen to me," Wesley commanded, his voice strained. "You know what happened to that girl at the party? The witches did that to her. It was no coincidence she looked so similar to you, Lowen. They were sending us a message."

Lowen gagged as she remembered the smell of copper

smothering the air, the thick black blood droplets slowly puddling beneath Blaire's lifeless body.

"Where w-would we go? What d-did you give m-me?" she asked, looking down at the blurry puddle of melted ice cream sitting in the cup on her lap as the air evaporated from her lungs.

"Where no one will find us. I'm sorry for doing this to you," he said. "I was afraid you'd try to run and that they would hurt you."

"Are w-we g-going to tell S-S-Sebastian?" Lowen asked before finally giving in to the drugs and closing her eyes.

"Sebastian will take care of himself. He always does," she heard him say, more to himself than anyone else.

Lowen heard the gears shift and gravel crunch under the tires as she and Wesley fled Moon Creek under the glow of a full moon.

Track 33 - "Invisible String" by Taylor Swift

Sebastian

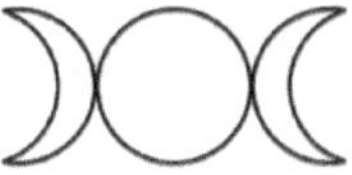

"HI, SEBASTIAN. IT'S Lowen's mother, Emily Lawrence. I know this sounds terrible, but is she with you?"

Sebastian could hear the faint edge of hysteria scraping against her vocal chords, although she was doing a well-enough job of hiding it.

"Hi, Emily," he said calmly. "No, I haven't seen her. She doesn't have her phone with her?"

He heard her sigh through the phone, a breath of worry coated in a thin layer of frustration.

"Yes, but she won't answer," she explained. "She and Wesley went out for ice cream at seven o'clock and are still not back. I can't reach him on his cell phone either. It's past curfew, and this is totally unlike Lowen. My mind just goes to the worst place after what happened to that poor girl, Blair."

Her voice choked as she tried to sputter out the end of the

sentence.

Sebastian looked at the time. It was after ten o'clock and the town was locked down. Lowen's mother should be worried; he would be, too, if he didn't know exactly what happened. Wesley took her. He knew he would do something like this. So instead of wringing his hands and pacing back and forth, Sebastian felt the comforting flames of rage course through his veins at Wesley's betrayal.

"Emily, stay calm," he said, his voice deep and gravelly, as if the flames had licked his vocal cords. "I'll look for them."

Where to begin, he thought, as he sat his phone down on his coffee table, crossing his arms against his chest in a furious calm. He may not have been included in Wesley's traitorous plans, but he did know someone who could figure them out.

Hello, Mr. Messing, Sebastian asked. *Have you heard from our shared treasure, Lowen?*

Silence rang loudly in his ears for a moment as he impatiently tapped his foot on the hardwood floor.

How are you in my head right now? Noah finally asked.

Upon hearing the boy's voice, Sebastian walked to his liquor cart and poured a generous serving of thick red liquid into a crystal rocks glass.

Noah, please. Now is not the time, he chastised. *Your friend is in trouble, so I am going to need you to tell me everything you know.*

I talked to her on the phone about an hour ago, Noah recalled. *But she had to go—someone was at her door.*

Who was it? Sebastian pressed.

Noah sighed with frustration before admitting, *I'm not sure.*

Sebastian tossed back the thick liquid in his glass, squeezing his eyes shut as it coated his esophagus.

Noah, I can feel you trying to hide something from me, he said, his voice lulling into a sing-song melody.

How are we able to do this?

You mean, how am I? Sebastian asked. *You know how you can read people's minds because you did the research on your family line as I asked. And what is that you uncovered, Mr. Messing?*

Noah

Noah had, in fact, gone home after leaving Lowen's house and researched his family history as Sebastian suggested. He had always known he was different—way before Taylor's spell and his ability to read people's thoughts—he just never wanted to admit it to himself. When he talked to the ocean when he was twelve, Noah knew he could hear her. When the geese organized and flew south for the winter, he overheard their honks from above and understood their frenzied conversations. When his dog was sick and dying in seventh grade, she told him she would rather be euthanized than suffer.

Noah would habitually rationalize the voices by believing he had an overactive imagination, and that this was some kind of only child mechanism to ward off loneliness. As he got older, he drowned out the voices with alcohol. The drinking never made them completely go away, but it did quiet them enough to not distract him. But when Sebastian lit the match in his mind that this could all make sense, Noah followed the flame. And the truth was astounding.

Noah sat at the family computer, a slow and bulky relic from technology's past, in the dark, claustrophobic room generously called the office. As he typed the name Sebastian had whispered to him, Wolf Messing, Noah was inundated with articles and stories about the man who had to be Noah's great great-great-grandfather. His head spun as he cross-referenced his own family's records with the articles in front of him until he was entirely convinced that he was related to the infamous man.

Noah read voraciously as puzzle pieces of his life snapped into place, the story of Wolf's life was truly astounding. As a boy, Wolf's family wanted him to become a rabbi, but he ran away instead. He didn't have any money for a train ticket, so he pulled out an old newspaper when the inspector demanded a ticket. The inspector saw a train ticket, not a scrap of paper, and let him stay on the train. It was his first instance of recognizing his psychic abilities, as he was able to make the train inspector see what he wanted him to, not what was actually in front of his eyes. When Wolf finally arrived in Germany, he had nothing, so he worked in kitchens until he found the perfect gig for his gifts: the circus.

Wolf's talents for mind-reading, finding missing objects, and predicting the future made him an instant hit for audiences desperate to witness magic. Among his admirers were familiar names such as Freud, Einstein, Gandhi, and Marilyn Monroe. Wolf's talents weren't just for the circus, though; Wolf predicted that Hitler would die if he went east, which turned Wolf's talents deadly. His prediction made him become Hitler's personal enemy, complete with a bounty for his head and Nazis on his trail. Using his gift of mind control, he was able to escape after being captured by mentally ordering the Gestapo to lock themselves in a cell and let him free. His escape led him to the Soviet Union, and to Stalin, where he became somewhat of a personal magician to the evil dictator. It was his price to pay for being given a safe haven from Hitler and the Nazis.

Noah's head unconsciously shook as he read his great, great, great grandfather's story, as if he mind refused to believe each subsequent fantastical fact could be true.

But his gifts, Noah thought to himself, closing his eyes to drown out the glow of the computer screen. The similarities between their two talents was undeniable. And now, he understood the weight of wielding such powers. Reading people's minds was dangerous work, even if he had yet to test his abilities to control minds. Honestly, he was too afraid to even try. But the power involved...

My great, great, great grandfather was Wolf Messing, Noah said, shaking himself back to the present moment. *Although I'm guessing you already knew that.*

Noah, you have untapped power. Your grandfather was powerful, Sebastian said, before adding, *He was also funny as hell.*

Noah blinked, unable to think properly for a moment. *Wait, you knew him?*

He gritted his teeth, suddenly frustrated by the mental conversation. He wanted to see Sebastian's face, to read his expressions. He also wanted Sebastian out of his head.

Now, how could I possibly know him? Sebastian asked, his voice playful, as if it were dancing in circles inside Noah's mind.

You know I know who you are, Noah said. *You've read my mind.*

Correct, Sebastian admitted. *But my mind-reading capabilities are nothing compared to your untapped abilities. I can help you though.*

Why would you do that? Noah asked, his eager swiftness giving him away as desperation washed over him.

Because you never know when you could use a friend who possesses great strengths, Sebastian said, his mischievous grin audible in Noah's mind.

So, you want to use me?

And teach you. Think of it as a transactional relationship.

Noah paused, considering the unknown risks. How many times had he read books or watched movies where a human made a deal with the devil? It never worked out favorably.

Are you dangerous? he asked.

Aren't we both?

Perhaps Sebastian really is the devil, he thought to himself. *He has an answer for everything.*

Remember, I can hear you, Sebastian interrupted.

Noah laughed, shaking his head incredulously before

answering, *If I do this for you—for me—no one gets hurt, right? You must promise me no one will get hurt.*

Sebastian sighed before saying, *You'll learn soon enough that you can never promise anyone anything when it comes to magic. So much of it is out of our control.*

Fair enough, Noah said. *When does our teacher/student relationship begin?*

Right now. Close your eyes and concentrate on an image in your mind. Do you have it?

Noah closed his eyes and blocked out Sebastian's voice. An ocean wave, blue and frothing, sighed as it stretched across the sugary sand on the shoreline.

Very good, Sebastian said. *Now, what did the ocean say to you?*

Noah's eyes flashed open, as if his body thought Sebastian was in his bedroom with him, peering into his brain.

How did you know she spoke to me? He whispered.

Magic, Sebastian said, reverence barely perceptible in the one word he uttered. *Now, let's try something a bit more difficult. I think you can do it though.*

Noah cracked his neck and loosened his shoulders, as if he were stretching before a football game. He could do this. He wanted to do this.

Close your eyes again, Sebastian commanded. *Imagine an invisible string connecting you to your best friend. Can you see where Lowen is?*

Noah pushed what seemed to be the invisible limits to his powers, squinting hard as he searched through his mind. Finally, a glowing, light blue string tied around his index finger tugged at him before going taut. His soul seemed to leave his body as it flew over the string it followed, leaving his empty vessel still standing in his bedroom with his index finger outstretched. His soul flew over the tops of fiery red and burnt orange treetops and over a gently winding river, all while following the glowing blue string. At last, he was led to a house in the middle of nowhere—a house he had never seen before. It was old and made of red bricks with small rectangle windows and black shingles. The warm glow of lights shone from each room. Noah knew with certainty that his best friend was inside this secluded house because the glowing string was closed in the front door.

Noah could feel Sebastian smile as he looked on telepathically.

You're going to be a great asset, Mr. Messing, Sebastian said.

Track 34 - "In the Air Tonight" by Phil Collins

Lowen

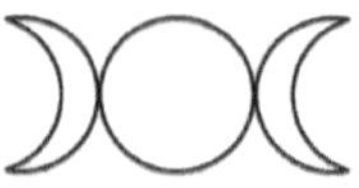

LOWEN WOKE UP in the passenger seat of Wesley's car, groggy and with a pounding headache. It took her brain a moment to wake, but once it did, it sent panic signals to each nerve ending and fired rapid questions to her consciousness. Frustratingly though, the most important and life-saving questions weren't the ones that picked away at her brain. Those were completely out of her control and, honestly, scared her too much to pay attention to. So instead of "Where are we going?", "Am I going to be safe?", or "What can witches do to me?", Lowen concerned herself with "What will I eat?", "Can I shower where we are going?", and "Can I get a change of clothes?" Finally, she settled on a question she felt confident asking out loud to Wesley, who sat silently with his hands gripped on the steering wheel.

"How long have I been asleep?"

"Only for about forty-five minutes. Again, I'm so sorry,"

Wesley said, turning to look at her with lines of concern sketched around his eyes.

Lowen couldn't muster the energy yet to be angry with Wesley for his drugging and kidnapping scheme, as the drugs still lingered in her system. Instead, she surrendered to the fate he had chosen for her for the time being.

"Should I text my mom and give her some kind of explanation for where I am? I really don't want her to worry."

"Yes, you should," he said. "Maybe you could tell her that you're spending the night at one of your friend's houses?"

Lowen sighed. It was the only logical lie to tell. As she reached for her phone though, Wesley gently rested his warm hand over hers.

"Before you call her though," he said, "I want to tell you I'm sorry. I didn't want to do this." He gestured toward the open road in front of them.

"What is 'this'?" Lowen asked. "Kidnapping?"

"I hope not, although I can see how it may look and feel that way. I just want to keep you safe. It's all I ever wanted."

Lowen watched as Wesley retreated into his own thoughts, his voice fading into stoic silence.

"Are we really in that much danger?" she asked.

"We are," he said with a certainty that made the hair on the back of her neck stand up. "But I promise I will do everything in my power to keep you safe."

The two sat silently in Wesley's smooth black Audi for a moment and allowed the tension between them to shift into something new. Something resembling trust based on a shared set of circumstances. Possibly the surrendering of each person's hurt feelings. Maybe even the beginning of a friendship.

Lowen's stomach knotted when she looked down at her phone and saw multiple missed calls from her mom. With a shaky finger, she pressed the button to call home and inhaled deeply.

"Lowen?" her mom answered, fear coating her voice.

"Hey, Mom," she said, trying to tame the shakiness in her voice. "I'm so sorry, I lost my phone and just found it."

"Where are you? Are you okay? I'm worried sick." Her mother's voice had never sounded so frantic, so frail.

"I'm so sorry, Mom," she said as a lump lodged itself in her throat. "Noah called and invited me to spend the night, so I just had Wesley drop me off. We lost track of time over here. I'll never do it again, Mom. I promise."

"Lowen, this is beyond irresponsible," Emily said, her voice switching from worry to anger. "You know I need to know where you are—especially with all that has happened this week."

Lowen leaned her head back against the seat and closed her eyes, a sad smile stretching across her lips. She could handle it if her mom was angry with her. Disappointed even. She just couldn't bear to think of her suffering in a frantic panic.

"I know, I won't do it again," she said, exhaling a large breath of relief. "But now, I'm kind of stuck here because of curfew. I promise we will stay in tonight and I'll call you right when I wake up."

She wished she had her phone charger, and then she wondered if where they were going would even have an outlet for a phone charger.

"Okay, I love you, too," Emily said, her voice softer. "Goodnight. And you're grounded when you get home tomorrow."

Lowen hung up and was seized by a sudden panic that this may have been her last conversation with her mother. Tears filled her eyes before she had a chance to realize they were forming. Using the sleeve of her sweatshirt, she wiped them away quickly.

"You should contact Noah to help you corroborate your story," Wesley said quietly.

"You're right. Thanks," she said.

At least someone has a plan, she thought to herself as she dialed Noah's number.

Before it had a chance to ring, she hung up, biting her lip. Perhaps she didn't want Wesley to hear her conversation, so instead, she texted.

Lowen: You up?

Noah: Lowen, where are you? Sebastian is looking for you. He said your mom is worried

Lowen: I'm with Wesley. Listen, I told my mom I was spending the night with you. Can you cover my story if she calls?

The three tiny dots bounced on the screen before disappearing. Lowen waited impatiently until they began to bounce again. Why was he hesitating?

Noah: Sure. What's going on? Are you safe with him?

Lowen: I can't really say, but I'm safe right now

Noah: Do you need me to come get u? Are you sure ur ok?

Lowen: No, I promise I'll be in touch though. Love u

Noah: Text me nonstop. Love u

Lowen looked up to see they were pulling into a massive gas

station. After over two hours in the car, she was relieved to get out and stretch, the blinding fluorescent lights becoming the beacon of normalcy she needed. She looked over at Wesley after he pulled up next to a gas pump.

"Grab what you think you'll need for a couple days: a toothbrush, snacks, water, whatever you can think of," he said, handing her a handful of twenty-dollar bills from his wallet. "Make it fast—they are going to be looking for us."

He looked around, seemingly surveying the area for any immediate danger.

Are witches easily spotted as such? Lowen wondered.

Lowen took the money and walked into the brightly lit gas station. Eighties light rock played loudly on the speakers as an elderly cashier greeted her. The woman, with graying hair pulled back in a sharp bun, stared intently at Lowen as if she were a shoplifter. Between the fluorescent lighting and the loud music, Lowen seemed as if she had entered a different reality after so long in the dark car with only the hum of the highway ringing in her ears.

Grabbing a basket, Lowen ducked from the unnerving eyeline of the cashier and searched for the hygiene aisle. She grabbed two toothbrushes, toothpaste and soap before locating a phone charger, some bottles of water, Nacho Cheese Doritos, Reece's cups, a red

Indiana hoodie, a few packs of gum, and a fleece blanket. No wonder Wesley had admonished her for not wearing a coat earlier—he knew he was going to take her far away in the middle of the night. As she walked down the aisles, a creeping sensation sent the fine hairs on her arms to rise. Someone was following her. With a chill crawling up her spine, she hurried to the counter to pay and get back to Wesley and the safety of the car.

The cashier scanned the items at a tortoise's pace, glancing frequently at the gas pumps outside. Lowen glanced over her shoulder, but the store was entirely empty besides herself and the elderly cashier. She jumped when the woman finally spoke.

"Miss, I think your car is leaving you. You came in with the Audi, yeah?"

Following where the woman's arthritic finger pointed outside, Lowen turned just in time to see the taillights of Wesley's Audi pull out onto the highway. How could he leave her? She ran to the entrance and swung the door open, her heart racing against her sternum as if she had just run a marathon.

"Lowen, I'm over here."

She looked to the right to see Wesley walking toward her.

"I thought you left me," she said breathlessly, tears springing into her eyes. "Your car…"

"I traded it for something they won't recognize," he said, his voice thick with guilt. "I should have told you."

She nodded as she wrapped her arms around herself.

"I'm sorry, Lowen," Wesley said. "I'm not used to taking care of someone else—not that you're a burden or anything like that—err, what I'm trying to say is I'll do better communicating my plans from now on."

"Thanks," she said, finally looking up at him from the dirty sidewalk outside of the gas station.

The two held each other's gaze for a long moment before Wesley pointed in the direction of an old wood-paneled station wagon parked in front of the gas station.

"It's not flashy, but then again, that's the point," he said.

"Oh shoot, I have to pay real quick. I'll be back in a second," Lowen said, jolting back toward the front door. That poor old woman was probably already putting back all of the items she had abandoned.

"I promise I'll be right here," Wesley called out over the bells announcing Lowen back into the bright store.

"Your sweetie still out there?" the cashier asked. "He gave us a scare."

"Yeah, it must have been another car that looked like his. How much do I owe you?"

Lowen tapped her foot and continuously checked the time on her phone, but the old woman didn't seem to mind and took her time ringing up each item. Finally, Lowen paid and grabbed the two plastic bags filled with what would keep her and Wesley alive for who knew how long. Did she get enough? She doubted it, but didn't know how to plan for something she couldn't expect.

"Have a fun evening, girly," the old woman croaked, as Lowen opened the door to leave.

She smiled broadly, revealing several black holes where teeth once were.

"Thanks," Lowen mumbled, hurrying out of the store.

"You ready?" Wesley asked as he opened the door to the station wagon.

He looked good. Steady. Confident. Despite everything that had happened between them, she thought she could trust him. She *wanted* to trust him.

"I think so. I'm not sure that I got enough though," she admitted, opening the heavy passenger side door.

Wesley turned the large key in the ignition. "We'll figure it out.

Hopefully we won't have to be there long." Surprisingly, the station wagon wasn't very loud, and the spacious seats were actually comfortable, Lowen thought as she fastened her seatbelt.

"Where is there?" she asked.

"We're going to a safe house. Well, sort of. It's about thirty minutes away, but we need to get rid of our phones before we get too much closer—it doesn't even take magic to track us with them."

Simultaneously, they turned the crank handles on their doors. With their windows rolled down, they both chucked their only connection to the outside world into fields in the middle of nowhere.

So much for texting my mom and Noah and letting them know I'm okay, she thought as her gut clenched with guilt.

Lowen rolled up her window and dug around in the plastic bags on the floorboard beneath her feet. She pulled out the fleece blanket and a package of Reese's. Tucking her feet underneath her, she placed the blanket over her body and opened the chocolate as a thought skittered across her brain: she should have texted Sebastian before throwing out her phone.

"You okay?" Wesley asked, seemingly sensing her unease.

"Not really, but I don't really have a choice, do I?"

"Not really, but you can trust me," Wesley said. "I've been

through a lot, and I'll make sure you're safe."

She noticed his eyes seemed to glaze over softly, as if his mind had left the present moment and traveled back in time. She thought about how his family had been slaughtered, and how he had continued living for so long, all alone. All for the promise of eternal life. If her life had been turned upside-down by merely knowing the truth of alchemy, she couldn't imagine how Wesley had lived for so long.

"I believe you," she said.

They locked eyes for a brief moment before Wesley turned his gaze back on the highway. As they settled into a comfortable silence, Lowen couldn't get Sebastian off her mind. She was puzzled by Wesley and Sebastian's apparent fallout. Wasn't Sebastian the one who taught him about alchemy? Why did they lose touch?

She decided to bring up the subject gently. "Will these witches go after Sebastian?" she asked.

"That's my hope," he said in earnest.

"Why would you want harm to come to him?" she asked without judgment.

"At this moment, I don't want harm to come to him," he said, as endless shadows of dark cornfields rushed past his window. "But

I do hope they follow him instead of us."

"What curse was broken the night of the Moon Water Ritual?" Lowen asked, hoping she hadn't overstepped the invisible tightrope to which she was clinging. "That's why the witches are specifically after us, right?"

Wesley's eyebrows raised; clearly he was surprised she had figured out so much on her own. "Yes, the ritual did break a curse, and specifically, Sebastian was the one who made it happen. He broke something that had kept him trapped under the thumb of the witches for far too long," he said.

"So, the witches are mad at him but also upset that you use magic and upset with me because I know about it?" she clarified.

"Pretty much," he said, unconvincingly.

"That's a start. Can I ask you another question?" she asked, opening the bag of Doritos.

"Go for it," he said, a smile tugging at the corners of his mouth as she chomped down on a chip.

"Why did you and Sebastian pretend to not know each other when I introduced you at the Halloween party?"

He sighed. "We have a complicated past. You'll learn the truth of it, I fear, but it's too much for this moment."

She considered his words but decided to press a bit further as she ate another chip.

"I read the letter you left for your parents. You were friends. Confidants. You planned on traveling together. What happened?"

Wesley's head turned in her direction, his eyes wide. "You read that?"

His sadness was so palpable it filled the car with a steady weight. Lowen cracked the window to let in some fresh air.

"Yes, it was tucked in the photo album Dr. Clarke found," she said softly.

The silence in the station wagon seemed infinite, her words echoing in her ears. She had intruded on something intensely private and wished she could shove the words back into her mouth. Not wanting to press the issue any further, she paused, but a thought occurred to her, one she wanted an answer to.

"Did the witches kill your family?"

If they did such a terrible thing to innocent children, would they do the same to her? Suddenly, her stomach no longer wanted the junk food sitting heavily inside it.

"Yes, they did," he said, running his fingers through his hair.

He gave no further details. No clarification. Nothing but silence. Lowen thought back to the newspaper article about how the

Vincent family had died. Now, fear gripped her throat so tightly she couldn't swallow. She wrapped the blanket tighter around her shoulders but knew that the trembling wasn't from the cold.

No longer able to stand the terror-filled silence in the station wagon, Lowen played with the archaic buttons on the radio, finding only one station that played soft rock from "the 80s, 90s, and today". A Phil Collins song whirled through the speakers, reminding her of car rides with her mom as a kid; she could imagine her mom singing along to the lyrics with the windows rolled down.

Leaning back against the headrest, Lowen let the memories flood her senses. She remembered her first slumber party when she was six years old. She was at her friend's house, and Jessica's mom had just tucked them in and said goodnight. Lowen lay quietly until Jessica's mom left the room, letting the small lump in her throat turn into a boulder. Before she knew it, she was crying and couldn't stop. Jessica, unable to understand what homesickness was, became so mad at Lowen for calling her mom and going home that she told everyone at school she was a crybaby. It took Lowen another year to try a sleepover again after that, with Noah and Taylor. She never felt homesick with them, but rather like they were an extension of her small family unit. She let herself think about the four faces that meant the most to her in the world until the boulder in her throat couldn't be swallowed down. She turned her head away from the road and rested her elbow on the passenger side door, covering her nose and mouth with her sleeve.

Right when Lowen felt the hot sting of tears well up in her eyes, Wesley interrupted her thoughts.

"We're here," he said, the turn signal clicking loudly in the night air.

Track 35 - "Tornado Warnings" by Sabrina Carpenter

Lowen

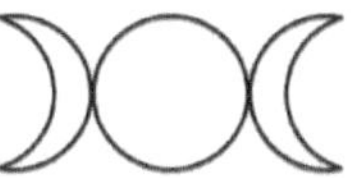

WESLEY PULLED THE station wagon into a gravel driveway about fifteen miles off the interstate. There hadn't been another car in sight since they took the exit ramp off I-70. An abandoned brick house sat at the end of the driveway, with what seemed to be miles of empty fields surrounding it before backing up to woods.

"Where are we?" Lowen asked, trying to conceal the tears falling from her eyes.

"I stayed here for a while after my family died. I was hoping that it was still abandoned." Wesley didn't look at her as he spoke but instead ran his hand through his hair and stared down into his lap.

"Are we staying in that house?" she asked. "Not to be picky or anything, but it looks haunted."

Wesley let a small laugh escape his lips.

"We have witches following us, and you're worried about ghosts?"

"He laughs!" Lowen teased.

She studied his youthful face and wondered if it would ever age. Would he naturally get older if he stopped taking the elixir of life or would he die quickly? She tried to push the intrusive questions from her mind.

"Actually, no, we aren't going to stay in the house. It is indeed a little old, but it isn't safe enough."

Wesley opened the glove box in front of Lowen, leaning slightly over in her space to root around. He smelled like oranges. She stared at the back of his slender neck, feeling an urge to reach out and touch it. To feel the short, golden hair at the nape. To comfort him. To tell him he could let go of his pain. She shook away the intrusive thoughts, her cheeks on fire.

"There we go," he said, pulling out a flashlight and testing it by flipping the button on and off. "Follow me."

Lowen grabbed the plastic bags from the gas station and followed him out into total darkness. Wesley opened the trunk of the station wagon and pulled out a backpack, two sleeping bags and two pillows. They walked around the side of the old, dilapidated house into an expansive field that backed up to nothing but trees. Lowen stayed close at Wesley's heels, feeling like a frightened kid in a haunted house trying to hide behind their friend before the monsters with chainsaws chased them down. Except the monsters chasing them were real this time.

"Here it is," Wesley said, pointing the flashlight toward the ground in front of them.

Beneath his feet was a tornado shelter from long ago. The steel door was rusted around the edges, but when he tugged at the handle, it opened to reveal a steep ladder. The hole below was concrete lined. Lowen couldn't tell how much room it included from up here.

"It's not so bad," Wesley said, studying the frown on her face.

"I take it you're not claustrophobic," she muttered, tipping her head forward slightly to get a better look at the hole. It looked extremely dark and extremely cramped down there.

"Are you?" Wesley asked, his eyebrows pinching together with worry.

"I am now," she half-joked.

"There is way more space once you're down there, I promise. I'll go first and help you down," Wesley said as he threw the sleeping bags and pillows down the hole.

"And chase out the rats, right?" Lowen asked, smiling as she teased him.

"There won't be any rats," he said seriously, turning backward to make his way down the ladder with the flashlight in his mouth.

Once he reached the bottom, he pointed the flashlight up at Lowen. "Okay, backing in is the easiest way to go. Just take your time and I'll be here if you need me."

Lowen did as he said and with shaky legs, made her way down the ladder. She was surprised by how quiet and dry the walls around her seemed. Maybe this wouldn't be so bad. There was no possible way anyone would find them in a storm shelter in the middle of nowhere. And she had to admit, Wesley made her feel safe; he knew what he was doing. The thought that he had survived the witches all of these years brought her a little peace.

When she reached the bottom of the ladder, she felt Wesley's hands reach up to her waist and lift her off the ladder with ease. He placed her down on the ground and withdrew his arms. She felt electricity surge within her as he touched her but guiltily pushed it out of her mind. She felt terrible that Wesley's presence affected her so much when she also felt an intense connection to Sebastian.

Lowen looked around; the storm shelter was narrow, but deep. One side had built-in concrete benches, but the floor was just dry, brown dirt. Wesley took off his backpack and started unloading the contents. He took out three battery-powered lanterns and hung them on hooks already screwed into the walls. He dusted off the sleeping bags and pillows and set them on the concrete bench, along with two canteens of water and a box of protein bars.

"You came prepared."

"Like I said, I've done this before. Just a second." Wesley climbed back up the ladder with a lock and attached it to the loop on the storm shelter's door. He climbed back down quickly and effortlessly. "It won't stop them if they find us, but at least it will buy us time."

"Wesley?" Lowen asked timidly.

"Yeah?" He seemed to hold his breath, anticipating her question.

"Where am I going to pee?"

Another rare smile escaped his lips. "There is an outhouse right outside of the shelter."

"Now, that's the scariest thing you've told me all night."

They looked at each other, smiling for a moment, then unrolled their sleeping bags side-by-side. Lowen silently prayed to some unknown god that she would survive the night.

Track 36 - "Twilight" by Elliot Smith

Noah

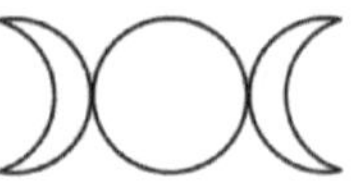

"WHAT SHOULD BE our superhero duo name?" Noah asked as Sebastian's car sped down the dark interstate.

"What?" Sebastian's green eyes darted to the passenger side seat, momentarily looking away from the road.

"You know, like the Psychic Boys or the Mind-Reader Men. I don't know, something like that."

"No."

"You're no fun." With a fake sigh, Noah tapped the screen to his phone and refreshed his Waze app. "We are about twenty minutes away." He felt excited, special even, that Sebastian had asked, well told, him to come along on an adventure to save Lowen.

"Save her from what?" he had asked.

Sebastian had not given him a response. When the flask of whiskey was halfway full, he had felt a little giddy and indestructible. Now that the flask was nearly empty and he had to ration his supply, anxiety and exhaustion took the wheel.

"I want you to focus. Close your eyes and think of Lowen. Concentrate on the smallest details you can think of: her fingernails, her eyelashes, her perfume. The more detailed and focused your mental image is, the more you will be able to get into her head," Sebastian coached.

Noah chewed his bottom lip, weighing the creeping guilt crawling up his shoulders. "I feel like I should get her consent before diving into her head."

"I feel like you should worry about her life a little more than her feelings right now," Sebastian snapped.

"Okay, Mr. Crabbypants, but who is this Big Bad anyway? The Hellmouth isn't opening, is it?" Noah quipped as he looked out of the passenger side window as dark, flat fields whizzed by.

"I have no idea what you're talking about," Sebastian said flatly, his emerald eyes concentrating on the empty, endless road ahead.

Noah smiled, knowing he shouldn't push Sebastian's buttons, but unable to control himself. "Is Lowen playing Buffy in this scenario? Of course she is. I always thought that I would be Buffy. I know I'm absolutely not a Xander, I could maybe be a witchy Willow though."

"Oh, I get it now," Sebastian said, slowly nodding his head. "A

Buffy reference."

"He knows Buffy! A man of the world!" Noah joked, his words slurring slightly as he turned to face him.

"I liked Spike," Sebastian admitted as he glanced in the rearview mirror.

"Of course you did," Noah laughed. "Are we becoming besties? I feel like we are."

He wondered why Sebastian couldn't just read Lowen's mind himself. It seemed strange to drag Noah along, who clearly had no idea what he was doing.

I can't read her mind. Wesley has blocked me from it, Sebastian explained.

Switching from thinking to speaking without noticing, Noah asked, "How did he do that? Why would he do that? Is Lowen in *serious* serious trouble?"

"Slow down, partner," Sebastian said. "There are spells to do just about whatever you need, as long as you have the money to buy them and a witch to buy them from. And as for why... well, that's something only Wesley can explain. And Lowen is going to be fine. We'll make sure of it."

Noah could feel the anger seething from Sebastian, noting how quickly his temperament changed. He hated the fact that Sebastian could slide into his thoughts whenever he wanted like a damn twenty-four-hour diner, but he was restricted from Sebastian's. If there was nothing to hide, why was he so clearly concealing something?

Noah began to suspect he might be in the Big Bad's car, and that the Scooby gang was in bigger trouble than he had originally imagined. Catching his own thoughts, Noah turned them off quickly the only way he knew how. He reached for his near-empty flask in his jacket pocket and finished off the warm whiskey.

Sebastian turned off of the highway onto a dark country road.

"We're here. But before we get out of the car, I want to address something."

Noah paused and looked into Sebastian's brilliant emerald eyes, his vision slightly blurred from the contents of his flask.

"You need to find another way to turn off your powers. The drinking will dull your senses permanently over time, not just when you want it to. You're better than... this," he concluded, swishing his hand vaguely to point out the mess that was Noah Messing.

"I hear you," Noah muttered as heat rose to his cheeks.

Turning to look out of the car window, Noah could make out the shadow of the brick house he saw in his vision. As they stepped out of the warm black car, his hair stood on end, and not just because of the cold. Closing his eyes, he searched for Lowen in his mind. A dark, cramped space appeared as a clear image. Claustrophobia strangled him as he realized the room was underground, but he focused on Lowen's tangible presence. The string connecting them had been pulled as tightly as possible, as if he could reach the end of it and touch her.

His heart sank into his gut as an overwhelming dread washed over him: What if he had gotten this all wrong? What if Wesley wasn't the dangerous one? What if Wesley was hiding Lowen from something or someone dangerous?

Oh no. Abort mission. No. Oh no. Did he hear me?

"Yes, I did. Thanks for the information. You've been a great help," Sebastian said. "Unfortunately, our duo days have come to an end."

Sebastian stepped from behind the open trunk, holding a long stick that looked to be a shovel. Before Noah could move his frozen limbs, Sebastian swung the instrument at Noah's skull, whipping it so quickly that it whistled through the still air before making contact. The white, hot flash of pain violently struck his body before the world faded into darkness.

Track 37 - "Season of the Witch" by Lana Del Rey

Taylor

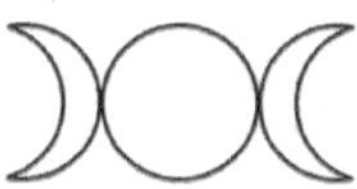

AFTER COMING TO terms with the fact that both her mother and father had been lying to her since birth about her mom's true childhood, Taylor couldn't help but feel excited about meeting them, even if the bitter pill she just swallowed left an aftertaste of distrust. The small flutter of nervous butterflies rumbled deep in her belly as she and her mother stepped out of the rental car into the dry afternoon heat of the Arizona sun.

"Don't be nervous, honey. You're going to love them and they are going to adore you," her mom said.

It was funny how her mom always had a sixth sense about Taylor's emotions. She knew just what to say and do, no matter how well Taylor stuffed down her emotions.

Maybe it is the witch thing, like a secret superpower to feel what others were feeling? she thought.

The front door swung open as a tall, elegant woman who looked to be in her sixties stood to greet them. Her smile was a carbon copy of Taylor's mom's.

"My girls," she all but whispered with glistening tears forming in her eyes.

She stepped out and pulled Taylor's mom into a tight embrace. They looked so very similar, tall and slender—if her grandmother's hair hadn't sparkled with silvery strands, she would have had a hard time telling them apart.

"Ava, I just..." Taylor's grandmother uttered, before her words caught in her throat.

"I know, Mom," Taylor's mom nodded as she looked earnestly at her own mother. "And here she is. Taylor, this is your Grandma Evie."

She stepped aside so Taylor was face-to-face with her grandmother. With no words spoken, her grandmother pulled her into a gentle, yet loving, embrace. She smelled of gardenia and freshly applied vanilla lotion. Her skin was so soft against Taylor's cheek that she thought she could go ahead and die in this embrace, and it would be just fine.

If Taylor had bet her robust college fund that the inside of her Grandma Evie's house matched the dated peachy stucco exterior, she would have been taking out a lot of student loans. Dark curtains draped over the windows, only allowing cracks of sunlight to enter the expansive living room. Multiple oriental rugs, detailed with rich burgundy and gold designs, were stacked and scattered across the cold white tiled floors. Plush velvet couches and chairs formed a U-shape in the center of the living room, all gathered around a large circular coffee table that held a collection of haphazardly scattered items: incense, tarot cards, books, moonstones, a large amethyst, candles, feathers, dried flowers and herbs. The living room gave off the distinct impression that many people used this room often. The sweet, yet earthy smell of old incense lingered in the air, evoking an unpleasant anxiety in Taylor's gut.

"I gather your mother told you about your family origins," Grandma Evie said.

"Yes, ma'am."

She didn't know what yet to call this woman, who was in fact her flesh and blood. It all felt too surreal, especially in this darkened cave, shielding itself from the palm trees and bright Arizona sun.

"There is no reason to be frightened. Being a witch isn't a curse, and it certainly isn't playing with the Devil's magic," her grandmother said, chuckling lightly. "You are simply a chosen vessel to channel the powers of the Earth. Also, you can call me Evie, child."

"Sounds so very simple, Evie," Taylor joked timidly.

"It is simple! But simple doesn't equate to *easy*. Or fun. The simplicity of being a witch is knowing you can harness the energy from the gifts of the Earth: plants, animals, the wind, the sun and moon, the tides, fire and ice. Everything contains energy—even the tiniest of objects," Evie explained as she tidied the coffee table.

She picked up a dried rose that seemed to be a leftover, discarded part of a spell someone had forgotten to throw away. Pinching it delicately by its stem between her thumb and pointer finger, she held the flower closely to her face. Taylor could see her mouth whispering something but couldn't make out the words. As she did so, the dried rose came to life. Red, velvet petals took the place of the wine-colored wilted ones before and even fanned out and bloomed like stiff limbs needing to be stretched. The yellowed thin stem between her fingers changed to a vibrant, sturdy green.

Taylor couldn't believe what she was seeing and turned to her mother with wide eyes. Her mother was watching Grandma Evie with a look that Taylor had never seen before: a deep, sorrowful longing. Until now, she could empathize with what her mother went through severing her relationship with her family, but she hadn't put much thought into what she lost when she made the decision to turn her back on magic.

Witnessing what her grandmother had just done with the rose, Taylor's perspective shifted instantly. Everything she thought mattered before didn't anymore. Everything she took for granted and overlooked was now teeming with importance. It was like Grandma Evie had flipped the "on" switch to the world; Taylor now looked at everything with new eyes, trying to see what energy it held: the lamp on the side table, the ladybug climbing up the wall near the window, the potted plants hanging from the ceiling in macrame slings. She felt like a newborn babe, not understanding anything and wanting to learn everything.

"We will get you all caught up, Ava," Grandma Evie told her daughter. "It's been a while, but it's just like riding a bike. We just need to gather everyone and get on with it. They will be so excited to see you—both of you."

She smiled at Taylor with a quiet, startling excitement.

"What about me?" Taylor asked. She was shocked by how small her own voice sounded, how desperate. "Will I be, like, reactivated, or something, too?"

"Unlike your mother, we never turned off your magic. We just withheld the tools to tap into it. You have probably already accidentally practiced magic without even knowing. Therefore, we just need to welcome you formally and teach you. Think of the next week as Beginner Witchcraft 101. Once the others arrive and we conduct the ceremony for your mother, we will get down to business helping you understand your gifts."

"What do you mean, 'welcome me formally'?"

Suddenly, the heavy weight of unease fell on Taylor's shoulders again. She wished she could push away the vague sense of dread she had felt since the moment she stepped into Grandma Evie's house, but it seemed to grow the more she tried to ignore it.

"Taylor, this is our heritage, our culture, our family. But it is also our responsibility. We need to formally articulate the proper weight, warnings, and rules for wielding such knowledge and powers." Grandma Evie smiled as she said this, but the smile didn't quite reach her eyes this time.

"Why don't you two take your luggage upstairs and get settled? I'll make some sandwiches and iced tea," she said.

Taylor's mom led her up the creaky wooden stairs to a small bedroom at the end of a long, empty hall, so stark and white in contrast to the dark, mystical living room downstairs.

"This used to be my room as a kid," her mom explained,

stopping to survey the room with her hands on her hips.

The bedroom was cramped, unlike the massive bedroom to which Taylor was accustomed. There didn't seem to be any relics of her mother's past, no teen posters or ballerina-themed jewelry boxes or old photos taped to the mirror, just a large four-poster bed draped with a handmade colorful quilt in the center of the room, accompanied by two tiny nightstands. Taylor rolled her suitcase to a corner and flopped down on the tall bed.

"Mom, are you okay? This has to be a lot for you to handle."

"Yeah," she sighed, "it is a lot, but it feels so good to be home. I feel like I've been missing a limb for all of these years and it's finally growing back to my body."

Taylor noticed a small difference in the way she and her mom communicated since the plane ride. It was as if they were peers, friends, open to speaking candidly about their feelings. The mother/daughter dynamic had shifted, and now Taylor understood that her mom needed her as a confidant as much as a daughter.

"Is this ceremony, like, going to be intense?" Taylor asked, fidgeting with the small silver ring on her finger that matched another one worn by Lowen.

She thought back to the night of the Moon Water ritual. The knives. The blood. How strong she had been despite the fear settling deep in her bones and reflecting in Lowen's eyes. She worried what real magic would be like if that was just an odd, small-town ritual. Suddenly, she wanted Noah and Lowen to be by her side. They kept her strong, and right now, Taylor Bell felt her weakest.

Her mom sat down next to her on the bed, taking her trembling hand between her own.

"Listen, Taylor. We don't practice magic just to bring flowers back to life," she said, her eyes fixed on her daughter with a quiet seriousness that made Taylor squirm. "It's not all potions and tarot cards, either. It's real. And it's powerful. We were given this gift centuries ago for a purpose, and that is why there are rules."

"What is the purpose?" Taylor asked, keenly aware something important was being kept from her.

"To maintain the balance of good and evil." Her mom said the words as if she had repeated them many times.

"What does that even mean?" Taylor asked. "Shouldn't we be trying to eliminate evil instead of balancing it?"

"If only it were that simple. Don't you agree there is a little good and a little evil in everyone? In everything? Even roses have thorns. We can't go around destroying everything just because they possess one dangerous quality." She ran her fingers through her hair as she continued. "But balance... we can do that. If someone is inherently evil, the bad outweighs the good. By eliminating that bad, we have balanced the scales a bit."

"Eliminate?" Taylor screeched. "So, you're saying you *kill* people? Like witch vigilantes?"

The room began to spin, the colorful quilt pattern becoming a manic kaleidoscope from which Taylor could not pull away.

"No, no!" her mother said, placing her hand over her heart. "Oh Taylor, there is a lot for you to learn about the world around you. What exists and what doesn't. Humans though—we don't take the law into our own hands. Humans have police, and courts, and jails, and karma. We don't mess with the human world unless we have to."

"Excuse me? What are there besides humans?" The uneasy knot in Taylor's stomach grew, twisting into strangling tendrils of ivy threatening to smother her.

Her mom sighed, letting Taylor's question float like a menacing storm cloud in the small, spinning bedroom.

Track 38 - "Possum Kingdom" by The Toadies

Wesley

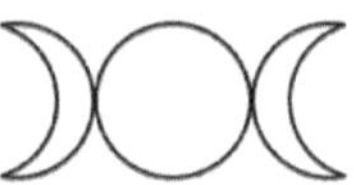

HIS INHUMAN HEARING could detect a car pulling into the gravel driveway above the tornado shelter. Two doors closed simultaneously, echoing in the still night air. He heard a muffled voice—a man's—speaking to someone else. His jaw tightened as a sickening crack screamed through the quiet, followed by the sound of a body hitting the earth with a light thud.

Sebastian is here.

He looked over at Lowen, who was miraculously sleeping soundly in her sleeping bag, despite spending the night in an underground bunker. He eased himself quietly out of his sleeping bag, and silently crept up the ladder. What was his plan? Did he even have one? At this very moment, he didn't quite know who his ally was and who was his foe. He did know that he had to keep her safe. It was all that mattered. As Wesley pushed open the door to the shelter, he heard the familiar voice humming a tune gently in the night air.

"Come out, come out wherever you are."

Wesley could practically see Sebastian's grin hanging from the words.

"Enough with the theatrics," Wesley said as he climbed out from the tornado shelter.

He used his body to guard Sebastian from the storm shelter where Lowen was sleeping innocently below. And despite thoroughly understanding how dangerous the situation was, Wesley couldn't help but want to childishly roll his eyes at Sebastian; the pettiness this man brought out in him still surprised him.

"Don't you even want to know how I found you since you broke my connection to Lowen?" Sebastian asked, with a shimmer of vitality flashing in his eyes. "How much did you have to pay for a spell to do that for you?"

The game never dulled for him. Wesley wouldn't entertain his craving for attention and theatrics, so instead continued to stare at him like a silent brick wall.

"Fine, I'll tell you anyway," Sebastian said, his grin widening. "Turns out our little friend, Noah, figured out his Messing power. What a fun little asset he was."

"Was?" A familiar, haunting emptiness crept into Wesley's

bones, as if someone had sucked out the marrow and left him entirely hollow.

This is what Sebastian did. It was his inherent nature—their nature: to use, to break, to shatter all that was fragile for their own gain. This was why, no matter how beautiful it was to actually feel, Wesley could never allow himself to indulge for too long. It was the heavy price he felt he needed to pay for immortality. He thought of Noah's half smile and the mischievous sparkle his eyes held, and what was left of his blackened heart broke for Lowen.

"You do know that you could *choose* to not think those thoughts going through your mind right now, my dear Wesley?" Sebastian said, taking a step closer to him. "I gave you this gift, and all you've done since is become insolent, and quite honestly, a buzzkill. I risked everything for you. All of this. Was for you."

Wesley held his ground above the storm shelter, unwilling to allow Sebastian to get closer to Lowen.

"I never asked for any of it. I never wanted it," he said through gritted teeth.

"Actually, if I remember correctly, you begged for it that night under the bent tree when you saw me in all of my glory," Sebastian said, his eyebrows raising. "And besides, you never stopped it, did you? You continued living, accumulating your wealth, living like a recluse in New Orleans. There are always ways, workarounds, to undo what was done. You could be buried next to your family right now, peacefully at rest, but you have chosen to remain. You have used your free will to stay alive, eternally and miserably."

Sebastian hissed the words at Wesley, spitting his venom angrily, as if Wesley's choices were a personal attack against him.

"Don't you think I thought of it?" he screamed, running his fingers through his hair with frustration. "Ending it all? But I knew what you were doing all of these years, trying to find her. Even if I didn't know her yet, I *felt* her. I had to keep her safe."

He pointed into the storm shelter that held the one thing he had stayed alive for all of these years. "I've been trying to undo the curse you set into motion," Wesley admitted, finally allowing the truth to free itself from his chest. "I couldn't die knowing I could have stopped you from doing to others what you did to me."

"Stop me? That's your plan?" Sebastian yelled before laughing bitterly. "You don't want to live forever? That's fine. I respect it, I really do. But it doesn't mean that myself and others don't deserve to enjoy our lives."

He kept with his persistent offensive attack, stepping closer and closer to the entrance of the storm shelter, as Wesley tightened his muscles, readying himself for battle.

"Who are you to decide who lives and dies? Would you kill me, Wesley? Would you feel justified? Because of who I am, what I am? Who decides which lives deserve more? You wouldn't kill a lion or a shark just for being a predator, correct? Isn't this the same?"

He allowed the questions to rapid-fire from his lips, disorienting Wesley with their mixtures of truths and lies. "Let me remind you, I didn't choose this either. I am simply living with what has been given to me just as it was given to you."

Sebastian's face now hovered millimeters from Wesley's, his familiar scent instantly transporting Wesley back to his family farm. Both men froze as Wesley's mind flashed with images of his parents and sisters, all while Sebastian intrusively read his mind.

"Wesley?" a small voice asked from behind him.

Lowen's eyes peered from the crack of the opened shelter door. She looked around, right through Wesley it seemed.

"Lowen, close the door. Lock it," he commanded, not letting his eyes off Sebastian.

Before she even had a chance to move, Sebastian ripped the shelter door off its hinges with one quick, easy motion. "Oh, thank God I found you," he said, rushing toward her to reach his arm down, like a prince saving a distraught and helpless princess from the evil villain's dungeon.

In horror, Wesley watched as Lowen placed her hand into Sebastian's as she was lifted from the shelter.

"Why would he keep you in such a dreadful place?" he asked as he brushed dirt from her cheek and snuck a quick smile at Wesley.

"Are you here to help with the witches?" Lowen asked, her eyes darting to the surrounding tree-lined fields.

At that moment, Wesley realized he should have told her the truth all along. This muddled version, this half-truth he had settled upon on the drive here, was a mistake. A dangerous one. She still trusted Sebastian, because she didn't know who he was. She didn't understand the danger she was in by being merely in his presence. All because Wesley couldn't stomach telling her the truth about his own identity. In the end, his own selfishness and shame would be both of their undoing.

"I know an absolute way the witches will never be able to touch you." Sebastian said, smiling as he brushed a piece of Lowen's hair from her face.

He held Lowen in a light embrace with his hands resting gently on her hips, a sight that made Wesley sick to his stomach. He was too close. Too comfortable. And the glimmer in his green eyes was the same as it had been all those decades ago in the woods as he stood over Wesley: wicked and self-serving.

Wesley tried to move his feet, but they were firmly planted in the ground, as though they were trees that had grown deep, tangled roots. He couldn't talk, couldn't yell at Lowen to run. How long had he been stuck like this? How did Sebastian get a hold of this spell? Wesley prayed Lowen could see his black pupils growing large, taking over the dazzling emerald of his irises. He should have taught her it was the first warning sign.

Speechless, Wesley? Good, you can just watch, Sebastian teased him telepathically.

Sebastian bent his head toward Lowen, kissing her passionately. She returned the kiss awkwardly, pulling away early by pressing her hands against his chest to create space between them.

"Where is Wesley?" she asked. Looking directly at him. Through him. Whatever this magic was, it was strong. It had made Wesley invisible.

"He didn't want to stay for this part," Sebastian said, gently fingering a strand of Lowen's hair near her face.

"What do you mean? What part?" she asked, instinctually backing away from Sebastian's body, inhumanly still.

"Lowen, can I ask you something? How long have you known that I'm immortal?" Sebastian asked, his voice becoming gentle.

She blushed, turning her body from him to scan the field for Wesley. "Since Dr. Clarke showed me your picture in the old Vincent photo album," she admitted.

"Are you scared of me?" he asked, delicately pulling her wrist so she would face him again.

"I thought I would be, but no," she admitted honestly, finally looking up at his face as he pulled her hips closer to his body.

Wesley prayed her instincts would kick in when her eyes locked on Sebastian's black irises. That she would understand there was nothing human about the man standing in front of her.

"Why not?" he asked, boldly running the tip of his nose up the side of her neck.

"Because I knew you wouldn't hurt me. I knew—know—that you care about me," Lowen said, squirming as she tried to remove herself from his tight grip around her waist.

Wesley yelled out to her despite knowing it wouldn't make a difference. His mouth, so close to her neck, made him want to jump out of his skin. Made him want to vomit. Or murder. He should have warned her how her blood could make him lose control.

"Does the idea of magic, of immortality, of turning a simple element into something so much more complex and valuable—do those things intrigue you?" he whispered into her ear.

Wesley watched as Lowen's body stiffened, as if she could now sense the danger she was in. "I guess. What's going on, Sebastian?" Lowen asked, her voice shaking as she pushed his arms away from her.

"Do you want to be a part of this world?" Sebastian asked, gesturing vaguely to the empty, star-filled sky.

"Aren't I already?" she asked. "I mean, I know all about you and Wesley."

"You are more than you know. One last question, do you trust me?" Sebastian asked, his voice choking on the words with a timid fear and gentle sadness Wesley hadn't heard come from the man's lips he had known for so long.

Lowen hesitated, opening her mouth and then snapping it shut. She turned around, scanning the open field surrounding them. "Sebastian, where is Wesley?"

Like a light switch, fiery jealousy ignited in Sebastian's eyes, a look Wesley knew well, as she scanned the field for Wesley, but for the first time ever, he didn't react.

Sebastian stared at Wesley, his pupils shrinking to reveal his dazzling emerald eyes. His true self. Instead of speaking directly to Wesley, he telepathically said, *She trusts you. Listen to me, Wesley. I know you don't like the choice I'm about to make for all three of us, but you need to at least understand.*

These witches will kill her without hesitation. And then they will come for us. We can keep her alive—forever. But I can't do this alone. She will never fully trust me, or forgive me, for what I've done and what I'm about to do. But with you on my side, she will learn to, and we can be a family, the three of us. Please, my beloved. Please take my side this once. It's for all of us.

Wesley discerned none of the charm or manipulation or careless attitude usually dripping from Sebastian's being. He was being truthful. And he was pleading with Wesley to save Lowen. Perhaps not in the way that Wesley envisioned, but definitely in a way that proved Sebastian did care about someone else, not just himself. Wesley knew loneliness was Sebastian's Achilles Heel. So, why did he find himself floundering with a decision? Honestly, what choice did he have? He could either be on board with this, or not, but either way, Lowen was going to be in danger from one side or the other, and Wesley was going to have to choose which one he would belong to.

Lowen

"Sebastian, are you okay? You look sad," Lowen said, adding, "And yes, I do trust you."

"Good," he whispered, a single tear falling down his cheek.

She caught the tear with her finger before it fell from his chin, watching as his lips parted to reveal long, sharp fangs growing from his top canines. Lowen screamed as Sebastian's eyes turned to pools of black, just like the monster in her dreams.

Track 39 - "Which Witch" by Florence and the Machine

Taylor

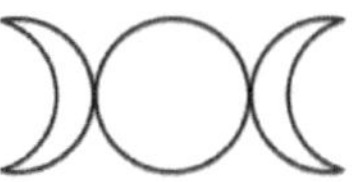

TAYLOR WOKE UP to what felt like the worst hangover of her entire life, the kind where she still felt completely intoxicated but also suffered the headache and nausea that permeated throughout the morning hours, except it wasn't morning at all. She rolled over on the bed she was tucked into—did she cover herself with the colorful quilt? It was 2:55 am. She tried to piece together where the time went. The last thing she remembered was having afternoon tea with her mom and grandmother on the outside patio.

Taylor sat up, letting the quilt slip from her shoulders to reveal she was clothed in a white, sleeveless nightgown she had no recollection of putting on. Standing up and walking quietly down the long hallway, she peered over the railing of the slightly curved staircase that ran along the gray textured wall. Below, she saw that all of the aunts and cousins had finally arrived at her grandmother's peach two-story stucco house. The downstairs living room was filled tightly with bodies, the heat rising from them making Taylor's gut twist. She descended the staircase to find her mother but was instantly caught off guard as woman after woman stopped her, shaking her hand, touching her shoulder, whispering how excited they were to meet her. She began to feel as if she were drowning in a sea of faces and hands and would never see the familiar face of her mother again.

The women weren't what she imagined when she conjured up the idea of witches; they were warm, they took her hand and introduced themselves or scooped her up into big bear hugs like they had known her for her entire life. She felt dizzy, as if she were walking in a hazy, slow-motion dream. The aunts and cousins didn't look like witches; most wore floral dresses or slacks and flowing tops, and none wore pointed hats or all black. They looked... normal, and welcoming, albeit a bit suffocating.

"Ladies, gather round," Grandma Evie said, gently tapping her wine glass with a sharp pocketknife. "Thank you all so much for coming this evening. We've been waiting so long for our daughters to be returned to us."

The room fell eerily silent. Taylor observed that not only did her grandmother easily demand the undivided attention of the room, but that this also felt like something she did regularly. Some women sat down where they could, while others leaned their backs against the living room walls, but all shifted their bodies to face Grandma Evie. Taylor's mother signaled for her to sit down next to her on the blue velvet couch in the center of the room, an unfamiliar twinkle lighting up her eyes that Taylor had never seen before. As if the house and these women had opened a part of her soul that had been buried.

"What happened to me this afternoon?" Taylor whispered to her mom. "I don't remember falling asleep."

"Don't worry, baby," her mom whispered back, signaling for Taylor to be quiet and listen as her grandmother spoke.

As Taylor attempted to focus on her grandmother, the room felt too hot. Too smothering. The thin cotton of her nightgown stuck to her sweaty skin as she closed her eyes and tried to catch her breath.

"Tonight, after eighteen long years of dreadful normalcy, both Ava and Taylor will be once again reunited with their true power and heritage," her grandmother said boldly. "It is a good time to remember our origins, and send blessings and offerings to the goddess divine, Hecate, who bestowed her gifts to our bloodline. We hold our powers as gifts to balance the world's good and evil. These gifts are a sacrifice, a sacrifice we give freely and with humble duty.

During this witching hour, we gather to invoke the Goddess Hecate, whose power and magic protectively cloaks us in the night's shadows. She guides our path by the light of the moon. She guards the doorway between the living and the dead and provides a torch to light the way to the underworld. She is our protectress from evil spirits and extends her power unto us to fight the evil here on Earth. Tonight, we use Hecate's strength to bring back one of her daughters to our coven and restore her gifts," she said, gently nodding her head toward Taylor's mother.

Suddenly, the women rose from where they sat, forming a loose circle in the room. As they took each other's hands, low hums began to form in the air, many in the same alto tone, but others harmonizing and layering their voices on top of the others. Taylor could feel the hum vibrate through her body, but sat as still as a marble statue, holding her breath as sweat trickled down her spine. She watched as her mother gracefully stood and walked toward Grandma Evie in the center of the circle. She wore only the same white, sleeveless nightgown, resembling a haunting angel standing elegantly in the center of the room.

"My dear daughter, tonight we welcome you back to the coven.

We welcome you back to be cradled in Hecate's strength. Do you understand the power of your magic?" Grandma Evie said, holding her daughter's arms lightly in her hands.

"Yes," her mother answered, focusing only on Grandma Evie's intense stare.

"Are you willing to serve Hecate as a connection between the living and the dead?" she asked, her voice rising as the collective hum became louder.

"Yes," her mother said, her voice flat as if she were in a trance.

"Do you recognize not all beings on Earth serve a purpose in line with our coven's mission, and there are many who seek to destroy us?" she asked, her eyes hardening as she stared at her daughter's face.

"Yes," she said, in the same monotone response as before.

"Are you willing to use your powers to fight a war that has been raging for centuries, for which is your life's purpose above all else?" Grandma Evie all but yelled over the oppressive hum of the women encircling them.

"Yes," Taylor's mother said without blinking.

"Will you sacrifice your life, and your daughter's life, for the coven's purpose?"

Her mother finally moved, glancing over at Taylor with eyes full of sadness before uttering, "Yes."

What the actual f—, Taylor thought.

She couldn't breathe anymore. The thick, hot air was swirling with too much incense, the bodies were humming and vibrating too loudly to think, and the room was spinning too fast.

"Taylor," her grandmother said, extending her arms for Taylor to join her.

Despite her fear and confusion, she did what her grandmother asked her to and stood to join her mother in the circle. Her legs shook, and she closed her eyes in an attempt to stop the room from spinning. Grandma Evie pulled the silver pocketknife from her sleeve.

"Palms up and open, and repeat after me, Hecate, we serve."

As the women in the circle repeated the three words, the room became darker and hotter. The flames from the candles began to flicker, but never completely lost their grips on the wicks. The women's voices became louder, the words feeling like drumbeats permeating every corner of the small house. Taylor swore she could hear snakes hissing the word *Hecate* in the walls, their thin bodies slivering behind the wallpaper.

And then she felt the searing heat of the sharp blade digging into her flesh. It was pressed much deeper into her palm than she had done to herself during the Moon Water Ritual, so much so that she had no choice but to utter a guttural scream in response. With wide eyes, she realized her mother and grandmother's hands were spilling just as much blood as hers, all of which was being collected into a gold bowl beneath their feet. The voices, the hissing, the flickering candles, the blood splattering into the bowl all came to a crescendo, before silence descended like a blanket to smother the flames.

The candles blew out the moment the women stopped humming. In the darkness, Taylor could only hear labored breathing by the women making the circle. She felt her mother's hands gently wrap her maimed hand with a cloth. The sound of a match strike. A lit candle glowing close to Grandma Evie's face.

"Welcome, my girls," she said, a smile stretching across her wrinkled lips.

The flickering candles created a shadow on her face, making the smile turn into a menacing grin.

Track 40 - "And He Slayed Her" by Liz Phair

Taylor

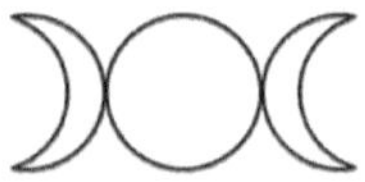

IT WAS AFTER five in the morning when the last of the aunts and cousins left Grandma Evie's house. The sun was rising, shining the glow of innocence onto the world. The witching hour was over. Taylor sat at the circular kitchen table, thinking of the neighbors turning off their alarm clocks, pouring cereal, and getting ready for work. It felt like a world so far out of reach to her now, and how she longed for it. She missed her friends. What she would give to be in her bedroom back in Moon Creek, sitting on the floor with Lowen and Noah, laughing and chatting about nothing. Her mother and grandmother had given her no indication when this trip would end, or when she would go back to the only life she recognized and now missed terribly.

Taylor's head throbbed from the previous evenings disturbing festivities and she couldn't stop her hands from trembling. There was still so much she didn't understand, and thinking about it transformed her fear and trauma to hurt and then to anger. Anger, such a comforting place for Taylor to go, like an old friend who always kept her safe.

"So, is anyone going to tell me what the hell that was and what the hell this all means?" she hissed harshly to the two women making breakfast a few feet from her.

"Taylor!" her mom chastised, although Taylor could sense her exhaustion as she scooped scrambled eggs from a pan onto three mismatched plates.

"It's okay, Ava," Grandma Evie interrupted. "Taylor, you have every right to be angry. We've kept so much from you, and now it's time you knew everything."

"Okay, so what's up with the whole sacrifice thing? And what about other 'beings'? And what are you talking about with the war analogies? What battle do we need to fight?"

Taylor's rapid-fire questions flew from her mouth, but one gnawed at her more than the rest. "And why now? Why, right after a girl was murdered at my house, am I swept away to be initiated into a coven? It's all connected; it has to be!"

Grandma Evie sighed as she hugged her coffee mug with her hands, both in perfect condition after slicing them with a knife last night and sat down at the kitchen table next to Taylor. She turned a vase of beautiful yellow roses around to point them toward the kitchen window's sunlight, fussing with their petals for a moment. Taylor was sick of seeing flowers. She felt the sudden urge to smash the vase against the wall.

Ah, anger, it's about time you joined me again, she thought.

"First things first, let's heal that hand of yours," her grandmother said, taking Taylor's palm into her own.

She used her other hand to gently hover over the cut, whispering words in a language Taylor didn't understand. Taylor could feel a tingle spread across her palm, along with the strange sensation of warmth, like an invisible warm jelly had been applied to her cut. She watched as her wound miraculously healed by only her grandmother's touch and whispered words.

At the same moment, the once-perky yellow roses wilted, some of which fell with a small thud onto the table, their stems still sticking out of the vase like bodies with missing heads.

"Holy crap," Taylor whispered.

"In order to take, you have to give," Grandma Evie said as she sighed. "Now to answer your most pressing questions, we have to go back to our history, so be patient because by the end of what I'm about to tell you, all of your questions will be answered."

Grandma Evie settled into her chair, and began weaving a tale Taylor would never forget.

"Hecate, the Greek goddess of magic, is our ancestor and ours alone. The gods created Her to be the guardian of the crossroads. Most simply, She was the connection between the worlds of the living and the dead. She protected the living from evil spirits, She could communicate with the dead and She was the goddess of the moon and night. Her descendants, the witches and sorceresses, have been able to invoke Her spirit to gain amazing powers and wield powerful magic.

"There used to be so many of us, healers and midwives, using the magic She gave us to do divine work here on Earth. But then, small men with big ambitions saw the power we had and did what they felt they needed to do to keep us down. Ah, how things never seem to change. But alas, they wielded their faith as a weapon to strip us of our power. The witch hunts of the fifteenth and sixteenth centuries, with their endless pyres for which to burn us, irreparably dwindled our numbers to what they are today.

"Every single one of us is a miracle, a magical gift, including you. But we aren't the only magical beings here on Earth. While Hecate tried to save Her dear daughters from the religious fanatics, She did not guard the doorway between our world and the underworld, and a demon was able to slip through undetected.

"This released demon had no ambition, only thirst for human blood, much like a dog's unyielding appetite for scraps. The demon didn't have a mind or a conscience, instead it purely acted out of instinct. It found a brightly lit castle housing a lonely man and sunk its deep fangs into his throat, sucking almost every ounce of blood from his veins, from his organs, from his tissue.

"Though, little did the demon know that the man he chose to drink from was one of the strongest princes in the land. As his fangs sunk into his neck, the prince took his muscular fingers and tore away at the alien-like red flesh of the demon. After the demon fed, he fled into the woods, injured and lost in this strange world's atmosphere, never to be seen again. He became a shadow with not enough blood or strength to survive.

"Meanwhile, the young, dying prince lay on his back on his cold marble floor, thinking about what it meant to die and listening as his breaths became more shallow and ragged. With all his strength, he lifted his hands to his face, for he wanted to know what it was that killed him. Could he make out what this beast was by the scraps left over on his fingers? As he lifted them, an overwhelming urge took over his body to feed from his own fingers. Disgusted, he held them to his mouth as he licked the sticky maroon blood.

"Despite the despicable taste, the prince found that the more he ate, the stronger he felt. Before long, he was able to sit up. The room looked different; every color dazzled brighter than before; every small noise was amplified. He could hear the cooks and servants in the kitchen below clearly, clanging dishes and boiling water. He stood up, stronger than he ever had felt before."

"Grandma Evie, I'm sorry to be rude, but what is the point of this?" Taylor asked, frustrated by the tales of demons and princes.

"Hold tight," Grandma Evie said. "I promise you'll want to know where this goes. Where was I? Oh yes. The man realized he was starving. Ravished. He stumbled, making his way to the kitchen, where the servants and cooks stood with mouths agape, shocked by the prince's bloody appearance. He ate everything in sight: the onion slices on the counter that were to go in the stew, the beef resting before being sliced, the lemon pastries with light sugar sprinkled on top. But none of it satiated his appetite.

"He then looked at one of his servants, a young woman with dark long curls and beautiful blue eyes. When those eyes met his, he could smell her terror, but he couldn't stop himself. He writhed as sharp canines cut through his bloody gums. His fangs sunk into the soft veins of her long neck before she could even gasp. By morning, the prince was alone in his castle, feeling nothing but self-hatred, guilt, and terror, while surrounded by the bloated bodies of his faithful servants. That wretched night, the first vampire was born, created from the pits of Hell."

"Wait, so you're telling me that vampires are real?" Taylor said, a laugh rising in her throat.

Even though her grandmother spoke with such detailed clarity, her rational brain couldn't make sense of it.

"It's true," her mother whispered, walking from the kitchen and setting a plate of eggs and toast in front of Taylor.

Taylor glanced back and forth from Grandma Evie to her mother, waiting for one of them to crack a smile and tell her it was all a joke.

Instead, her grandmother only shook her head before continuing her grotesque tale.

"Oh yes, vampires are very real and very dangerous. When that escaped demon fed upon a human man, he forever tampered with the very DNA of his bloodline for eternity. The poor prince, Vlad, became a monster, and to his credit, it was no fault of his own. He didn't even know what he was or what he was doing, he was simply overcome by his insatiable appetite for human blood.

"For a time, he fed eagerly, but the overwhelming guilt ate away at what was left of his soul, so he attempted to suffer and starve, but the demon coursing through his veins wouldn't let him give up so easily. Instead, it whispered to him that he could easily erase the misery and guilt he felt; all he had to do was get rid of his soul. The demon told him of the ways to do it, and Vlad listened eagerly, desperate to try anything that would end his suffering.

"At the same time, the demon taught Vlad the wonderful tricks that came with being a magical creature: he could move at incredible speed, he could hear even the smallest of sounds, he could jump higher than the tallest trees in the forest, he could break marble with barely a closed fist. Vlad did not fall ill or feel coldness, and he would never age. He would also never die. As an apex predator, he could charm any of his victims with ease, luring them into unknowing, deadly traps. He could read minds and turn off his soul if only he surrendered to his new life, both the good and the grotesque. Vlad finally relaxed as his soul quieted its miserable suffering. For all the downfalls of this demon's curse, Vlad also felt truly alive. And he could live this way forever. So, bit by bit, day by day, Vlad allowed his soul's anguish to quiet until eventually he could no longer be victim to its incessant ramblings of guilt. After a time, his soul simply vanished.

"With his soul's disappearance, Vlad felt euphoric and wanted to embrace who he was. He wanted to share his power, his life, with someone else. The idea of an eternity alone was almost too much to bear. He sat with the puzzle in his mind: how could he create something like himself? The idea hit him like a lightning bolt: if he had been changed into who he was by drinking the blood of the demon, then couldn't it be possible to change a human by tricking them into drinking his blood? Surely it would work as the demon's essence and blood coursed through his veins. Would they need to be on the brink of death as he had been? He decided, with not much more thought, to give it a try."

"Wait, wait, wait. Now, you're telling me a vampire matchmaking story?" Taylor exclaimed. "What does this have to do with me? Or Blair's death?"

"Patience, dear," Grandma Evie said. "Don't you want to know how vampires still exist today?"

Taylor's mouth dropped open, speechless.

Grandma Evie smiled. "As I was saying; that night, he left the castle to visit the largest local church to find someone who would suit his desire. He sat next to the statue of Michael in the very last pew and watched. And waited. When she walked in, he knew immediately she was the one. Her blonde curls bounced as she walked, and her eyes sparkled innocently, while her mouth curled up into a mischievous smirk. She looked from the corners of her eyes, without moving her head much, which very much added to her delightful, yet almost sinister demeanor. The girl laughed unashamedly in the church, and very shortly upon entering had many women surrounding her. They were all taken by her, but out of the corner of her eye, she snuck a sparkling glance at Vlad. He raised a handsome eyebrow to her slightly and then slipped out of the cavernous building into the night. You see, Vlad had become an expert at stalking his prey. He caught her scent as she walked past him and knew which carriage she would be escorted back to after the service, where she would finally be alone within its confines. He would be waiting.

"As Claudia Cel Tradat settled into her carriage seat, Vlad watched her body jolt when she noticed him sitting across from her. Without a word, he leaned over to give her a soft kiss. He moved his soft lips over and onto her neck, lust taking over any feelings of self-preservation. As he bit into her flesh, she didn't gasp in pain, only a single tear dropped from her eye as she understood that her death was coming. As her eyes began to close, Vlad trickled hot, sticky blood on her lips before pressing his wrist down firmly against her teeth. With the same natural knowledge that sheep must be herded, Claudia knew to drink.

"And that is how the vampire species began, and how it continued. The blood from one demon who escaped from the pits of Hell created all the monsters who kill humans, who feast upon their blood, and who create more of their wretched souls with their blood magic."

Taylor sat frozen at her grandmother's kitchen table, staring at her cold, yellow eggs.

"Are you okay?" her mother asked, gently touching her hand with her soft fingers.

"How? Why? What?" Taylor asked, unable to form a complete thought.

"Do you mean, 'What does this have to do with us?'" her grandmother asked, her eyebrows raised as if she enjoyed the secret onto which she held.

"Yes," Taylor said, irritably. "Exactly."

"Obviously, Hecate was not happy. Not only did She feel a sense of responsibility for unleashing the demon, She also intertwined the unbearable pain of losing her daughters to the witch-hunt fires with that of the unnatural gain of a new beast unleashed into the world.

It felt unfair to lose such beautiful creatures who were healers, and in exchange, live in a world with blood-sucking demons. Hecate made it Her mission to rid the world of vampires, and Her witch daughters were to be the soldiers to carry out Her orders."

"I'm a soldier now?" Taylor said, pointing to herself. "A soldier to fight vampires?"

"I know this a lot, dear, but bear with an old woman as she passes down the oral tale that was once told to her," her grandmother said.

Taylor sighed, crossing her arms in front of her chest. "Go on," she said irritably.

"That brings us to today, and the 'why now' part of your questioning. But before I get into specifics, I must start at the beginning of another story and explain some things about your town of Moon Creek.

"You see, for centuries, all sorts of mystics—healers and witches—were drawn to Moon Creek for its interesting topographic properties. Moon Creek is the only place on Earth where the sun and moon are opposite each other at their most perfect placements during monthly full moons. This means the power harnessed by the full moon is infinitely greater in your small town, and the energy lasts much longer. Therefore, many magic workers are drawn to Moon Creek, but so are more dangerous and sinister beings, for most powerful magic draws upon the power of the moon."

Taylor's stomach dropped as she listened to grandmother speak of things that hit way too close to home: full moons, magic, and powerful rituals.

"Centuries after the demon created the first vampire, and in turn, Vlad figured out how to create more of his kind, many vampires walked the Earth, each losing its soul a little sooner and with more ease than the last. Of course, the witches, at Hecate's command, work their magic to take the vampires out, but much like cockroaches, after they killed one, a hundred more popped up.

"The witches decided to create a complex spell that could at least eliminate some of the time that these creatures were able to roam the Earth and drain the blood from their innocent victims. The spell bound the vampires to eternal darkness; even stepping foot into the sunlight for more than a moment would turn them into ash. You see, those damned souls were able to hide in plain sight, pretending to be innocent mortals before the spell. One of their greatest strengths is their ability to woo humans, to come across as beautiful and strong and the daylight only helped them blend in. Therefore, they needed to be stopped from roaming like normal humans as the sun shone upon them.

"The spell itself was to be cast under a full moon by the strongest coven on Earth, our coven, and the curse would be triggered when the next vampire took his next victim and turned that human into a vampire. This first caveat was for a simple purpose—to warn the vampires of what would happen if they decided to not play by the rules the witches set. You see, the witches, although powerful and immensely skilled, were worried the complicated spell wouldn't work. It required difficult magic on a massive scale, and they worried what the ramifications would be. Remember, to take, you must give—and this spell would require taking a lot.

"The witches hoped the threat of the curse would curb the vampires' reckless creation of new vampires. Their plan worked, and the vampires seemed to heed the warning, but the witches stayed in Moon Creek to utilize the strength of the moon just in case the curse was triggered.

"Years passed with this fragile agreement between the witches and the vampires. The vampires were free to live in the daylight and feed, but they could not create new vampires. The witches held up their end of the bargain by not activating the curse, although they did still individually hunt and kill vampires for Hecate. This harmony, if you could call it such a thing, was broken on a cold winter night in 1894. A notoriously arrogant vampire whose reputation for living amongst humans with very little regard to the secrecy of vampirism was catching the eyes and ears in both the witch and the vampire communities.

"Both clans found him to be exceptionally dangerous; neither witches nor vampires were safe if humans found out about their existence. Secrecy was the one unifying code of conduct, for the witches knew what happened when humans acted out of fear. The pyres would be erected once again. The vampires also knew that although they possessed immense strength, there were ways in which they could be killed, and they would rather not have humans possess that knowledge."

"How does one kill a vampire," Taylor interrupted.

"A great question!" her grandmother asked, smiling. "Decapitation, stakes through the heart, and fire are the three ways to kill a vampire. Well, and stepping into the sunlight, of course."

Taylor nodded, silently amused by how accurate the movies and books had been.

"Continuing on," her grandmother said after taking a sip from her coffee mug. "This brazen vampire befriended the most powerful and elite humans across the globe, becoming an eccentric guest who was wined and dined—although he never ate or drank."

"Why did he do it, then?" Taylor interrupted again. "What's the point in befriending humans if he was only going to put himself in danger?"

"For the adoration and attention granted to him. Living as a vampire, especially after the glory days of creating your own vampire family ended, could be tormentingly lonely. This vampire had never known his sire and was instructed by passing vampires to never trigger the curse; therefore, his coping mechanism for isolation and loneliness was to seek the attention of others.

"After getting into political trouble in France, this vampire fled to America where he seemingly stayed under the radar. It wasn't until he triggered the curse that the witches even knew he was here! The moment he drained his victim's blood and forced that wretched soul to drink from his demonic blood, the curse was triggered, and our coven completed the spell. The man who died that cold night and came back to life as the undead was the first vampire to never be able to step into sunlight."

Grandma Evie paused dramatically, allowing Taylor to understand the weight of her words.

"The spell worked, and the witches collectively took a relieved breath, for it established them as the more powerful of the two groups. It also meant humans were all the safer, as vampires would have to hide away during the daylight hours, only to be left creeping down deserted streets in the deep, dark night. No longer could they pretend to be human and walk amongst the living. They were destined to live an existence in the shadows. And although it seemed that the witches had at last won, they were also very aware of the second caveat of the spell in which they had created."

"A second caveat?" Taylor asked, unease seeping under her skin. She could tell this story wasn't going to end with a happily ever after.

"In order to take the strength to bind vampires to the darkness, the witches had to give," Grandma Evie explained. "And this is what they gave: a loophole to break the curse. Don't fret though; the loophole was difficult; it wasn't even bound by time. You see, every person on Earth has a twin flame, a soul's other half. Most people go their whole lives never encountering their twin flame, and still live lives full of love and beauty. Honestly, meeting your twin flame can be a curse; they are the mirror image of you, showing you your deepest insecurities and fears.

"The loophole was one in which daylight could be restored to vampires in the form of a twin flame, specifically the human twin flame of the last vampire created before the curse took place. Since vampires are eternal beings, one's twin flame could be born at any point in a vampire's future. It was what could have been an eternal loophole, a person harder to find on the time spectrum than a needle in a haystack.

"But on the physical location spectrum, much easier and very specific. The twin flame would be born where their first flame died and became a vampire. Wouldn't you know that that incredibly arrogant vampire who decided to ignore the warning of the curse killed and sired his vampire directly in Moon Creek?"

"Moon Creek? Why was he there?" Taylor asked, a tingle crawling up her spine.

"No one knows. But we did know that when the twin flame was born, that is where they would be. More than that, our coven was the only coven who knew exactly how to break the curse—it would require a spell, a ritual, and witches' blood in order to work. Therefore, we didn't worry much moving forward. How on Earth would a vampire ever have the tools to break such a thing?"

The kitchen began to spin as Taylor listened to her grandmother. Pieces started fitting into place, and the picture in the puzzle was becoming clearer. The Moon Water Ritual. Her blood, witch's blood, in the creek that night.

"Grandma, I think I broke the curse," Taylor finally uttered without looking up from the table. Instead, she studied the grains in the wood, wishing herself to shrink into a size that could fit and live in one of the crevices forever.

"You did, honey, but it wasn't your fault. You were tricked. Tricked by the notorious vampire. He tirelessly spent a century learning what the curse was and how to break it. We're not sure who he blackmailed, bribed, or killed, but he somehow coerced someone in our coven to give him the information he needed.

"From there, he watched and waited. To his credit, he was clever. He even made the town believe they created a quirky ritual for good luck with the moon water. It was a nice bit, honestly. Without any blood on his hands, pun intended, he was able to get not only a witch's blood for the ritual but also the twin flame's.

"It was easy for him to find out who *you* were, but the twin flame was harder. The only pieces of information that he had were that: a. the person would be from Moon Creek and b. they would not be able to break the curse until they were eighteen. I'm still not sure how he found out without using the blood of every eighteen-year-old in town. His persistence paid off because you and Lowen finally broke the curse he activated all those years ago."

"Lowen?" Taylor finally looked up in shock. "Did you say Lowen?"

"Yes, dear, she is the twin flame. And she is the key to reactivating the curse, which is why your mother brought you here."

"What do you mean? Is she okay? Is she safe?" she asked as she pushed the kitchen chair away from the table and stood up.

"She is by no means safe. The vampires know she is the reason they are able to once again walk in daylight; therefore, they won't let her out of their sight, and who knows what they might do to her," her grandmother said firmly. "Their nature is to feed, and they don't have to kill her to enjoy her blood. They could even attempt to make her immortal, that way the curse would stay broken indefinitely. From what we know, her twin flame and his sire are holding her prisoner."

"What? Prisoner? How do you know all of this?" Taylor's mind reeled, images of Lowen flashing through her mind. The first day of kindergarten. Handing her the blade down in the bed of the creek. Anger burned in her belly, searing away any trace of panic. How could they keep this from her?

Grandma Evie sighed, pausing for a moment to let her words marinate. "Ever since you broke the curse, we've been following you and your friends. We knew the vampire would show himself to you;

he's vain and brazen, yes, but also because he would want to keep Lowen close. He knows we are looking for her," her grandmother said.

"Wait," Taylor said, looking at her mom as she studied the floor guiltily. "Do I know this vampire?"

Her mother remained silent, letting the air grow thick with tension.

"Well, of course you do," Grandma Evie said. "He is your friend's paramour, Sebastian St. Germain."

Taylor closed her eyes. She needed a moment to wrap her brain around these truths. How did Lowen meet Sebastian? At the bonfire where he "saved" her from an almost terrible fall. When was the bonfire? The night after the Moon Water Ritual. He had basically become Lowen's shadow ever since.

It all made sense now, this beautiful and charming stranger coming into town and sweeping her best friend off her feet. Did Lowen know who he truly was? Taylor couldn't be sure, but she wanted to believe Lowen would never continue a relationship with him if she knew, right? Lowen had a habit of wallowing in dark thoughts, but she would never take it this far and put herself in danger.

"Why would Sebastian know you are looking for her? Isn't it all over now since the curse is broken?" Taylor asked suddenly.

"Not quite. The balance between good and evil will crumble if we don't find her and recast the spell."

"Is it possible to recast the spell? How would it work?" Taylor asked, still standing frozen next to the kitchen table where her grandmother and mother sat.

"We will always have to give in order to take," her grandmother said, pausing before looking up at Taylor with apologetic eyes. "We will give Hecate the blood of the twin flame in order to take daylight away from the vampires again. There will always be another twin flame somewhere in the future; that's simply the nature of the spell, but we can stop vampires from walking in the daylight for now."

"So, what you're telling me is that you intend to kill Lowen?" Taylor growled, her voice deep and shaking.

"It's what must be done, my dear. I'm sorry. We told you there were many sacrifices as witches who wield the power we do. Our own individual needs must be ignored for the greater good. It's part of the oath we take."

"This is bullshit. I'm not going to let you kill Lowen." Taylor's anger shook her entire body as she looked down at her grandmother with disgust.

"It's been decided. Members of the coven are already on their way to her and Wesley as we speak," Grandma Evie said, folding her hands in her lap as if the conversation were complete.

"Wesley? What does he have to do with this?" Taylor asked, shaking her head in disbelief.

"You didn't figure it out? He was the last vampire to be turned, and who therefore triggered the curse. Sebastian is his sire. Lowen is his twin flame," she said. "It's so very unfortunate for him. I usually don't pity vampires, but he always seemed to truly suffer his fate, and never once was tempted into the carnal urges that mark those with the demon blood. As soon as Sebastian turned him, he cut all ties from his sire, finding a way to not feed from humans and living most of the last century in sad isolation.

"It's hard to live the life of a vampire and keep one's soul intact. Did you know Sebastian murdered Wesley's entire family, tore them limb from limb, before he turned him? I can't imagine the terror, or the immense grief and loneliness that young man felt. We knew he would come looking for Lowen as soon as the curse was broken. Like the witches, he wanted the curse to remain so Sebastian and others like him could never do what was done to his sisters and parents."

"Are you suggesting that Wesley is working with the witches to kill Lowen and redo this whole daylight curse?"

Taylor felt as if she may vomit. She had welcomed both Wesley and Sebastian into her house. She hadn't questioned their presence enough. Hadn't gotten to know them the way she should have to protect her friend.

"That is exactly what I'm suggesting. The price of Lowen living is too high. Many more innocent people will die if she stays alive, even Wesley knows this," Grandma Evie said.

"I don't want to have to make that choice," Taylor said, her voice a low growl.

"No one does, but it's the choice that must be made."

Taylor ran from the kitchen to the small bathroom in the hallway, falling to her hands and knees in front of the cramped bathroom toilet. She struggled for air as she released the vomit that had crept up her throat.

She remembered throwing up in the hallway in kindergarten after seeing her bully smash out his teeth. Because of her magic.

For a moment in her grandmother's small bathroom, she felt relief followed by a moment of clarity. This was her family; how could she ever go against them? She had possessed these powers her entire life, and they served a purpose. She knew what she needed to do.

Using all of her mental power for a moment, as she had watched her grandmother do when healing her hand, Taylor imagined the bathroom door opening without using her hands. As she did so, the brass doorknob turned to the right and opened quickly and efficiently. She pulled herself up from the cold, tiled floor and stared at herself in the dirty mirror.

It's what must be done, she thought.

Track 41 - "Vampire" by Olivia Rodrigo

Noah

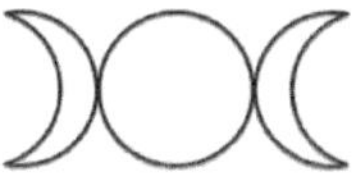

NOAH'S EYES OPENED to the stars twinkling above him. His body was stiff, as if it had been laying in this uncomfortable position with his legs splayed out and left arm stuck underneath him for hours. His head throbbed and a high-pitched ringing in his ears made it virtually impossible to hear anything else. Slowly, he was able to sit upright and take in his surroundings.

That's right, I'm in the middle of nowhere, where I came on my own free will with Sebastian, he thought as he looked at Sebastian's car parked behind him. *What a psycho.*

Noah touched his hand to the back of his head, his fingers sticky with thick blood. *Don't freak out, don't freak out. You're awake and alive, and you need to find Lowen.*

Shakily, he got to his feet and reached into his jacket pocket for his flask. As he tipped it back, he realized it was empty. With a sigh, he listened for any sound that might tell him which direction to go.

Cutting through the incessant high-pitched tone ringing in his ears, Noah could faintly hear deep voices coming from behind the brick farmhouse.

Keeping along the tree line on the edge of the property, he tried to avoid being seen. As he approached the large open acreage behind the house, he could make out the figures of a man. Definitely Sebastian. His knees shook as the memory of something being smashed upon his skull came flooding back.

Noah winced as he remembered the violent incident, and gasped when he saw Lowen climbing out of storm shelter. He sighed a breath of relief as he realized she was unharmed, and almost ran across the field to embrace her, but a voice deep in his gut told him to wait and listen. He watched with horror as Lowen and Sebastian embraced. He wanted to shout at her to stop, to warn her, but what would he say?

Where is Wesley? Noah thought to himself. He knew Wesley had brought her here. Probably to protect her from Sebastian.

I'm right here, Noah, Wesley said, his voice floating into Noah's mind. *You can't see me?*

Wait, I can hear you! Noah said, relieved to hear a familiar voice besides Sebastian's in his head. *So you can communicate telepathically, too?*

Yes, but I don't have time to explain, Wesley said with urgency. *Sebastian is going to hurt her. You've got to stop this, I can't. He's used some sort of spell that has me frozen here, invisible. Noah, listen to me. You've got to stop him.*

How the hell am I going to do that? Noah asked, more to himself than to Wesley as he watched Sebastian and Lowen's intimate conversation from across the field.

Squinting into the darkness, Noah witnessed Sebastian's face change. His once universally gorgeous eyes turned black and his expression went cold. He smiled, sort of, maybe more of a grimace, and stretched his lips back to reveal long white fangs. Fangs?

Is he a vampire? Noah asked Wesley, not believing his eyes.

Now, Noah! Do something now! Wesley screamed.

"Stop! Stop, Sebastian," Noah yelled, revealing his whereabouts that were just safely hidden in the shadows of the tree line. "You can't hurt her. Take me instead!"

It was a stupid and cliche thing to say, but it worked because Sebastian stopped momentarily, looking over with a mild surprise at Noah. Noah ran toward the two of them, recognizing the shock and horror in Lowen's eyes as Sebastian began to cackle.

"Take you instead? What movie did you get that from?" he

snorted.

There was a terrifying sparkle in Sebastian's black eyes as they darted predatorily at Noah and then back to Lowen.

Listen to me, Noah, Wesley said. *The witches are coming, and they will undo whatever this spell is that has me invisible. Just stall him until they get here. And for God's sake, shut your mind off!*

Noah concentrated on his mind, trying to sever the connection between himself and Sebastian without the help of his flask. He stood frozen, concentrating only on his mind and Lowen's wide eyes, the two friends both seemingly unable to move.

Noah, stall him! Talk to him, ask him questions. There is nothing more that Sebastian loves than talking about himself, Wesley directed him.

"Sebastian, what are you?" Noah asked, Wesley's words breaking the frozen fear coursing through his veins. It was his way to stall, but also a genuine question.

"I thought you were St. Germain, the alchemist," Lowen whispered. "This isn't alchemy at all, is it?"

Noah hated seeing how pale Lowen was, how all of her limbs trembled with fear. She looked like she was going to puke. Honestly, he wasn't too far from it himself.

"Well, in a way it is," Sebastian said. "The practice of alchemy was never really *real*, now was it? The science behind the magic, something anyone could do with the right formulas and work ethic—that was utter nonsense. Humans need science to rationalize magic, so it made sense. But the principles of alchemy, now those are very real. The immortality, the elixir of life, the ability to cure disease, they are all very real and completely possible, just not in the way in which you think."

He paused dramatically before continuing.

"What do you think the elixir of life consists of that provides immortality? It's certainly not something that can be concocted by a human on Earth. Something so powerful goes beyond science, well into the realm of magic. And with magic, there is always a price to pay," Sebastian explained, entranced by his own oration.

"What price did you pay?" Noah asked, glancing at Lowen, a signal for her to hold tight as he slowly stepped closer to where the two stood in the field.

"You make a deal with the devil if you want to live forever. The only elixir of life is found in the blood of a demon from the pits of Hell. It's an ironic bargain; you must die to live forever. And drink a little demon blood," Sebastian said, letting his tongue run over his sharp canines.

"So, you're saying you are an actual vampire? Like a dead, then immortal, blood-sucking vampire?" Noah asked, his voice remaining calm, but feeling completely detached from the rest of his body.

"I mean, we've been called so many names throughout the centuries: shriga in Albania, vrykolakas in Greece, and strigoi în România, but I suppose vampire is the most universal label. For me though, vampires are synonymous with evil and death, therefore I came up with my own sort of name for us: alchemists," he said, proudly lifting his chin into the night air.

"Yes, it was I who created the myth of the alchemist in order to be welcomed by the human world while still allowing parts of myself that are different to be seen as eccentricity, rather than remain ashamedly hidden away. These parts of myself are gifts: I can live forever which grants me unfathomable knowledge and I can acquire bottomless amounts of wealth. By the way, the whole turning base metals into gold was always a fabrication; the elite loved their gemstones and gold, so why wouldn't I pretend to be able to turn their subpar baubles into things of immense beauty. I merely swapped out their trinkets with relics from my personal collection," he said as he paced slowly in front of the tornado shelter like a professor lecturing in front of a chalkboard.

"Like I said, my wealth was bottomless, and it made them all so very happy. I'm often surprised people never caught on to the schtick, but people will believe what you want them to believe. Even you," he said, lightly brushing his hand against Lowen's cheek as she reactively shuddered.

Noah thought he caught a look of sadness flash in Sebastian's eyes as she flinched. "So, you mean to tell me alchemists were never real? You invented the term so you could be a vampire who people like and accept?" Noah asked incredulously, now close enough to see the full extent of Sebastian's transformation.

"Simply put, yes. But of course I did have to leave out the fact that I only survive off human blood. That would have really put a damper on my friendships," Sebastian said as he laughed, mostly to himself.

"There has to be more to it than that," Noah pressed, glancing at Lowen intermittently as they worked out an unspoken plan together. "With all that wealth and power, you didn't have to go to those extremes unless you wanted something you didn't have. You wanted companionship. You were lonely. That's the reason why you do all the things you do, isn't it? You pretend it's all just cruel fun, but deep down you care."

Noah's voice rose as he continued to uncover the truth, anger bubbling to the surface that he and his friends had been used in whatever game Sebastian was playing but also seething because of his smugness in explaining it all.

They're here, Noah. Watch out, it will get ugly with the witches, Wesley warned.

Out of seemingly nowhere, at least thirty women walked silently from the woods beyond the field in a horizontal line. They all looked vaguely familiar to Noah, but he couldn't place where he would have known any of them. Some were very old, while others looked younger than himself. Noah had the impression none of the women were frightened, and all looked ready for battle with eyes transfixed on Sebastian and Lowen.

"Well, hello witches," Sebastian yelled with bitter glee, opening his arms wide as if he were ready to embrace them with warm generosity. "I knew you all would arrive sooner or later."

"Speaking of broken spells," a slender woman with graying hair said as she took large strides to close the space between herself and Sebastian.

She never finished her sentence aloud, but instead muttered a language Noah didn't understand and moved her hands in a fluid, rapid movement. When she finished, Wesley appeared directly behind Lowen and Sebastian.

"It's time we repair the spell you've broken, Sebastian," the woman continued, not breaking her intense gaze from the vampire.

"Ruthless witches," Sebastian said, stepping in front of Lowen. "You really do plan to kill her, don't you?"

"Kill me?" Lowen gasped.

"You do realize the hypocrisy, do you not? You can justify killing an innocent but make me the villain if I do the same!" Sebastian yelled, his eyes wild with fury. "I would never kill her!"

"Kill me? Why?" Lowen shouted, her eyes full of fear and fury as she hid behind Sebastian's broad shoulders.

"She is the twin flame, so she must die," the woman said, with no hint of emotion.

Lowen peeked out from behind Sebastian and stared at Noah, who barely nodded to her. She blinked, affirming she understood.

The witches rapidly approached Noah, Lowen, Sebastian, and Wesley, as if they were floating over the cold, dark grass.

"Now!" Lowen yelled.

Noah instinctively pulled Lowen to his side while the witches distracted Sebastian. Wrapping his body protectively around her, he watched as Wesley moved with superhuman speed, knocking

Sebastian to the ground. He gasped as Wesley's eyes turned black and white fangs extended from his mouth. Wesley bit down onto Sebastian's neck, ripping it open with ease. Without taking a breath, he lifted his head from his neck and ripped the flesh away at both of Sebastian's wrists as Sebastian quietly looked on in shock and sadness.

It all happened so quickly that Sebastian hadn't even put up a fight. His blood spilled onto the cold grass below, leaving him unable to find the strength to move. Although his wounds would have killed a human instantly, Noah could still hear his ragged breathing and see the slight sparkle still in his eyes that had changed back to their brilliant green. Sebastian, near death, moved only his eyes, looking frantically before finding Lowen.

Tell her I'm sorry, Sebastian whispered in Noah's head, his voice ragged and weak.

The ringing in Noah's ears was almost too much to handle, and as he reached his hand to cover them, he realized the sound was actually Lowen screaming by his side. Upon seeing Wesley turn into a vampire and watching him rip Sebastian apart, Lowen lost her mind. Like, truly lost her mind.

It was pretty much the same response Noah felt flash through his veins internally, but Lowen's fear overpowered any emotion he could conjure for himself. He wanted her to stop her horrendous scream. For her to turn it off so they could pretend the horrible thing they just witnessed didn't actually happen. Noah closed his eyes for a moment to remove himself from the scene and when he did, the screaming stopped.

The field was so quiet, it was almost peaceful as he kept his eyes shut. When he finally forced himself to open them, he saw Lowen sprinting across the field away from the witches. They didn't even move, not one of them. They just let her run. It wasn't until Lowen's body slammed into an invisible wall that Noah understood why they hadn't exerted the energy into chasing her. They didn't have to.

Magic, it seemed, could do all of their hard work for them. Poor Lowen. How she struggled. She looked like a hamster in a glass tank, trying to crawl her way out, just to slide back down again. The barrier the witches had created utterly trapped her.

"Come back, Lowen. You have to face your fate," the gray-haired witch called.

Her voice had softened a bit. The tenderness only made Noah realize he and Lowen were defeated all the more. Lowen must have sensed the same thing, as her limp body slid down the invisible wall and sat in a crumpled ball in the grass and wept. In less than a second, as if he had traveled through the air, Wesley stood in front of Lowen on the other side of the field. His fangs were now gone, his face completely human and beautiful once more, despite the red stains of Sebastian's blood still visible on his chin.

"Stop!" he yelled, his teeth gritted as he faced the witches. "Sebastian's right. What right do you have to kill her?"

"We will not be killing her; we will be sacrificing her," the witch said. "There is a difference, Wesley, and you know this better than most. The breaking of the curse will only bring more death and destruction. So much more. Wouldn't you and Lowen rather sacrifice her life than be the reason thousands more will die, or even worse, turn into monsters like yourself? The curse protected so many lives, and can again, as long as Lowen's blood is no longer on this Earth. I thought you, of all people, would agree, and maybe even help us with this matter."

"I can't. I won't be a part of this," Wesley said, shaking his head as he stared at the ground.

"The twin flame connection is stronger than we thought," the witch mused, her eyes darting back and forth between Wesley and Lowen.

As Wesley and the witch continued to talk, Noah snuck over to Lowen's side, a lump rising in his throat. He stood in front of her next to Wesley, blocking her body from whatever was coming. If this was the end for Lowen, she wouldn't experience it alone.

"You'll have to kill me, too," he interrupted with a shaky voice, but he held his chin high.

"Noah, don't," Lowen pleaded as tears streamed down her face.

"Yeah, Noah. Don't," a flat, sarcastic voice said from behind them.

Noah turned around quickly upon hearing the familiar voice, warmth washing over him for the first time since he woke up in a puddle of his own blood.

The resemblance was uncanny. Noah instantly realized the reason all of these women looked so familiar was because they all looked so much like his best friend.

"Taylor, what are you doing here?" Noah asked, bewildered.

"So yeah, guys, this is my family," Taylor said as she walked from the tree line, gesturing to all of the women standing in a line in front of her. "Turns out my parents have been lying to me my whole life and I'm a witch. So that's cool."

Taylor stood tall, her body still, and Noah couldn't help but notice the determined, cold look in her eyes. The look he knew so well. Anger. Raging, seething, fury.

"Your grandmother did not want you here. That's why she and your mother stayed behind with you in Arizona," the lead witch admonished. "Why did you come? Not to stop the sacrifice, I hope?"

"Actually, finding my family has really helped me figure out what I am and who I am supposed to be," Taylor said to no one in particular as she stepped to join the witches in their line. "I came to do what I promised when I became a part of this family."

Noah's heart sank. He couldn't believe Taylor was willing to be an accomplice in murdering Lowen because of some pact she made with her witch family, a family she had only known for a couple of days.

"Noah, I'm sorry, you're just going to be in the way," Taylor said, finally meeting his eyes as she waved her hand in his direction and whispered unintelligible words.

Noah then sunk into the deepest pit of unconsciousness, unable to find his way back to the top.

Track 42 - "Burn the Witch" by Radiohead

Lowen

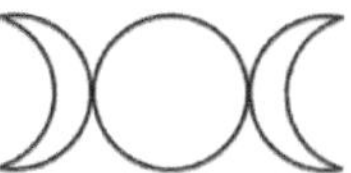

"WHY WOULD YOU do that to him?" Lowen screamed at Taylor as she watched Noah fall to the ground.

Scrambling to her feet, she lunged toward the girl she used to believe was her best friend. Wesley held her back firmly by wrapping his arm around her waist, although he seemed to exert very little effort. She knew she looked at him like a wild animal, which warmly covered the paralyzing terror threatening to seize her. Her body filled with justified rage: the rage that this situation had painted her as the weak, helpless thing in need of saving, the rage that she just watched Wesley slaughter someone she cared about, the rage that someone she cared about was able to fool her so easily. She felt stupid and small and insignificant, and nothing pissed her off more.

"Why did you kill him?" she screamed at Wesley as she pointed to the crumpled, bloody heap that was Sebastian.

"And why are you willing to kill me?" she screamed at Taylor.

"You're all monsters!"

"I'm sorry, Lowen. I'm so, so sorry but you've got to understand, we're all just doing what we're destined to do," Taylor said, a tear sliding down her cheek.

As Taylor spoke, Lowen noticed the witches quietly forming a circle around her. Multiple fires, glowing with shades of green and orange, sprung up from seemingly nowhere inside of the circle of human bodies. The warmth was comforting in the cold, midnight air until the heat felt suffocating. Lowen tried frantically to wake up Noah, slapping his cheeks and nudging his lifeless body, but his eyes refused to open. Checking his neck with her two fingers, she was relieved to find a pulse.

The witches began to chant in unison something foreign to Lowen's ears, the buzz of their words vibrating in her chest. Lowen's rage was amplified when she saw Taylor standing directly in the center of the circle, chanting along. She seemed to be looking each one of the women in her eyes, making connections with them as they chanted their incoherent words.

Lowen watched as Wesley attempted to break free from the circle, but the spell seemed to hold him in place, leaving him utterly useless. She felt pity for him despite everything he had just done.

They were both trapped. Both apparently, twin flames with no say on how others would use their predestined identities.

She suddenly thought about the reality of dying; she didn't want this to be her last day on Earth. She so desperately wanted to see the sunshine one last time, to hug her mother, to hold her sister's hand, to walk in the woods of Moon Creek and watch the deer.

The spell began ramping up in the air around them, the chanting grew louder as fires blazed brighter. She knew it was going to come to a crescendo soon and found herself holding her breath. She was so damn pissed that this was going to be it for her. She prayed Noah would be okay. She hoped whatever magic they performed to kill her was as gentle as Taylor's spell to make Noah fall asleep.

The witch with gray hair drew out a long silver blade as she stepped toward her, and Lowen realized with dread that her death would be much more gruesome. She closed her eyes. This was it. She held her breath.

The chanting ceased suddenly, but the silence only lasted a few seconds before the sounds of bloodcurdling screams filled the air, one after another, like dominos falling in a line. Lowen wondered if she was hearing herself scream for a moment. Was this what it sounded like to die?

With fluttering hesitation, she opened her eyes. She didn't want to see her own blood, her own slow death unraveling around her. What she saw instead was entirely different. The witches were screaming, some silently with mouths agape, some like wild, wounded animals. At first, Lowen couldn't understand why until blood gushed from each woman's throat, as if each one had been sliced with an invisible blade. Blood poured everywhere, filling the air with a nauseating copper scent that reminded her of Blair. It seemed like it took hours for them to stop screaming and drop, even though it couldn't have been more than a few minutes.

Then, silence. Lowen turned to see Taylor standing, moving her hands in a rhythmic motion, her whole body shaking as she completed the spell to kill her coven. She finally crumpled to the ground and sobbed into her hands.

"I told your grandmother you would only be trouble," the slender witch with gray hair snarled, seemingly untouched by Taylor's gruesome spell. "You've been without us for too long. You don't know loyalty. You don't understand sacrifice."

"I do know loyalty, and I'm loyal to my family. These people are my family, which is something you'll never understand," Taylor wept. "And don't talk to me about sacrifice, I know what you intend to do."

Taylor looked up from her knees and nodded to a gleaming blade the witch clutched in her palm. As the witch hovered the blade over her head, gripped by both of her hands and intending to use momentum to swing the blade down upon Taylor, Lowen quietly crept up behind her, quickly slid the knife out of her hand, and stabbed it directly in between her shoulder blades. She heard a soft pop deep inside the woman's chest, her ragged breath filling the silence in the air as she crumpled to the ground. Lowen stared at the blade in her back as she fell like a heap of laundry onto the soft earth. Her wet, final inhalation seemed to fill the night air, as if the bubbles of blood had escaped her lungs and rocketed into the sky. Death was everywhere.

"We can still save him," Wesley said, pointing over to Sebastian's lifeless body. "But we're going to need your blood, Lowen."

Lowen, Taylor, and Wesley ran to the heap that was Sebastian's body across the field. As they approached, Lowen noticed bright crimson blood still flowed from the gaping wounds on his neck and wrists. His eyes seemed to be looking at her, although he didn't move at all.

"Are you sure he's still alive?" she whispered.

"Yes, I can feel it," Wesley said. "When someone is your sire, you have a natural connection to them. You can feel their feelings, you can sense their senses, and you can tell when they're dead. He is barely hanging on, but he's still in there."

Lowen nodded, trying to make sense of a world now containing vampires.

"He needs to feed," Wesley continued, wincing as the words fell from his lips. "Blood is what makes him strong. It's up to you though, Lowen. He was never going to kill you, but he was going to turn you. I couldn't watch him do that to you, but I understand why. He didn't want you to die. He thought he was doing the right thing."

"He wanted to turn me into a vampire?" Lowen asked, staring into Wesley's amber eyes with terror.

"Yes, he thought it was the only way for you to live," Wesley said, unable to meet her eyes.

"Will he kill me if he feeds?" she whispered, crouching down to the ground closer to Sebastian.

Taylor shifted uncomfortably from foot to foot next to her, her arms tightly crossed over her chest. None of them were going to be the same after this.

"No, I'll stop him before it gets that far," Wesley promised, crouching down next to her. "But this is a sacrifice and it's going to hurt. He could easily take you to the brink of death."

Lowen inhaled and lowered herself down into a lying position next to Sebastian. If Taylor could kill her whole family for Lowen, she could sacrifice some of her blood for Sebastian. She scooted close to him, like their bodies were spoons, with her back pushed up against his chest. Feeling the pool of his warm, sticky blood, she thought about what Sebastian planned to do to her. He was going to make her become like him—immortal. In his own warped mind, he thought he would be saving her. Was it all his own personal gain? Was their entire relationship just a ruse to break the curse so he could walk in the daylight again? In her heart, she didn't think so, but she knew there was only one way to find out.

With a shaky sigh, she moved the hair away from her neck as Wesley adjusted Sebastian's head so his mouth lined up with her skin. For a moment nothing happened, and a wave of panic washed over her that he was already dead. Suddenly though, she felt a light kiss on her neck, like butterfly wings against her flesh. And then the pain began, deep and throbbing. Her life was slowly being sucked from her body in a sleepy haze. It almost felt euphoric, like an intimate surrender. She closed her eyes, feeling him come back to life. As she felt his strength return, hers drained in exchange. All she wanted to do was sleep. She felt like letting go, like floating up to the twinkling stars in the black velvet sky and becoming one of them. She could vaguely hear Wesley tell her not to go to sleep, but he was too far away for her to care. A heavy cold settled over her body, and Lowen let the black nothingness and deep, aching throb wrap her up and carry her away.

Track 43 - "Murder in the City" by The Avett Brothers

Lowen

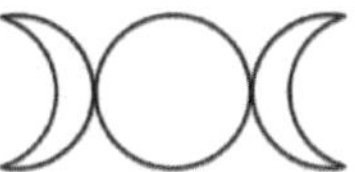

LOWEN LOVED THE way Noah's living room made her feel, especially as the first large snowflakes of winter fell outside. She nuzzled into the soft, velvet couch and watched the orange flames crackle in the fireplace. Inhaling deeply, she took in the sweet aroma of chocolate chip cookies baking in the kitchen. She turned her head, watching as Noah walked in, holding a plate of his from-scratch goods.

He looked worse for the wear: his bleached blond hair growing out, revealing his natural black roots. Swollen, dark bags hung under his eyes as if he hadn't slept in days. Even his smile had been damaged in the battle; it still dazzled with his bright white teeth but had become slightly haunted by little lines of sadness pulling down at the corners.

"Do you think we'll hear from Taylor?" he asked, sitting down next to her and pulling the yellow blanket over both of their legs.

"I don't know," Lowen admitted. "She slaughtered her family, Noah. *I* killed her family. I don't know how she'll be able to face what she's done, what we've done. I don't know how she'll face her mother."

"Her mom calls me every day asking if I've heard from her. She's worried sick."

"We all are, but we've got to trust she can handle this in her own way. And if she needs some space, we have to respect it," Lowen said, although she didn't know if she believed what she was saying.

Deep down, she felt at fault for what happened, for the choice Taylor was forced to make. She wondered if Taylor hated her for all of it. She would understand if she did. A part of her hated herself. Lowen's gut twisted when she remembered how excited she had been about her dark adventure in the beginning. She loved the mystery of Sebastian, falling for him selfishly even though she knew he could be dangerous.

Lowen had put all of them in harm's way for her own sick, twisted fantasy. To punish herself, she hadn't spoken to Sebastian since that night. Plus, she didn't have the energy yet. The side effects of having a dying vampire drain her body of most of its blood were more intense than the movies portrayed. The past few weeks had required a strict regimen of eating, sleeping and watching television as she allowed her body to fill back with the precious blood it needed for survival. The blood Sebastian had drained from her. Many times, she had to shake herself from the memories of his soft lips brushing her neck and the euphoric pleasure that washed over her body as she was slowly drained.

"It would have happened whether you fell for him or not," Noah whispered, reading her thoughts again.

"I thought we were following the rules of consent, Noah," she reminded him, playfully nudging his arm before leaning her heavy head on his sturdy shoulder.

"I'm sorry, it's just hard to turn them off when I'm not drinking—which I'm not. Seventeen days and counting," he said, smiling sadly at her.

"Do you know how much I admire you?" she asked, taking his warm hands and squeezing them.

She leaned back gently against the sofa and closed her eyes, exhaustion taking over. The lies piling up to keep her mom and sister in the dark didn't help with fatigue, either. Noah watched her close her eyes and let his own mind drift momentarily.

"What's next, Lowen?" he finally asked.

"Who knows," she admitted. "But right now, we have two

bodyguards watching our every move. No vampires or witches will be able to hurt us," she said.

Remembering that the world held magic and darkness, like vampires and witches continually hit her like a ton of bricks. She sometimes wished she could go back to not knowing, but understood wasting time on wishes would only make her more miserable. Noah squeezed her hand and stood up from the couch. He walked to the large living room window, peering out into the darkness. She knew he was looking for Wesley's car, which would be predictably parked across the street. She would have known he was on duty for the night even if she hadn't seen him.

Since she found out they were twin flames, Lowen realized their bond was so strong that she could not only sense his presence, but she could also anticipate what he would say or do. She now understood why his physical proximity had flustered her so many times before. It was also why she was drawn to the ground in the Moon Creek woods and had nightmares about the bent tree; it had been where Wesley died. Where Sebastian had killed him and then brought him back to life, eternally cursed.

If she lingered too long on the thought, she felt death creeping into her own body, cold and heavy. It was unnerving, so she tried to keep her distance from Wesley, too. She didn't know the specifics of their relationship, but it seemed Wesley and Sebastian had come to a fragile truce and were working together from this point forward.

"Did you hear that?" Noah asked, leaning his ear closer to the window.

A faint cry echoed in the distance, cutting through the silence of the falling snow. A few more cries followed suit.

"Coyotes?" she asked.

"Must be," Noah answered, as he pulled the heavy curtains shut. "They give me the creeps when they howl during a full moon."

"Let's not wish for any more monsters," Lowen teased half-heartedly.

The two friends situated themselves on the large couch in the dark living room surrounded by blankets and pillows as they were lulled to sleep by the sounds of haunting howls echoing through the Moon Creek woods.

Sneak Peek at Book Two
of the
Moon Creek Saga

HE WOKE UP to silent white giants falling onto his burning face. The snowflakes instantly turned into sizzling teardrops sliding down the sides of his cheeks. He hadn't cried since witnessing his father strike his mother for the first time when he was five years old. The melted snowflakes rolling down his cheeks triggered the jarring memory that he had long assumed was dead and buried. In order to stomp it back down into the pit of his gut, a sort of backpack that carried all of his trauma, he decided to focus on something else, like figuring out where he was.

The bare branches, stretching like skeleton fingers above him, gently swayed in the bone-chilling December morning sunlight. The snowflakes had begun to stick to the ground, an outline of his body visible on the ground as he sat up. He was naked. Where were his clothes? Why was he so hot? Hadn't his mother told him when he was little and sick that a high fever could make one see things that weren't really there?

He sat in the quiet woods and tried to focus on the memory tickling somewhere in the back of his mind.

He remembered staring into yellow eyes—not his own, burning heat and blood-pumping fear. Hunger and running. A dog, maybe. Its fast, soft paws barely skimmed the surface of the ground, stretching its rhythmic limbs so that its ribs opened and pulled inside its muscular frame like an accordion. He remembered the ravishing hunger in his stomach the most.

When Nate Dillon woke up naked in the Moon Creek woods, he felt satiated for the first time in months.

Acknowledgements

Writing my first book was such a rewarding, yet incredibly difficult, experience. There is no way Meet Me in the Woods would be what it is without the help and support of so many kind and talented people.

First, I'd like to say thank you to my husband, Brent, and my daughters, Izzy and Lauren. You guys openly encourage my craziest dreams and have always given me the space (and quiet) to turn my imagination into stories. I love the three of you more than any words I could string together.

Next, I have to thank everyone at the Wild Ink team: Abby, thank you for taking a chance on my teen vampire story. Andie and Nicole, I could have never made it through edits without your valuable insight. The entire team, as well as my fellow Wild Ink Authors, are truly some of the most talented humans I've ever worked with.

Finally, I have to thank some very dear friends. Hollie, thank you for agreeing to read the earliest drafts of Meet Me in the Woods and giving the most valuable and gentle feedback. Shannon and Tara, thank you for being the best friends a girl could ever have. Meg, your daily texts of encouragement keep me going. Mom, thank you for the daily morning phone calls that keep me sane and for always believing in me more than I could ever believe in myself. Thank you for always having a book in your hands and for always encouraging me to fall into a story of my own as a little girl--you changed my life by doing so.

Thank you to the writing community as a whole; there are many wonderful authors and agents who have been so encouraging along the way. Your support and feedback has taken the isolated task of writing a book and turned it into something communal and sacred.

Thank you to my dear friend, Jessie Knuth, for creating such a beautiful cover, from serving schnitzels at the Rathskeller to working together on this project; I'm so lucky to have had your friendship for so many iterations of our lives.

Last, but certainly not least, thank you to my former students whose own stories and lives still live in my mind in vivid detail. I hope you find some of the most beautiful parts of these characters and know that you inspired them. I'm so proud of who you all have become.

About the Author

Courtney grew up and still resides in Indiana, where she graduated from Indiana University and obtained degrees in Communication & Culture and Telecommunications. After a few years of working in the event planning space, she felt called to get back in the classroom and surround herself with books and learners, so she earned her teaching degree in Secondary Education and became a high school English teacher at the largest public school in Indianapolis. Courtney now works freelance as a social media designer and has authored her first YA novel, *Meet Me in the Woods.*

In her free time, Courtney spends as much time outdoors as possible with her husband, two daughters, and three dogs: Tyson, Andy, and Teddy.